DRACO

AN ALIEN WARRIOR ROMANCE

HATTIE JACKS

ACKNOWLEDGMENTS

All my thanks go to everyone who believed in DRACO and backed it as a Kickstarter.

In particular I would like to thank the following backers:
Emilie Kunz
Chance C. Hightower
Hillary E Spencer
Natasha Wimmer

AMBER

The blank white wall in front of me is not the worst of my problems.

It's the sound from behind me, part snarl, part guttural horror. Wet, sharp, and as I've already seen, emanating from something with far too many limbs and eyes.

If it wasn't for the pain in the cuts on my arms and legs it has already inflicted, this could be a nightmare brought on by too much cheese.

But it is absolutely not a nightmare. This is completely real and most probably deadly. I slam my hands on the wall, leaving red streaks from my blood as I run my fingers over the surface. This can't possibly be a dead end.

It can't possibly end like this.

The screechy snarl comes again, only louder, and although I don't want to, I look over my shoulder to see the thing.

Bright reds, greens, and iridescent blues. It could be beautiful like a butterfly. Only it's not. It is bladder emptying terrible.

I scrabble at the wall, and my finger finds a small depression which I push.

The ground gives way. I hear a long, low howl as I drop into a chute. Looking up, all I can see is spiny legs, scrabbling but failing to follow me.

I've escaped.

So, when I land and the wind is expelled from my body, the first thing I do is laugh. This is not a nightmare. This is my life.

I think the creatures that chase me are aliens. I've been running from them for...I don't know how long. Given the healed and healing injuries I have, it could be two weeks, maybe. I have no concept of time. From the moment I woke up suddenly, gasping, screaming, and believing he had found me, caught me, taken me, to the realization that it actually was much, much worse.

Not only do aliens exist, but they really do abduct humans. There's just a lot less probing involved.

Instead there is an alien maze, and I'm the mouse.

My only reprieve is that, so far, whatever is controlling this place seems to want me alive. But my near death experiences are getting fractionally closer every time. I'm beginning to think anything would be better than this place, even being back on Earth, in my old life, racing around my home town of Newcastle as a photographer for our local paper.

Dealing with all the rituals I had to go through in order to ensure he didn't find me, my ex who decided he just couldn't accept that we were over and had to continue to stalk me across the North East of England, from city to city, town to town. Until I no longer had a home, or friends, or family. Rituals which have become singularly useless to me now.

I finally catch my breath and check my surroundings.

I'm back in a cell. One door, no obvious windows, even though I always feel like I'm being watched. Metal walls. Metal floor.

I look up at the ceiling. The hole I dropped through has gone.

There is no escape for this mouse. I'm not sure there ever was. Despite myself, despite my intentions not to cry, a tear slips from beneath my eyelid, running over my face and dripping into my ear.

And then the floor gives way again. This time, because I was on my back, I'm falling headfirst down a chute, and I twist as much as I can, because I refuse to die here, and if I do, it's not going to be by dropping on my head.

This fall is taking a long time, the chute less of a dead drop and more of a slide, allowing me to finally turn myself around. Ahead, I see a block of light, rapidly getting larger as I barrel towards it. I put out my arms and legs to attempt to slow my descent, but the walls are coated in something which is incredibly slippery, so it doesn't matter what I do—I'm going to slide out at speed, whatever happens.

It's then the smell hits me. So far, most of my time here has been devoid of scent. The strange wafers I was given to eat both smelt and tasted of nothing, the liquid I drank, again, nothing.

But this is a stink, rank and nasty and almost making me gag. Now I do not want to end up wherever I'm going, and I redouble my efforts to slow down, to no avail as the odor envelopes me and, with an unpleasant plop, I drop out of the chute and onto something spongy.

Which makes a change. Usually my poor bum takes the brunt of any fall, and I have the bruises to show for it. Especially as my clothing has been replaced by what can only be described as a set of bandages which leave little to the imagination.

This time the laugh which escapes me is one of relief.

Until the sponge beneath my butt cheeks moves.

I look down.

I've landed on a monster. Neon orange, it has two heads on long, individual necks, one of which is twisting to look at me with its eight black eyes, each eye the size of a fist. It makes a snickering sound like metal being rubbed together, and a mouth splits what I could call its face, revealing too many teeth.

They make a snap for me, but my time as a mouse has made me even more wily, even more ready to run than I ever was on Earth. I tumble off the thing, hit the floor, and jump to my feet, looking around wildly for an escape.

The walls are no longer white. Instead, they are a rough dull gray, like concrete and metal mixed together. In places, there are patches of moldy yellow and moss green. But as I stare, I become aware of eyes popping out to stare back.

The neon thing growls. It has no legs, so it's slithering towards me, leaving a green trail. Both heads are snapping in my direction as I take in my surroundings which are increasingly familiar.

I'm still in the maze, only it's much, much larger, and now I'm not a mouse anymore.

I'm a bug, and I'm going to end up squashed.

DRACO

"Not good enough." I release a stream of smoke from my lungs, which feels good, but not good enough to assuage my rising anger.

The Jiaka cowers at my feet. I run my tongue over my teeth and look up at the ceiling of the ante-room in my extensive quarters.

A gilded cage.

My prison.

My domain.

"I told you I needed weapons, and you brought me useless trinkets." I get up from my dais and grab hold of one of the spears he has brought.

Only the bones know where he got the nevving things from, but I can only think they were made as decoration, covered in jewels and of no actual value, not here. I snap one in half with one hand. The metal shears, as if it was waiting for this moment to be destroyed by a Sarkarnii.

The Jiaka's three eyes widen in his pale blue face. I bend down to him and puff out more smoke, making him blink.

"I should just throw you into the pit," I snarl, and he squeaks slightly. "Just as an example of what happens when there is failure."

My skin aches. My head aches. All of me wants to shift, to stretch, to be in my dragon form. But the collar around my neck buzzes a warning, and all I can do is heave up some sparks which splatter on the Jiaka, singeing his clothing.

"But you've shown an atom of ingenuity somewhere in there." I point a vicious claw at the side of his head. "So, I'm going to give you one more chance. Find me some proper weapons." I straighten and then fire out a kick.

He rolls over and quickly gets to his feet. "Yes, Draco," he jibbers and then races to the door.

It doesn't open, and he hops from foot to foot. I'd find it funny if I didn't have a hide which I want to claw off my body and a need for the weapons he's failed to find.

Jiakas are supposed to be good at this sort of thieving. It's why they're in the nevving prison in the first place.

"Open," I growl out, and the doors snap into the walls, the Jiaka falling through them in his haste to get away and keep all limbs attached to his body.

"Still making friends in here, I see." Drega strolls through the open door.

My brother's skin shines with fresh bright blue scales compared to my dull gold. The lucky nevver must have recently shed. I don't know how he manages it, given that the process eludes me most of the time until I'm just about ready to rip it off.

"I'm not here to make allies, brother," I snap, throwing myself back onto my throne.

He snorts and drops onto another large chair nearby. "I'm worried about Draxx," he says.

"Draxx can look after himself."

My brother, the general, could always look after himself. He was the strong one, before everyone we ever knew was killed. Before he lost the female who was to be his mate.

"Draxx has taken leave of his mind. When did you last see him?" Drega grumbles.

"He was with us in the last run." I drum my claws on the arm of my throne. The sound echoes around my quarters.

Quarters I obtained by making sure I was bigger and badder than all of the other convicts incarcerated in this prison. Quarters I fought for, destroyed for. Quarters I killed for. Quarters which belong to me, like the rest of this quadrant in the galaxy's most dangerous, most feared prison.

Kirakos.

The word strikes fear into any law-abiding species.

But not me and not my brothers. We have nothing to fear anymore. Not least, time spent incarcerated in the maze prison where the galaxy puts its most troublesome species.

"For all of half a seccari," Drega says quietly. "You do know how much time he's spending in the pit, don't you?"

"Like I said, he can look after himself," I growl. "As can you. We need to prepare for the next run, and so far, all I have are those." I point to the remaining spears.

"Toothpicks?" Drega smiles, revealing his sharp teeth. Subconsciously, he trails a claw over the collar.

They would have been, if we could shift into our Sarkarii forms.

"Your job was to find a way to get these nevving things

off." I tug at my collar and ignore the sharp spike of pain I get from 'interfering'.

Drega sighs. "They weren't designed to come off. You know that as well as I do. It's what's driving Draxx to distraction, and it's not something we should be worried about."

"Oh." I lean forward, blasting out smoke and sparks. "You think they'll just release us if we're successful in a run?" I snap my fingers. "Just pop these things off and wave us goodbye?"

Drega rolls his eyes and growls low in his throat. "You know what I think, Draco."

My brother, once a healer, now a destroyer. Like me. Like Draxx. Although Draxx was always the dangerous one.

This den, my quadrant, contains the last of our species.

"Which is why we need weapons, *Drega*." I echo his use of our full names. "I'm not leaving without it and without blowing this place to atoms."

"It isn't here. We'd have found it by now. Someone would have found it." Drega turns away from me and starts rooting through a platter of meat left out until he finds something he likes and pours out some ale-wine into a golden goblet.

There are luxuries in the maze prison, if you're prepared to gouge eyes out and take them.

"The map is here. It's the reason we got ourselves sent to the Kirakos."

"That and all the piracy," Drega mutters.

"You enjoyed it as much as I did." I laugh at his haughty expression. "And we're not doing too bad out of it all, anyway, are we?" I gesture around, knowing his quarters are as opulent as mine.

It helps you are a feared species in a place like the Kirakos. It means we get what we want, when we want it.

Drega doesn't answer me.

"The next run is going to be soon. It's been half an ev already since the last one. If I don't have the weapons I need, I'm going to use it for information gathering. Are you in?"

"I'm always up for a run." Drega gives me a feral grin. "Nice to stretch a few muscles other than knocking heads together."

I extend my claws. They've not been used much in a while, and I miss tearing through flesh. If I can't shed and I can't shift, killing is the next best thing, and the run provides the perfect opportunity.

My scales ripple with the need to shed, itchy, irritating. I want to roar out my flame and frustration. Shedding is awkward and uncomfortable. I hate most things, but I hate them even more right now.

We might be providing entertainment to those who have incarcerated us in the Kirakos, but every run brings me closer to my objective.

I don't want to get out of this maze prison. I want to gain control of it. The map is the key.

A squealing alarm rips through the air. I frown at Drega. "Draxx?" I query as the noise sounds like a pit escape.

"Unlikely. He doesn't trigger alarms."

I get to my feet. "This could be fun."

I love new. New is a threat, and I love to deal with any threats in my quadrant. Each one I put down just enhances what I already have. It gives the other inmates another reason to fear me.

"It could also be deadly." Drega stares into his goblet with a frown. Like he's ever been afraid of anything.

I ignore him. He loves to play as much as I do, and if I'm right, we'll have something to take our mind off things until the next run.

My mouth curls up in a smile as I head out into the maze.

AMBER

I have my back to the crumbling wall. It is incredibly tall, so high I can't even see the top. Exactly the same as the one opposite. The mottled surface looks like it might be climbable, until you get close and it has a weird smoothness which would make such a thing impossible, unless you have suckers.

Not going to rule out something in here having such things. The neon orange, two-headed snake is still coming. It grumbles rather than hisses as it weaves its way towards me.

I don't get the chance to consider what the point of all of this is as the two-headed snake lunges at me, and I dart to one side. It hits the wall with a "splat" sound, and I don't hang around to see if any damage has been done.

Instead, I run. I wasn't a gym bunny before I was, presumably, abducted by aliens, but the amount of running I've done lately? Definitely improved my cardio. Turns out alien abduction has some benefits for a thirty-three-year-old couch potato.

Well, it has one benefit. The rest is pretty awful.

The walls go on forever. I can hear slithering behind me as I continue to run and run until finally, something changes. The color darkens, and I can see a junction up ahead. I don't risk a look behind me as I dive to the right and find myself in exactly the same sort of massive corridor I've just exited. It fades away into the distance.

"No!" I cry out in frustration.

There's no way I'm going to get away from the neon snake if there is nowhere to go other than to keep running.

I can hear it slithering, sliding, the sound getting louder and louder like someone turning up the static. I know I can't possibly run any more. I will end up running forever. I flatten myself against the wall, hands outstretched, hoping it might decide I'm not a worthy meal and give up.

A foul head appears around the corner, hissing through all the teeth. My hand dips into a small alcove. As I turn my head in surprise, I see them. Multiple holes in the surface. Hand holds. Foot holds.

The neon snake hisses again, and I swing myself up, climbing as fast as I can. Hand, foot, hand, foot, not thinking about anything other than going up, getting away. Not thinking about the height or what might happen if I fall.

All I think about is the fact the hissing is growing fainter and the neon snake isn't following me. All I can think about is getting away, about the drumming of my heart, the sick feeling which never seems to leave me.

That I don't want to run forever and it was the reason I was running the night I was taken. Heading to London to get lost in the metropolis. To hide in plain sight from him, my ex. The stalker who made my life a misery for the last three years. Traveling in a hurry, in the dark, over the empty moorland. Lights, not from anything earthly, blinding me and causing the car to crash.

I reach the top and heave myself onto the flat surface, panting and panting. And all I can think about is getting air into my lungs and for the red hue covering my vision to leave. For my heart to stop racing.

Finally, I get to my feet and find I'm staring out over the strangest landscape. Only it's not a landscape at all. It's the most enormous maze. Huge blocks, like the one I'm stood on, disappear into the distance in every direction. Somewhere high above is light, but not like any light I've ever known from a sun. It has a strange, otherworldly feeling, as if it's artificial somehow. As I stand and attempt to take in the enormity of the maze, some movement catches my eye. One of the blocks in the distance is shifting position, changing the layout.

From within the deep chasms, I hear howls and other noises. Chittering, metallic sounds, roars, and other noises which have no earthly equivalent. The maze is changing, and those stuck in it are not happy.

The thought sends a chill into my bones. If I was in some sort of training maze before, just how long am I going to last in this one?

I drop to my knees and peer over the edge. Way, way down below, I can see an orange splotch. The neon snake can't get me, but it appears it's willing to wait. I need to find another way down.

I also need to find food and water, possibly shelter or something, although as I stand and stare around, I'm guessing the odds of me surviving very long here are pretty slim.

Which is when the next trap door opens under me, and

I just have time to think "not again" whilst weightless and falling, when I'm suddenly spat out, rolling over and over until I hit something hard and unyielding. All the air is expelled from my lungs, and I can't move.

All I can do is look up at the dark shape looming over me. A shape which resolves into, quite simply, an enormous creature.

I follow his two huge legs upwards until I get to a heavily muscled torso. He has golden scales which ebb and flow like a tide over his skin. A cruel, handsome face, sharp cheekbones and burning eyes with slits for pupils. And when his mouth opens, he has sharp fangs like a snake. Sparks of light rage between the reappearing scales and over the shaved portion of his head, his dark hair a Mohican lit by flames.

A clawed hand reaches down, and before I can scramble backwards, it has me by the throat, and I'm being lifted into the air.

And this alien is absolutely male. I can tell from the acres and acres of muscle on display as, clutching at his unbelievably thick wrist with both hands, I am dragged up his body until I'm staring him directly in the face, my feet dangling because he has to be close to seven feet tall.

Smoke curls from his nostrils.

He is everything my mother warned me about.

He is what the word "run" was invented for.

He is one hundred percent bad news.

"What do we have here?" he growls, in a voice which has been borrowed from the devil.

And even though my brain is screaming at me to get away, my body isn't paying any heed. He shoves his face into my skin, and the heat from him makes me catch my breath. He inhales deeply before shoving me away from him again.

"Female." His mouth parts, a tongue, a *forked* tongue swipes over his lips. "Mine."

If I wasn't in trouble before, I most definitely am now.

DRACO

The female is a strange one. She has no scales, only a pinkish, soft skin covered in downy hair. Her eyes are stormy with black round pupils, and they are wide as they take in the enormity of a Sarkarnii warrior.

Clawless hands grasp at mine. I lower her to the floor. She is slight, short, curvy. So unlike the female Sarkarnii, who would not stand for being handled in this way, given I'd most likely be on my back, at risk of a venomous bite.

The thought causes my cock to stir, the head pushing at my pouch, wanting to emerge.

I can't possibly be wanting to mate though. Females are rare in the maze. Those controlling the Kirakos use them as rewards or as bait.

Bait!

I release her suddenly and take a step back, a snarl crossing my lips as I take in the state of her dress and body. Multiple cuts require healing, and the tiny scraps she wears will not protect her from the night.

The only thing in this maze which will protect her is me. It doesn't matter if this female is bait.

"Mine," I snarl.

"What?" She coughs. "How can I understand you?" She slowly starts to back away from me, heading in the direction of the trap door, one of many, from which she came.

Right now, all I want to do is shift and stop her from ever moving again unless it's at my behest and over my cock. But her accent is strange and her question most odd.

And I forget myself.

"I am Draco of the Sarkarnii, ruler of the fourth quadrant. What are you doing here?" I stomp towards her, grabbing her arm and holding it tight.

Her hair, the color of my scales when I'm not desperately needing to shed, flips around her shoulders and catches the light.

"My name is Amber, not *female*, and I'm not doing anything," she fires back. "And I'd much rather not be in anyone's quadrant." She looks down at my hand gripping her and swallows.

There's a shadow there, like someone has held her like this before, only they left a mark. It makes me want to destroy something, anything. My blood boils, my fire rising.

No one touches this female but me.

A cracking sound above us indicates this part of the maze is on the move. From the way she looks up, she understands what's happening, and I wonder just how long she's been here.

And who else might have a claim on her.

"Well." She puts her hands on her hips and glares at me. "If you're the ruler, then stop this thing from moving."

"I control the organic, not the inanimate," I reply, amused at this little spitfire of a female, so unlike the

Sarkarnii. "And if you don't want to be eaten, I suggest you pay your dues to me."

I put my finger under her chin and tip up her face as I lean down. Her lips part, and her round pupils turn to pinpricks.

"So, what have you got, treasure? What can you offer?"

The walls are swinging around us, moving without care for whatever is in their way. The female's eyes dart from me to the movement.

"We have to get out of here before we're crushed!" she says, attempting to keep her voice even, but I can hear her heart beating out of her chest.

She struggles against me, but, still mindful I don't want to hurt her, I keep my grip firm.

"We can go once you let me know what you have to bargain with. Nothing is for free in the maze, female."

The struggle ceases while, all around us, the ground shakes and the walls rumble on their slow, inexorable movements, changing up the maze in anticipation of the run.

She draws herself up, and her gorgeous eyes flash at me. "And I told you I don't have anything." She opens her arms to demonstrate her distinct lack of belongings.

And instead demonstrating exactly what she does have to trade.

"Oh, I'd say you have just the thing." I huff out a smoke ring. She immediately wraps her arms back around herself, but what has been seen can't be unseen. "I require a bed warmer and"—I twist her around, checking out her back and front carefully as she makes the most delicious sound of annoyance—"you're a little small, but you'll do."

"I...what?" Her mouth opens and shuts again in a thin line.

"Do you accept?" I lean into her, smoke curling from

my nostrils as I repress the urge to shift, to mate, to do anything other than control myself.

"Accept what?"

"My bargain, little treasure."

There's a loud scraping sound, and the wall closest to us begins its turn. She looks around wildly, her chest heaving, and I can almost feel the fluttering of her heart.

"If you can get me out of here, then yes, yes I accept!" She attempts to move, but I still have her at my mercy.

Something akin to enjoyment spreads over my black-ened heart.

"Then it is done." I grin at her. "You are mine."

AMBER

Draco is the first alien I've spoken with. The first alien which didn't want to kill me. The first sentient alien I've encountered.

Apparently, that means I belong to him. Or at least it means he got to trick me into belonging to him.

It appears he wants to do other things with me, and I'm wondering if I should have taken my chances with the neon two-headed snake.

I'm lifted as if weightless and slung over his shoulder.

"Hey! Wait! No!" I call out, my voice strangled from my position. "I can walk, and I can run."

"And you are far too small to do either efficiently." His growl rises up to me, dark and sinful. "So I will carry you."

I bristle at his words, but a small part deep within my stomach quakes. I've survived this long without Draco. Other than making me a bargain I couldn't refuse, why the hell should I trust him?

I'm absolutely certain I should not be bouncing along uncomfortably on his shoulder as he strolls...*strolls* away from the moving walls.

I attempt to push myself upright. His scaly skin is smooth and hot under my touch. The little bright zaps which trail through pulse slightly between the golden shards of his scales. A wall swings towards us, and despite myself, I flinch.

Which means I get a sudden, hard hand slapped on my essentially bare bottom.

"Stay still, female," Draco says, his pace increasing from a stroll to a stride.

His hand doesn't move. It continues to grasp the globe of my arse cheek, and I can feel my face heating up. Everything about this alien is so wrong. The way he just allowed destruction to happen while he bargained with me and I obviously had nothing...

Well, I had something. I have a lot of skin on display, and I'm not exactly small in the chest and bum departments. I had considered what my uses to aliens might be... and I had been hopeful it might not be for my body. It was a mere hope, however.

As it turns out I am an object, and my flesh has currency.

Fucking great. I've been stalked, abducted, and now I belong to an alien and all by the time I'm in my thirties.

Draco is jogging now, and I'm flopping up and down on his broad shoulders, starting to feel sick when I spot it.

The neon snake.

"Draco!"

He doesn't respond, just continues at his unhurried pace as part of the maze slams shut and the neon snake lurches closer.

"DRACO!"

He halts as I batter my fists on his back, and there is a

familiar snarl just before I'm dragged unceremoniously onto my feet.

"I warned you, female..." he says.

"The neon snake." I point behind him. "It followed me!"

As Draco turns, the snake attacks. He puts his arm up to shield himself from one head, which latches on while the other slams into his hard abdomen, teeth sinking into the scaly skin.

He lifts his head and roars with a volume that makes me cover my ears with my hands. The snake head on his torso lifts away and stares directly at me, the tail coming around and lashing in my direction. The maze is still changing, still moving, and where I might have had an exit, I'm backed against a closing wall which is pushing me inexorably closer to the neon snake, one head biting at me while the other continues to rage at Draco.

I jump to one side to escape the thrashing tail, but I'm not quick enough this time, and it lashes across my torso. The tip is sharp, and it slashes through the thin clothing I'm wearing, and I stagger away, clutching at the wound, worse than any other I've had while I've been a mouse in the other maze.

Draco's eyes snap to me. His nostrils flare, a single wisp of smoke curling from one. With practiced ease, he clamps a huge *clawed* hand around the neck of the snake creature. What I thought were just long black nails turn out to be weapons of mass destruction as he slices his way through the neon snake and, with a soggy wrench, the neck is free of the body and lands on the ground, twitching.

The remaining head flicks backwards, and the entire creature starts to spin and writhe. Draco snorts at it with derision and is by my side in a single stride.

Smoke huffs out of his mouth in a perfect O. His eyes are feral, claws dripping with bright green blood as the neon snake expires with a horrible death rattle behind him.

"I told you I'd protect you, treasure," he says, those slitted irises checking me over as I attempt to hide my injury. "You did the right thing submitting to me."

I open my mouth, just about to tell him to go to hell, when pain spikes through me and takes my breath completely. The last thing I see is a pair of burning eyes and a mouth filled with smoke.

DRACO

The female goes limp in my arms, and as she does, she exposes her torso, a long livid line streaked across it from the Melabuk's stinger.

Every living thing in this maze knows to avoid the sharp end of a Melabuk. They're easy to kill, provided you don't get stung.

Except this female. But as I look her over, her pink skin, her shiny gold hair, no scales, no claws, nothing. She is defenseless, and she reminds me of a species I once saw on our old planet.

Could this be another human? A defenseless creatures stolen from her distant home world?

I gather her up in my arms and head for the nearest passageway. I can't believe the alarm was about her. It must have been related to the movement of the maze in advance of the run. It's changed considerably, meaning I have only a short while to reacquaint myself with the new alignment before we get our chance at sanctioned escape.

Fortunately, I discovered the underground tunnels, or

rather, I extracted the information about the tunnels from the relevant parties when we first arrived.

Space pirates are universally disliked, and the galaxy council sending us here after one too many raids on wealthy Caison ships was expected. And I was a very good pirate.

I just didn't expect it to be so nevving hard to find the map. The one star map which is supposed to provide the location of every species in the universe.

The map which should tell us if there are any Sarkarnii left alive after the arks carrying most of them were blown to atoms.

I came here believing if I could find any of my species, then maybe I won't have completely failed as a Sarkarnii warrior. But now, having lived in the Kirakos, having tasted what it is to be more, to be a ruler, to be better, maybe the map isn't to find my fellow Sarkarnii. Maybe it's for revenge instead.

Maybe I can have it all without compromise.

"What in the ever-loving bones are you doing with a human?" Drega says, confirming my suspicions as I enter my quarters.

Without warning, I curl myself around her, my fire rising as I eye my brother.

"She is mine," I snarl out.

"I never said she wasn't." Drega narrows his eyes. "What's wrong with her?"

"Melabuk sting." The words are a growl. I want to help her, protect her. *Consume her*.

I want to breathe my fire on my brother for even looking in her direction.

"You'll be needing my services then, brother." Drega folds his arms, lifting a brow, pierced in the old fashion.

"If you don't get the anti-venom for her in the next

secarri, you will end up with fewer limbs than you came in with, brother or no," I snarl, all my attention focused on my mate.

I hear Drega huff his smoke and his feet beating a retreat.

I gently lay Amber on a couch. She is covered in injuries, some old and some new. The tang of her blood is so strong I'm unable to help myself, my tongue laving over her skin, cleaning up where I can. She tastes like I've been delivered to the ancestors, and when I'm done, it's abundantly clear why I destroyed the Melabuk for touching her.

This female is my *szikra*. From deep within, something starts to beat. Something rises, more than just fire, more than flame. This is it, this is fate.

"Draco?" Drega's voice is deadly quiet behind me.

I turn with a roar to see him holding up an injector in one hand and the other empty for me to see. "Let me give it to her. She's too small to hold out for long," he says with remarkable evenness rather than his usual bluntness.

The war for control is incredible. I want to shift so nevving much. I do not want to let Drega anywhere near her. But I want her saved too.

My collar shrieks, sensing the shift as my tail extends, flicking back and forth. With a huge shudder, I pull it back and step to one side. "Do it and get out. Don't let anyone in here again, understand? Put Drasus on guard."

Drega hurries forward and injects Amber with the serum. Almost immediately, color returns to her cheeks, and her tense body relaxes onto the soft cushions underneath her.

I rise, facing Drega with a growl I've dredged up from our ancestors' bones. He's staring down at her, and I want to rip his head from his body.

"I said leave."

He shifts his gaze from her to me as I open my mouth again. This time, it's not words which issue forth, it's my flame, my fire. Roaring from me uncontrollably.

Drega takes two paces back. Like any Sarkarnii, he is mostly immune to flame, but the fact I chose to breath fire means he knows just how much danger he is in.

"No one is to come in here. I will come to them, if I'm needed."

"The run?" Drega queries. "You can't run if you're in rut."

My scales prickle alarmingly. I've never been in rut, but this cannot be a rut. I simply need to shed.

"We can't rut. You know we can't, not without a Sarkarnii female. I am not in rut." My teeth are gritted. It's a struggle to speak. "Get out, Drega, before I do something to you we both regret."

He backs away, dipping his head in respect. "As you wish."

The door opens, and he leaves. I gather Amber into my arms. Her scent, not of her blood but of her and me together, invades my senses.

She is the wind on the plains. The sharp sky. Fresh scales, warm furs. She is what I want to bury myself in. She is what I want to be able to shift again for. I want to be a full Sarkarnii. I want to take her as a full Sarkarnii.

"Who?" Her eyes are half open and her little brow furrowed as I carry her through my ante-room and into my bedroom. Here is where I sleep with my treasures.

"Draco, my *szikra.* I am Draco, and you are mine."

AMBER

All I can hear is growling as I attempt to open my eyes. Every single part of me feels like it's been on fire, put out, and then trampled on.

Only when I look down at myself, I can't see any new damage. I'm still in my ripped clothing, if that's what you can call a couple of bandages held together by mesh. The slash in the middle is edged with my blood, and it makes me feel slightly sick.

I sit up.

I wish I hadn't.

I'm in a bed. A very big bed which, frankly, takes up much of the round room. The walls curve in and hug the furniture, and the ceiling is also curved, so it's a little like being in an egg. There is a distinct scent in the room, musky and masculine, like leather and cigar smoke. It's oddly calming, oddly familiar. I rub at my eyes, my arm muscles screaming at me.

I haven't seen a bed in weeks, let alone one with what appears to be silk sheets. The entire place is filled with stuff which twinkles, and stuff which doesn't, and certainly nothing I recognize.

The snarling gets louder, and where I thought there was a blank wall, an opening snaps into existence and a huge silhouette stands, blocking much of the light.

"You are awake," it rasps, a voice like the night.

For a brief second, I think I see a tail, extending out, lashing behind the figure. And then it's gone. Draco steps into the light.

His severe chiseled cheekbones and chin are covered in a dark scruff, his incredible jewel-like eyes glitter, reflecting the strange lights which dance over his scales and skin. They are both there and not there, darting like fireflies, until suddenly the light show is cut off and he steps towards me again.

"Where am I?" I shrink away from him, the reality of the bargain I made with him yesterday—or maybe yesterday. I'm not sure of the time—coming flooding back.

I agreed to be his bedwarmer.

I am a complete idiot. My guts are a block of ice. What have I done?

"My quarters," he says with a grin that easily shows a set of fangs where his canine teeth should be...if he was human...and this behemoth is absolutely not human.

I swallow down the fear which is rising within me. I survived the attentions of my insane ex, even if it did mean I ran from him. I do not have to be defined by how he made me feel. I've survived here, or at least in the other maze, until now, and I'm still not dead.

"I meant generally."

He tips his head to one side, looking both birdlike and reptilian. "You mean the Kirakos?"

"This planet?"

"Kirakos is not a planet." Draco's eyes flare. "*The* Kirakos is a prison."

I had questions. I had a million questions all battling to get free, so I could attempt to understand my circumstances. Only now I have none. Now I just have indignation.

"But I've done nothing wrong! I shouldn't be in an alien prison. I was abducted, brought here against my will." I want to carry on, but I realize what I'm saying is exactly what anyone in my position would say.

Draco's smile is predatory. Smoke curls from his nostrils, and he blows out a long, insolent white cloud of the stuff. "I'm sure you were. The wardens occasionally toss the inmates something sweet to whet our appetites, innocence does not factor in their choices."

My breath catches. "You were expecting me?"

His slit pupiled eyes rove over me. "We haven't had any treats for a long time. Probably because the Sarkarnii are troublesome." He rumbles deep in his chest with something which could be a laugh. "Maybe you weren't meant for me."

I pull the silky sheet up against my ripped clothing as his dark tongue slips from between his lips slightly before retreating.

"But you're mine now."

My blood chills.

And he produces a dish from behind his back with a flourish.

"Mine to enjoy." He takes a step towards me.

I shuffle away, but my back hits the wall, and there's nowhere to go.

"Mine to feed."

He's on the bed. It dips under his weight, and I'm acutely aware of just how enormous and powerful he is.

But also the massive dish he has put on the bed is full of

brightly colored objects, is steaming slightly, and is releasing an incredible savory aroma.

It's my turn to lick my lips. I haven't tasted anything decent for such a long time.

"I don't belong to anyone. Not you, not anyone." I hear the words leave my mouth before I can stop them.

I don't have to be the Amber I was. I can be stronger. I can be a survivor.

Draco blinks.

I stare.

He's never been told 'no' before. His huge bulk shifts uncomfortably for a second, then a fang appears as his lip lifts.

"We made a bargain. Surely your species understand how binding that is?" He studies me carefully.

"You know what I am?" I spit out, anger I didn't know I had in me rising up.

"I have met a human female before," he says haughtily. "Although she was nothing like you." His voice drips with sin. "You are far smaller."

My voice cracks as a bitter laugh springs from me. I'm a mouse. I was always a mouse in a maze, hiding from my ex. Running from him. Terrified, blocked. Trapped.

Nothing changes. Even at the far end of the universe.

"Humans are a commodity, it seems," Draco continues, his sharp gaze intense, like a laser. "And I wonder why?"

"Humans are a commodity to you," I mutter.

Draco scratches absently at his side. Clothing, it would seem, at least on the upper half of his body, is optional for this alien.

"I like having something to bargain with."

"It's not me."

"No." The predatory smile is back. So much fang, so

much claw. "I'm not going to bargain with you because you're already mine."

His attention is brought back to the food.

"But you should eat." He pushes the platter at me.

Any appetite I have has long gone. Now I know what I am to him. He considers me a possession. All the agency I might have had—and it was limited, when I managed to escape my ex, leave my home, make a new life—it was all for nothing.

I am a belonging again.

"I'm not hungry," I say, pulling my knees up to my chin and hugging them.

Again, Draco blinks at me. It's almost as if blinking doesn't come naturally. Or someone responding in the negative also doesn't happen regularly. Or at all.

"You should. The poison will have affected your system. You need food," he finally says, after a few more blinks.

"Poison? You poisoned me?"

Okay, so my situation might have looked like it couldn't have got worse. It has got worse.

"No! I didn't..."

There's a pounding somewhere, and his attention is diverted away from me.

"Nev!" he growls. "I told them I was not to be disturbed." Draco looks back at me, his eyes burning in his head.

But the pounding gets louder.

He huffs out a massive puff of smoke, growls, and then flings himself off the bed. His feet thump as he hits the floor. Feet which I see are not booted. Feet which are basically claws and scales.

If I wanted any reminder I'm not on Earth and Draco is not human, I just got it.

DRACO

I am going to kill them.

I don't care who they are, whoever is banging on my quarters, attempting to get my attention, will die. I suck in plenty of air, filling my fire sacs with accelerant.

I didn't ask to go into rut this close to a run. All I can think is the wardens knew, somehow, that the little human female would trigger my mating instinct.

But nothing should trigger it other than a Sarkarnii female, or at least it's what I was led to believe by my elders. Only a Sarkarnii female can flip a male into a mating rut, avoid our fangs, send us into a mating trance, and tame the viciousness which is a male mid-shift.

Sarkarnii females can also sting worse than a Melabuk. The only thing which can stop a full grown male Sarkarnii, females are to be treated with the utmost care. We might enjoy other willing species, if they dare, but a mate bond can only ever exist between Sarkarnii.

Or so I was told, when being a warrior was something I aspired to. Long before being what I am became important or desirable.

And yet this little human, this tiny scrap of a female who I could snack on and still not be full, has made my hide itch, my cock hard, and every single part of me burn.

For her.

Except I need this run. I don't need a rut. And the inconvenience has to be engineered because nothing happens in the maze without the wardens being part of it.

And I really, really need to shed. My skin is so nevving tight I think I might just explode.

I pound towards the door, and it opens with a snap. I release all of my pent-up fire directly at the insolent creature who dares to ignore my orders.

"Have you quite finished, brother?" Draxx growls at me. Unaffected by my blast, he glares.

"Nev off." I unsheathe my claws. "I'm in no mood, Draxx."

"There's a run. Drega says you might not be on it." Smoke curls from his mouth. He's bulked up a lot since I last saw him, his collar biting into the scales around his neck.

"Like you give a zar about the next run. You disappeared during the last one. Either you want to best this place or you don't." I retort.

I need to shed. I have to get out of my skin, or I will do someone some serious damage.

And Draxx might have just put himself in the firing line.

"I need to get out of the Kirakos," he snarls, ignoring my ire. "I want this run to be successful."

"And I want the map."

"You want it all, Draco. You always did," Draxx snarls. "We got in here for a reason. You still haven't fulfilled it, and I want out."

"If this run goes to plan, we'll get everything we need. If not, then there will be other runs." I turn my back on him. "Do not come here again. Not unless I ask for you."

I spin back, grabbing him by the neck and shoving my claws under his eye.

"Don't test me, Draxx. Don't even think about it. I am still your commander. I am still your elder. If you need to shed"—I look at his drab scales, worse than mine—"then shed, but don't take it out on me. This is your only warning, brother."

Draxx is very still. He knows what I'm capable of. He's been through it all with me, with us, since we were forced to leave our planet. Since we were forced to do everything we were brought up to eschew. Commanders, generals, healers, none of those titles matter any more. We are all the lowest of the low now.

"Yes, Draco," he says, still filled with all the fire in the universe.

I release him immediately, unwilling to expend any more energy on my troubled sibling. I have a sweet female I need to charm. I shove him in the chest, and he takes a measured step back.

"Don't come back unless I give a direct order." I walk away from him, the door closes, and I activate the lock, for all the good it will do.

Should the wardens wish to exert their power, I am powerless to stop them. The emasculation burns at me like a thousand flames.

I stride through my quarters to where I left Amber, the tasty treasure I should get all to myself. Now I can feed her, find out what she likes. Claim her completely.

Only she isn't in my bedroom. Neither is the food I left.

The entire place is filled with her scent. Fresh, piquant, perfect. But no Amber.

Females do love their games. I lift my head to follow her scent.

It seems she looked around my room, but not finding it to her liking, she has exited. I trail her easily through my quarters, up through the carefully constructed stairs, and out into the small enclosed courtyard which affords me a little air not recirculated, but privacy from the rest of the maze.

"Can humans fly?" I lean against the doorframe after watching her looking up at the high walls.

She jumps, and inwardly, I cringe. In her hand is the receptacle of food I procured for her, some of which, I note with some satisfaction, has been eaten, despite her earlier protestations.

"Not without help," she says.

"Sarkarnii can fly." I tap a claw on the collar, and it bleeps at me. "When we're not collared."

And when we're not stuck in our unshifted skins, unable to shed.

"Why are you collared?"

I'm across to her in a couple of strides. She backs away until her back is against the wall, her face upturned to me, my hand on her throat, encompassing it, caressing, feeling her against my skin.

"Because I am very dangerous, my treasure, and a tasty little snack like you shouldn't be left alone with me."

AMBER

Draco holds me against the wall. I honestly should be freaking the fuck out right now with this massive, seven-foot, dominant alien and his hand around my throat, except somehow I don't feel afraid, and I don't know why. He has no grip on me. All which flickers in his eyes is mischief. So, when he tells me he's dangerous...

My core clenches.

Smoke wafts from his nostrils as he hitches up one corner of his mouth revealing a fang and looking very much like a bad boy alien. One who delights in being wicked.

One who lives to be the epitome of sin.

"I don't believe you." The words come out as a whisper.

Draco releases my neck and a single claw traces down my skin, hot and cold at the same time.

"You should, little human," he rasps. "I only offered to protect you because of what I am."

"And what is that?"

"I am Sarkarnii. I am Draco, leader of the one hundred armies, high commander of the great warrior horde, the last of my line, the first of the galaxy captains." His lip lifts higher. "Pirate, brigand, spacesnake, all of these things, but most of all, *szikra*, I am yours."

He leans into me, and the scent of smoke and musk is incredible. He breathes out a slow stream and sucks it back up his nostrils.

My knees go weak.

"Pirate?"

He throws his head back and laughs. "Of all the things I am, you pick pirate." He fixes me with his slit pupils. "But then, trouble knows trouble."

"I'm not trouble." I can't help myself. The words come as a reaction. Something I know I should say in order to avoid drama.

"If you're here, with me, you're trouble," Draco rumbles. "The wardens saw fit to give you to me, and that makes you the most dangerous thing in the Kirakos."

"I was just running away from the horrible neon snake."

Draco furrows his brow. "Neon snake?"

"The thing you...killed." I shudder at the memory of the head coming off.

"The Melabuk? It stung you, and those things are nasty. One less is a good thing."

"What I mean is, I was running from it. I wasn't given to you."

"Anything which runs in my quadrant is mine. The wardens know." Draco licks his lips, the tips of a dark forked tongue sweeping over them and making me feel...strange.

His gaze trails down me as I shiver under his scrutiny. I'm nothing special. Not very tall, probably a bit too wide, certainly in places. Boring dirty blonde hair, watery blue eyes. I'm not wearing much, and what I have on is pretty well ruined.

The claw flicks at the slash on my outfit, the blood now dark. "This will not do. Not for my female," he rumbles.

"It's all I've got," I reply, clutching at the damaged fabric.

"We'll see about that," Draco says, the slit pupils in his eyes narrowing farther. "But in the meantime, you need to feed."

What is it with him and his desire to make me eat?

"I had some. Thank you."

Draco releases a stream of smoke, and a growl lurks in his throat. "Not enough."

A hand encloses mine, a tail encircles my ankle.

A tail?

My eyes fly to his face, and the second I look back, the tail has gone.

"I am not what you think I am, Amber," he says in his forty-a-day voice. "This is not my only form."

He takes the dish from my hand where I've only just been holding onto it and stares at the food contained in it. I've eaten a few items which turned out not to be a shrimp, a tomato, or a samosa. At that point I became a little scared to try anything else. That furrowed brow is back, and the imposing chiseled face softens.

"I'll eat more if you answer my questions."

I can't believe I've been so bold. I haven't been for such a long time. Before my ex decided stalking me was the way to win me back. I never wanted to be in my early thirties and looking over my shoulder. That wasn't my plan when I left uni and started working for my local newspaper as a photographer.

Back when I was happy in my skin. Back before I met John and he tore my life apart. When running seemed the only option, and my life, the job I loved, all had to be left behind.

Draco rumbles deep in his chest. Lights spark through his scales for a second before winking out, and a smile plays over his lips.

"I should eat *you* for such insolence to a commander of the hundred armies and *pirate*," he says, backing off from me a fraction.

I draw in a breath. He absolutely does not mean to actually eat me, that much is clear in his eyes and in his stupid bargain for me to be his *bedwarmer*. If I thought being a mouse in a maze was terrifying, the mere thought of what this alien has in his pants...given I've already seen a disappearing tail...it's unthinkable.

"No..." I stumble over the words. "I'll eat. I just meant I wanted to know more about this place."

Draco huffs out a smoky laugh. "Ask me your questions, Amber."

"First off, how can I understand you?"

He looks first at my hand, then at the platter, then back up at my face.

"Oh!" I scoop out something which could be a blackberry, but when I put it in my mouth, it isn't. I chew and swallow the savory item, which tastes like bacon. Draco smiles with a large portion of fang at my action.

"Language-nanos will have been injected into you at some point. You'll be able to understand, and if they're decent quality nanos, you should be able to read all the galaxy's known languages." Draco shrugs, as if this is the most normal thing ever.

"Something was injected into me?" I lean back against the wall, yet again my appetite disappearing.

Almost immediately, Draco is towering over me, gently

supporting my weight with his arms. "I did not mean to alarm you, little jewel," he murmurs in my hair, and this time, the scent of him nearly overwhelms me. Draco is like a night next to an oak log fire mixed with spice. "The nanos will not harm you in any way. But it seems like the wardens wanted you to be able to interact with the inmates."

"That doesn't sound good."

"It isn't."

DRACO

I did not bargain for Amber. I bargained for something small and fragrant to warm my bed, a female of a species I knew nothing about and did not care for. What I have in my arms is far, far greater and far more precious than I realized.

And the wardens are involved in delivering her to me. Of that, I am sure. They did not let a female filled with the best translation tech loose in the maze if they did not mean for her to be used to their own end.

Her appearance just before this next run cannot be a coincidence. Her falling into my arms cannot be a coincidence.

But my bargain with her, to provide protection? That was all my own doing. And I should not have let my sense of honor cloud my judgement. I'm stuck with protecting her now.

And it's the last thing I need.

I stretch out my neck. There's still no sign of shedding, and I want to scratch myself to the ancestors. I'm only not doing so because I want my female to eat.

Another reason her appearance is poorly timed. I'd make a trip to the aquium, the hot waters being the only place where I can shift enough to encourage a shed, only I can't risk it, not with Amber requiring my attention and protection.

"Come." I lift her into my arms and carry her back inside, through to my bedroom where I place her on the bed. "Wait."

She opens her mouth to speak, but I cut her off. "Eat," I growl.

Her eyes widen, and I scent something new. Sweet musk, as if it's been sent from the ancestors to taunt me.

Arousal.

Nev it all! I cannot be tempted by her!

Instead I head into my den where I keep those things I hoard. It's a good thing anything shiny takes my fancy, and I pick up some Zio silk which shimmers like scales in many hues. As I head back through my ante-room, the doors snap open for me.

Drasus is stood just outside, his strong shoulders squared as he takes his job seriously.

"Draco." He sweeps his arm towards the floor. "Commander."

"Draxx?"

"My apologies, sire. He told me I was allowed to leave for my meal."

I roll my eyes. Just the sort of thing Draxx would do. Drasus is one of my most loyal and most feared warriors, his hide criss-crossed from his many battles. Even so, he knows I requested him as my guard. For him to leave his post should result in punishment.

"You take your orders only from me," I snarl and shove

the silk at him. "Have this made into a garment for a female."

His eyes widen.

"Not a Sarkarnii, a human."

Something tells me it will not be difficult for this to be done. The Kirakos might be the galaxy's prison, but it is not exactly large, and Amber's presence will not have gone unnoticed, even if she's only been here for half a tick. Anything, or just about anything other than weapons, can be obtained for a price. That includes clothing for my female.

"Yes, commander." Drasus gives me another bow.

For an instant, I feel something which might indicate I've eaten an enemy who isn't agreeing with me. A rising in my gullet, something which hasn't been there for a long time. Then it's gone.

"Tell them Draco sent you." I tap the collar around my neck, the exact same as on Drasus. "This doesn't mean anything, and they know it. Tell them I am unimpressed with recent tributes, and unless I see respect, I will be ensuring those who have failed me will not see the start of the next run."

Drasus nods curtly and hurries away. The collar seems to suppress our ability to shift in different ways. Some of my form will shift without warning. I still retain my ability to flame. But others, like Drasus, have to rely on only their Sarkarnii senses and increased speed and strength, the collar hindering any shifting at all for him, including his fire.

I hate what we have become. I hate what I brought us to. Most of all I hate...

"Draco."

I don't have to turn to look at where the voice is coming from. I have disabled all of the viewscreens in my quarters.

But it has been impossible to shut down all of the screens in my quadrant. The wardens have ways of installing them, even if they rarely send guards into my quadrant. Collared we may be, but caged Sarkarnii are still deadly.

There are limited options to manage me and my den warriors.

But what they can do to us means a species which doesn't play well with others has to play the game, regardless.

I stride out of my quarters to the screen opposite.

"Warden Gondnok."

"I hear you might not be undertaking the next run."

I bunch my fists. It's bad enough having Amber in my quarters and having to resist the worst temptation which has ever come my way. It's bad enough being so nevving close to gaining my prize, and it's worse knowing the obstacle in my way was placed there by the one set of creatures I abhor more than anything.

The viewscreen is projecting a holographic image of the head warden because I really need to see more of him. The poor quality image does nothing to hide the foulness of the Belek. His sallow yellow undulating skin, bulbous and worm like. His three eyes are flat black whereas I know in person they are wet and runny.

"I will be on the run."

"And yet you have a female?" He knows exactly what I have.

"There are plenty of females in the Kirakos under my protection. You will need to be more specific." I manage, just, to keep my tone even.

If he wants what I know he wants, he is going to either have to admit he put Amber in here for me or he's going to have to admit one of the other wardens did.

"I mean the *Uman* in your quarters."

"*Uman*?" I furrow my brow but blow out a long stream of smoke which swirls through the holo until it hits the screen. "You mean my little bargain? My bedwarmer?"

Belek believe they don't have emotional tells. It's the one thing which has gained them superiority and power in the galaxy. It's the reason they are the wardens of the Kirakos and the vast wealth it brings them. The thing is, they do. He shifts food from one pouch to another, the dark coloration moving down his segmented body.

Warden Gondnok doesn't know what I have in my quarters. He did not release Amber into the maze. Someone else did.

"I don't want anything distracting you. Not this time, Draco. If this run is not successful, I will make sure it is your last," he says.

"If this run is not successful, I will ensure I make it to the warden quadrant, and you will breathe your last," I threaten casually, feeling the accelerant rising.

I lean over to the viewer, through the holo, until my face is right next to the view screen.

"Don't forget, I am the one on the inside, Gondnok. This is my show."

"You look like you need to shed, Draco," he says with a sneer. "Perhaps you should visit the aquium, get rid of your skin before the run, and make sure you're in tip top condition."

I let rip with my fire, burning the entire wall black and, despite the warnings from the collar, my tail extends and thrashes as I march back into my ante-room where I fling myself onto my chair, scratching furiously at the skin on my throat, desperate for the shed to start.

"Are you all right?" Amber's soft voice interrupts my murderous thoughts. "You look in pain."

I can't remember the last time anyone cared how I felt, apart from not wanting my anger. And yet this tiny little scrap of a female wants to know my wellbeing.

So, what exactly is a human anyway?

AMBER

Draco has a large section on his very muscular neck which is raised and flaking. It looks inflamed, and I can smell burning.

The last thing I want is to be in the debt of this huge male alien. I do not want to be dependent on anyone ever again. Except this is not Earth, this is some sort of weird prison and, despite the fact I'm not a prisoner, it doesn't matter.

I'm here, I'm defenseless, and I have no options left, other than running...and that went so well last time I tried it.

I know it's not possible to run forever. Sometimes you have to hide and, despite everything, if I have to hide behind this massive scaly alien, I will. Plus it means I can ogle his very nice, muscular bum.

Did I just think about Draco's bum?

This whole situation must be getting to me.

I became adept at hiding once John started stalking me. I knew our relationship was doomed the moment he told me I should go to the gym more, make him "proud," as he put it.

And yet leaving him wasn't so straightforward as I always told myself it would be.

Because you always tell yourself you'll just walk away. Only when you share a home, a vehicle, a life—walking away isn't just a matter of closing the door and posting the key through the letterbox. So, I kept telling myself I would go next week, or tomorrow. I took bags of belongings to work and hid them under my desk. All the time, he chipped away at my confidence, at my ability to walk away at all.

Until he went away to a conference. And suddenly the door was wide open.

Or so I thought.

"I need to shed," Draco rumbles in his sinfully dark voice.

I'm still trying not to think about how I felt when he caged me earlier. Every instinct within me should have been screaming to leave, to run.

Only I didn't run.

My brows knit. "Shed?"

"My species has to shed its skin once every half ev." Draco shifts uncomfortably on his big chair, as if he's trying to rub himself against the surface surreptitiously. His eyes hit mine and then slide away.

I'm not sure what an "ev" is, other than a period of time, but I understand a little better. Draco is scaly. I know reptiles have to escape their skin every so often, so it stands to reason Draco's species also need to do this.

I think what surprises me more is that it bothers him. He's so self-assured, powerful, in control. But he's not in control of his body, and I find it a little bit amusing.

He scratches at the area on his neck around the collar he wears, his massive claws scraping like stone on sandpaper, only a lot, lot louder. He looks miserable. My heart drums out a beat I didn't know it had.

"Why not have a bath? Do you have such a thing as a bath? That might help. I mean, I don't know much, but when I was younger, I had problems with eczema, and my mum used to give me a warm bath to help." I burble on like an idiot, trying not to see Draco's multi-faceted eyes and slit pupils trained directly on me.

He's stopped scratching and has his chin propped on his hand, leaning on the arm of his chair, gazing at me.

"I could have a bath," he rasps. "But I need a companion."

"Oh...Oh?" I sound like a bloody owl at his suggestion.

Draco has his lip hitched over his fang in the most illicit smile I've ever seen.

"To help me with the shed, of course," he says in such an innocent voice I feel like looking around to see if anyone else has entered the room. "A shed is always better with some assistance."

It is really getting quite hot in here, and I'm hardly wearing anything.

"So." Am I really going to say what's on the tip of my tongue? "Why not have a bath?" Heat flows over my skin in waves.

"It means I have to go to the aquium, and that's just not possible right now." Draco sighs.

"Aquium?"

"Hot baths. Provided for all the"—he waves his other hand in the air as if searching for the word—"inmates."

"If it was me, I'd go, rather than being uncomfortable," I suggest.

Now it sounds like I *want* to see this alien naked, and I'd quite like the floor to swallow me up.

"You know what, little *szikra*? You're quite right. We should go to the aquium, as long as you don't mind a trip through the maze?"

"I have to come?" Immediately, the thought of going back into the maze tightens a grip around my guts.

Even having the so-called protection Draco claims to be offering, even after having seen him kill the neon snake with his bare...claws. That place is dangerous and maybe we got lucky.

Or maybe it's dangerous to stay here with an uncomfortable alien who is eyeing me with a look which could strip paint. He shifts again in his huge chair, all ornate and all badly worn. And yet, he still manages to look regal.

"If you think I'm leaving my little bedwarmer on her own, you're very much mistaken," he rasps.

Oh, the bedwarmer thing. I thought he might have forgotten. From the glow in his eyes, he has absolutely not forgotten my rash bargain with him.

Because jumping in with both feet is something I still don't seem to have been able to master. Now I'm bound to this huge alien with his beautiful scales which ripple with light. No choice, only the one I made in a rush.

"Come with me, heartsfire." Draco beckons me with one of his huge hands tipped with sharp ends.

And for the first time, I wonder if there is a mistake with my translation nanos. I'm his bargain. I'm his belonging.

I have nothing to do with his heart.

DRACO

Pulling Amber close to my body, I scan outside of the door to my quarters before we move out. The maze may have shifted, but the scent of the aquium is all I need in order to direct myself to the place, regardless of what has changed. The Kirakos was not designed for Sarkarnii, even if the collars were.

I do not want to take Amber into the maze. I do not want to expose my *szikra* to anything which might harm a hair on her head or a scale on her body...

Only she is not Sarkarnii, and I'm not supposed to find a mate, let alone a fated one. I swore on the bones of my ancestors on the day I left Kaeh-Leks I'd not stop until I'd conquered the galaxy which allows the destruction of a species.

And yet I already know I am not leaving her. Not until I have buried myself in this beautiful female and she has dominated me, taken my seed and scent. Until the entire universe knows she is mine and mine alone. Even then, the chances of me leaving her alone are slim to none.

Amber will be mine. Of that, I have no doubt, and one day soon, she will see my full form.

For an instant, there's a chilling in my blood. One which shouldn't be there, one which evolution pulled us out of many millennia ago when we gained our fire and our unshifted forms. What if Amber does not like my shift?

Then the chill is gone. If she can bind me as a *szikra*, she can do anything, and she will accept what I am. Humans cannot be that different from Sarkarnii, or she would not have triggered my rut.

Wait?

Rut?

I can't possibly be in rut. Drega only said that to annoy me, with his shiny recently shed scales and irritating attitude. He always was a smug nevver.

This isn't a rut.

It isn't.

The maze has moved considerably since I was last abroad. It looks like it has changed in order to make the upcoming run particularly arduous, which would suggest either the wardens know my plans or they are anticipating them.

"How long have you been...here?" Amber asks me, trotting a little to keep up with my larger stride.

Her eyes dart around as I attempt to move as quickly as I can and also keep both the scent of the aquium in my nostrils and try to scent any other inmates.

All of which is made doubly difficult my Amber's deliciousness, invading my nostrils with every step. I'm a Sarkarnii commander, one of the elite of my species, I cannot be this nevving distracted.

I've tracked herds of Herabeasts across the plains, sought out enemies and eliminated them. Other warriors used to sing of my exploits. Keeping track of some hot water and the lesser beings which beg my mercy to inhabit my quadrant is as simple as breathing.

And yet I'm struggling to fill my lungs at all. Including my flight lungs.

But my senses are not as dulled as I feel they are. A flash of silver and I'm raking out with my tail, the vicious barb on the end making contact with a soggy thud as the Xicop guard leaps for me and my mate.

"That was a very stupid thing to do." My tail has shifted away before the Xicop can blink or register the large hole in his thigh. "Since when are guards allowed free access to my quadrant?"

"I heard you were indisposed, Draco." He snivels from his position on the ground. Best place for the creature.

"I am not, and neither are my brothers, especially Draxx. He is in a particularly pleasant mood and would be more than happy to attend you."

The Xicop's chest heaves, his four eyes blinking discordantly and his hairy skin slick with oil. "I'll be leaving, Draco. I must have taken a wrong turn since everything moved."

"You are a spy," I growl. "There was no wrong turn." I shift position until I'm standing over him. "And no unauthorized beings leave my quadrant. You know that as well as the next guard."

"Please, Draco, I'll leave. I didn't see anything," he gibbers.

But one of his pairs of eyes darts to Amber, still in her ripped outfit.

She has been seen.

With me.

Anger the likes of which I've never felt before flows

through me. It's something which has been dredged up from the very depths of my being. I want to ensure this Xicop is not only punished but his ancestors feel my rage.

"Draco," Amber says, her voice trembling.

My name on her lips makes me hesitate, and the Xicop takes instant advantage. He flips himself upright, his leg unstable but unfortunately useable given I wasn't able to hit his egg sacs on the outer thigh. He attempts to slam a silver dagger into my abdomen.

But I haven't shed yet. My scales are not soft but hard, almost brittle. The blade slides sideways as I catch his arm and casually break it.

He howls. I slam my claws into the sensitive thigh area and the howl stops. He knows what I can do. I drag him close to me, attempting not to inhale his stench.

"Whoever you are reporting to will find you saw nothing. Won't they?" I pull down slightly on his thigh. "Or I will finish the job I started here, and you don't want to lose your precious young, do you?"

"They won't hear anything." His voice is high-pitched and terrified, eyes rolling in his head. "Not from me. Nothing from me."

"If I hear a single whisper, I will know it was you, and I will come." I don't even need to snarl when I scent his emission and feel his legs shake.

Shoving him back, I grab hold of Amber, spin her around, and propel her as fast as I can in the direction of the aquium.

I couldn't assuage my irritation with some gentle killing due to her intervention, so an aquium needs to be worth exposing Amber to the maze.

The Xicop might not talk, but all the other walls with

eyes...they will. The sooner I get her out of sight, the better my heart will feel.

But this is not a rut.

This is a bargain I made with a pretty female to warm my bed.

Because I am Draco, Commander of the Hundred Legions, Captain of the *Golden Orion,* and ancestor of the High Bask.

And the Kirakos is mine.

As for the creatures in it? There's only one I will accept. Amber.

No one, nothing, will take her from me.

AMBER

I feel numb. Draco's response to the other alien, the one which looked like a warthog but with four eyes, was violent in the extreme, but then he is also bleeding from his abdomen, his assailant's blade having hit home.

But also, and this is the big one, he definitely has a tail. I distinctly saw the thing uncurl in a riot of gold and black scales, ridged like a fairytale drawing of a dragon but barbed with a vicious spike on the end which he used to knock the warthog alien onto the ground. Then, as quickly as it was there, it was gone.

Obviously, Draco is not human, but he is more alien than I could possibly imagine.

"You're bleeding," I comment as I'm hurried down another, slightly narrower passageway.

Draco looks down at himself and huffs out, sparks shooting out of his nostrils in a very alarming manner. "Nevving Xicop," he mutters before he looks at me. "I'll be fine, *szikra*. It's a scratch, nothing more."

I want to say it doesn't look like a scratch, but Draco has

just demonstrated his different physiology. Maybe it is a scratch to him.

What's bothering me more is why I care.

He's tricked me into a bargain, out of which it seems all I get is to see him inflicting violence on anything which comes our way. He's grumpy, dominant, possessive. Everything I should loathe.

Except Draco holds himself differently. He's not trying to impress me or frighten me into compliance. He's purposeful, intense, directed. None of this is about him. He doesn't need assurances from what goes on around him. He's not self-centered, merely centered.

And for that reason, I don't want to run. Instead, my curiosity, so long un-piqued on Earth, has been given a jostle, and I'm drawn to Draco unlike I've been drawn to any human in a long time.

He lifts his head, scenting the air before gently but firmly pushing me towards a blank wall. I know it's not going to actually be a blank wall because the mini-maze never had blank walls. Only Draco furrows his brow, handsome features settling into confusion.

"It should be here. I can smell it," he says, his voice a pit of gravel.

"Smell what?"

"The aquium. The water," he growls. "It should be here."

I take a step in front of him, but a massive hand grabs my shoulder.

"Stop."

I shrug him off. "There's no one here, Draco. It's safe."

To my surprise, he doesn't try to get hold of me again, instead standing back and watching me, leaning his shoulder against a wall, arms folded, eyes glittering as I approach the flat surface, running my fingers over it until I find what I'm after. With a click, the hidden door within the wall swings open, inwards.

Draco is immediately ahead of me, his massive back, just as muscular as his front and really quite delicious, blocking my way. He turns his head to one side, lips hitched to show a long fang.

"Well done, little treasure. Looks like I might have got more than I bargained for."

"If you want more of me, Draco, you're going to have to bargain harder."

I'm initially stunned at my confidence, my ability to tease seemingly stripped away with the rest of my personality when I found myself hiding from the unwanted attention of a man who refused to consider I might not want him.

Only, that was a tease, wasn't it? I just teased a seven-foot alien with enough power in one of his clawed pinkies to rip me from gizzard to throat.

"I might just do that, female," he rumbles, the lip hitching higher and a twinkle appearing in his eye. "If you ask me to reopen negotiations."

A huge hand comes out and grasps my arm, gently pulling me behind him as Draco lifts his head and sniffs the air again, two long plumes of smoke coming out when he exhales.

"The aquium is close," he says, and I'm not entirely sure, but I think I might hear a hint of relief in his voice.

He's a big, bad alien who has no compunction about breaking bones, but the thought of a bath to soak his itchy skin...it makes him happy.

And for some reason, I find that far too cute. Especially as Draco is anything but cute.

Isn't he?

DRACO

I'm not sure what to make of Amber. She draws me in like a tiny dancing mothar to a spark, ready to consume it, feed from it, grow larger and greater until it becomes one of our ancient ancestors, the unshifting Sarkar, small and fierce, fire breathing and loyal.

I want to eat her. Lick my way over her body until she groans with pleasure. I need to be tamed by her, see her riding me, impaled on my cock.

I shake my head, hard. My stomach screams at me because the stupid Xicop has tried to burn me with a poison-tipped dagger, and it's merely served to irritate me even more. I need the aquium, I need to shed and heal, and I need to know this female is safe. One is unlikely to follow the other, and it irritates me further.

Except this female is a key. A rumor which occasionally circulates the maze. The suggestion there is a creature which is able to open up the hidden passages, make their way through the Kirakos unhindered, and it appears my treasure, my bargain, is just such a key.

The passageway is filled with vegetation which has a

lush scent. I risk a quick check on my little *szikra*, who is staring, wide-eyed, around her.

She has no idea what she is.

"I thought this place was a prison?" she says, her voice melodious and calming to my unquiet soul.

"It is. The Kirakos was built around a small moon. In the depths, some of the original parts of it survive."

"It's not on a planet?" Amber's breath seems short.

"It's somewhere between a ship and a planet." I shrug. "It can be moved if necessary, but in the main, it stays in one place, far enough from any part of the galaxy where the inmates might have supporters who wish to let them out."

"A space ship prison?" she says slowly. "I'm not sure whether to be impressed or horrified."

"Be horrified."

"Thanks," she grumbles.

I risk another glance at her, and she's folded her arms over her pleasant chest. I wonder if she has nubs like a Sarkarnii female or something else instead.

Because I want to pleasure her, take my calm from her, bury myself in her. I want to be tamed by a female, made to be hers, made to worship her.

Be made to burn this place out of existence for her. Females have always provided a counter to the viciousness of the Sarkarnii male, but it's been too long without them. We are already too feral to be reprieved.

The scent of water increases as I push aside a swathe of plants, streaked black, gray, and green as they take their nutrition from the glowing hearts of gems, bioluminescent, that stud the walls of the aquium.

"Wow," Amber says, yet again pushing in front of me, ignoring any risk to herself. Again. "Is this it?"

"This is one of the aquiums," I say, again inserting

myself between her and anything which might be lurking in the water. "Not the best one. I will take you. Stay close."

Amber's little brow creases, but she does as I ask, and I lead her through the three pools until I reach the final one.

"Okay, I admit, this is better," Amber says to me, and, for the first time, her lips are curved upwards in a smile.

My heart booms loud in my chest. Loud, as if I'm shifting. Only I'm not shifting. All I've done is please a female.

This female. My female. My heartsfire, my *szikra*, my Amber.

Mine.

My entire being roars the word as I put my back to the large rock next to the entranceway and heave, shoving the thing slowly into the groove I created when I first came to the Kirakos and found this place.

"Bathing and shedding are something best done in private," I say to Amber in the hope she is watching me with awe at my strength.

Only she's not watching me. Instead, she's staring at the large aquium. Three interlinked pools, bright with their glowing gems. In one corner, water trickles melodiously down through several falls until it enters the pool. She kicks off her footwear and balances carefully in order to dip in a toe.

"It's hot!" She smiles. "Underground springs?"

"Probably all which is left of the original moon," I reply as I shuck off my pants.

My scales are vibrating with the desire for a soak, rattling almost as loud as my heart. My need is so great, I can almost tear my eyes away from Amber to the water.

Then I'm free of my clothing to a gasp from my female.

She is now unable to take her eyes off me. Of one particular part of me. Despite all my need, I put my hands on my hips and return her gaze.

"Well, female. Do you like what you see?"

AMBER

Almost as soon as he's pushed the huge stone over the entrance to the three pools, Draco divests himself of his clothing. I've already seen plenty of him. Enough to know he's built like a carved Greek god, a stunning scaled six-pack which drops to a neat "v" at his waist, then the rest covered by a pair of leather-like trousers.

Trousers which are now long gone and instead I have a very confident male alien, hands on his hips and entirely naked.

Very naked.

Completely naked.

I've seen men naked, of course, but not quite as blatantly as Draco. A blush which could start a forest fire creeps over my face, but the eyes want to see what the eyes want to see and, as I drop my gaze, both intrigued and terrified, I take in the view, the muscular male form, neat, huge, powerful until I reach his waist.

"Well, female. Do you like what you see?" Draco puts his hands on his hips.

There is a very large bulge expanding the scaled skin

over where I would expect to see his junk. It seems heavy as it hangs slightly between his legs. But it is entirely smooth and scaled. There is nothing else on show.

Absolutely not what I was expecting.

"I...er...." I stumble out.

What exactly do you say when you expected alien male parts and there aren't any?

It appears Draco takes my speechlessness for approval as he smirks, raises an eyebrow, then jumps into the pool with a tremendous splash, water firing out in all directions and washing over my feet.

"Hey!" I call out when he resurfaces, flicking his head to shed the water from his hair.

Instead, I get a wicked grin, one filled with sinfulness, as he reaches the side of the pool and looks up at me, water beading on his eyelashes and on the scruff around his chin.

Cute.

I punch the word away in my mind. Draco is many things, but he is not cute. He is a killer.

My killer says nothing, continuing to stare up at me, chin pillowed on his heavy muscular forearms.

"What?" I ask with some annoyance, but mostly at myself.

The last thing I need is to feel anything for this alien or for anyone. My heart is a shriveled thing which will remain so until the end of time. I can't trust, I can't care. I just can't. Not before, not now, not ever again.

Not for a cute, vicious alien.

"I'm just wondering what I have to bargain with in order to get the rest of your secrets, little treasure," he purrs.

God dammit. Just no, universe, no!

"I don't think you can afford me this time." I walk around the narrow edge of the pool away from him to explore, but he follows me in the water, tracking my progress. "After all, I had my life to think about before, but now"—I gesture to my surroundings—"what more can you offer me?"

Draco pushes away from the side, arching his back over, and I see the swish of a tail as he doubles under the water, all glittering scales and male muscles (save for one, apparently), before resurfacing on the other side of the pool where he puts out his arms, resting them on the edge and leaning back with a puff of smoke.

"Then perhaps you are the one with the bargain. What do you want, treasure? Jewels to match your eyes? Fine clothing? The best food the Kirakos has to offer?"

He looks so smug now he's in the pool, his skin and wound to his abdomen obviously isn't bothering him as much. A big, gorgeous, smug alien with cheekbones I could cut myself on and eyes I could lose myself in.

"Can you actually get me any of that?" I fold my arms and mock tap my foot. "Or are you all mouth, big guy?"

This time, I only just see the wake of water as he dives under and explodes out of it next to me, arms wrapping around my waist. I just have time to squeak out a brief exclamation before I'm pulled into the bath hot water, all the time my head kept carefully above the surface as Draco holds me in strong arms, my back against his chest.

He puts his lips on my ear. "I can get you whatever you want. This place is not a prison for me, and you, my *szikra*, are my key."

I wriggle in his arms, and he releases his grip, meaning I can turn around to face him, my legs unaccountably straddling his waist as he holds us both easily in the warm water. I can't deny it feels good. I haven't been able to bathe other than the occasional strip wash to make myself slightly more fragrant since I got to the maze prison.

But Draco is slippery, and I find myself sliding down his muscled abdomen and landing on...

This is not a bulge.

This is not his tail.

I risk a glance down and see the most enormous appendage shimmering under the water. The water is clear enough I can see the monster between his legs. It's heavily ridged, large scales covering the entire thing, each one making it look almost armored. Each one making it look like a dream sex toy. The tip—I'm not entirely sure I can make it out, but it seems to have a sort of hook.

And the entire thing was not there when he dropped his pants. But boy! It's there now.

"But how?" I gasp at him.

A slow, lazy, dirty smile spreads over Draco's face. "My cock is always safely pouched, my sweet, until it is time to use it."

My mouth drops open. *Pouched?*

"And you want to use it?" My voice is hoarse, hardly audible.

"I want to give you the utmost pleasure, Amber. I want to worship you until you can't scream my name anymore," Draco rasps.

It's then I realize the scrap of material I'm still wearing has gone completely see through, and Draco's eyes are blazing like he's about to burst into flames.

DRACO

My mating gland is pumping in my chest as if it's about to break lose and batter its way out of my body. I can feel the mix filling my bloodstream.

I am in rut.

My cock, so nevving uncomfortable in my pouch, burst through my slit the second I took hold of Amber. The second my gland enlarged, the second I sucked her sweet scent into my nostrils, untainted by the maze, by anything at all, the warm water amplifying it.

My need to shed is so great, I thought my pouch sealed shut and I was safe from the need to mate her.

Except, I am in rut.

I can't believe I'm in rut.

Amber shudders in my arms, her huge, beautiful, stormy eyes blinking at me, her long hair plastered to her head. By the bones of my ancestors, I want to bury myself in her.

Because she is my female, and females need to be worshipped before they are mated, or else a Sarkarnii male risks losing parts of his anatomy. So, I carry her over to the edge of the pool and lift her out of the water, parting her thighs so I can take a look at what smells so glorious, even under the water.

All Sarkarnii warriors are given lessons on female anatomy because if you get things wrong, your female will not be best pleased, and the chances are, not only will you be unable to mate, but she will insist you grovel at her feet for ticks on end, with a raging pouched cock and all the mating mix extruded by the gland filling your system, setting you ablaze with no respite.

I run my hands up the inside of Amber's thighs, and her breath huffs on my head. As I touch her, my tail uncurls, my scales harden, becoming completely visible, and my horns extend.

"Do you want this, little treasure?" I'm bound, stuck, staring at her gorgeous pussy, but I need to know what she wants. "I rut for you, and I have to taste."

I need to know she wants me. I bargained with her for her life.

Amber is different to my lessons. Her pink slit is hairless like a Sarkarnii, but that's where the similarity ends. It is filled with pretty folds I want to explore and already moist with her desire. I will still need to dance for her, but not yet.

"Yes." The word hangs on her breath. Her eyes are closed, and her body vibrates under my touch as I slide my hands farther up her thighs, parting them even more so I can drink in my fill of her delicious scent.

When my tongue whips out, gently swiping over her skin, she shakes and gasps.

"Draco! You really do have two tongues!"

I lift my head away from her gorgeous cunt and smile

up at her, the tips of my forked tongue popping out from between my lips, and hiss.

"All the better for devouring you, *szikra*." I bury myself back between her legs, and she cries out.

My horns lock into place and instantly, Amber's hands are on them. At the same time, the collar whines under the pressure of a half shift. I know it's a risk. The last thing I want is to be rendered insensible with a shock, not when I'm so close to giving pleasure to this delicious morsel.

But I can't help myself in the presence of this female, of my Amber. I want to give her everything I am, as much as I am.

By the bones, I want to give her my cock and seed! But females have to be prepared, and I will have to settle for tasting her deliciousness instead.

This time.

I lap my way through her soft folds, my forked tongue ensuring I get as much of her in my mouth as I can. Amber arches her back and her grip on my horns increases, causing my un-pouched cock to release a stream of pre-cum into the water. She gets instantly wetter, her moisture like nectar on my tongue.

Who knew females could taste this good? She is intoxicating. I have no recollection of who I am or where I am. All I have is this perfect cunt and my tongue, sliding inside her, finding a sweet little pearl of delight under a protective hood which makes her squeal with delight. The more I touch it, tease it, enjoy it, the more she floods me with her essence.

I slip in a digit, to find she is incredibly, incredibly tight. Too tight to take a Sarkarnii male maybe? Then, as I delve deeper, my tongues working at her little bundle, my finger curling inside her, exploring her heat, Amber cries out my name, and her entire body convulses. Her sweet, sweet cunt clamps onto me, then expands, then clamps again, her spasms growing more and more intense, as moisture covers my fingers, my tongue, and my hand.

Amber exhales with a low moan, her body continuing to pulse. I carefully, slowly clean her up, savoring every last drop, and I can turn my attention to my hand and fingers.

She looks at me from under heavily lidded eyes, her face a mask of pleasure.

"I would worship you like that every time we mate, my perfection. If you wish it." My words are slightly slurred with the pleasure of consuming this treat, this female. *My mate.*

But I can't possibly take a mate. Not here in the maze, in this prison. It would be suicide for her and for me.

And yet when she blinks at me, her eyes still clouded with the delights I gave her, I know I have no choice. Amber is mine, regardless of what I want or how I want it.

Which makes the anger roaring within me, already loud, grow to a deafening level. I have her.

Nothing will take her from me.

AMBER

I'm dazed, wrecked with pleasure, with everything Draco has just done to me, wringing me out as if he's tasted human all his life. Until a whining sound brings me somewhat back to my senses. It's coming from Draco, from his collar.

"What's happening?" My voice is hoarse with screaming out his name, and my cheeks are already too hot to flame more.

"I am in rut," he rasps, licking his lips with his incredibly naughty tongue. "I have to shed, and I have to mate. The only way I can shed is to shift. The collar prevents me from shifting."

"Oh," I say, and his eyes flare as my mouth forms the words.

He takes in a deep breath and manages, for a second, to tear his eyes away from mine.

"I am Sarkarnii. I have two forms, the one you have been seeing and another, larger form, very different. Without my collar, I could shift between each form at will. With the collar, attempts to shift are punished, and it is also supposed to continually feed a narcotic into my bloodstream to suppress the shift, although we disabled that part a long time ago."

I can see him attempting to get his tail under control as the collar continues to sound. He pushes away from the side, away from me, and dips under the surface. The noise is muffled, and I see him start to writhe, and individual scales pop up onto the surface of the water.

When he comes back up, he uses his vicious, vicious claws, raking down his torso with a low groan of pleasure as some of the skin slips free. Slowly, sensually, he moves his claws over his arms, and the sounds increase as more scales slide away. His voice echoes around the pool chamber, deep and warm. As if I needed a reminder of what he just did to me, my pussy clenches.

"I feel like I should leave you alone," I say in an attempt to cover my embarrassment at yet again allowing my body to yield to this huge alien.

"Or you could help me," he suggests with a wicked glint. "After all, you did agree to be mine."

Yet again, he's brought up our bargain, the one which seemed to have me attending to him rather than the other way around.

Only the incredible orgasm he just gave me with his double tongue—I've never experienced anything like it.

I can see that some of the skin is stuck, just at the back of his neck, and because I'm British, I feel it would only be polite to do what he asks, given what he just did for me. So, I slip off the side of the pool back into the water and make my way over to him.

Draco's chest is heaving as I reach him. I'm not sure if it's because of the watery acrobatics he's just been performing, but I bump up against him, and he closes his eyes, a rumbling deep within him I don't really understand.

So, I put one hand on his shoulder, and with the other, I reach around to the back of his neck. Almost instantly, his skin begins to slither off him, dropping away as he bucks against it, finally slipping free. He bursts from the water, his tail, seemingly huge, firing him upwards in a riot of black and gold.

He is magnificent, powerful, and he just brought me to almost oblivion with only his tongue...his two tongues.

I am dependent on him. I belong to him.

After everything which has happened to me.

I shove myself away from Draco as hard as I can, not wanting him to see the tears in my eyes, even if he understands for a second what they are. For some reason, I managed to kid myself that being with him meant I wasn't alone.

But I am alone. I am as alone as I ever was. Trapped in an alien prison with a huge reptilian alien who controls this place.

Who controls me.

And in that moment, his of distraction, mine of horrible realization, it doesn't matter what words he says, how sweet they might seem. I am a mouse in a maze regardless.

I heave myself out of the water and run down the edge of the pool. I have no idea where I'm going, and given Draco locked us in, there isn't anywhere for me to go, but I have to run.

It's the only thing I've ever been any good at.

I reach the waterfall, not even able to take in how pretty it is, sparkling with water and jewels. All I can see is the dark alcove behind it, and I dart inside.

It's warm, like the rest of the place, and it leads into a

passageway, a little like the others Draco led me through on the way here. I scrub at my face, attempting to clear my eyes of tears, but it doesn't work. My vision remains blurred because my heart is a stone and my life is a disaster.

The passage opens out into a small chamber, one lined with stone shelving. The light is lower in here, but I still have nowhere to hide. From Draco or myself. My legs shake hard, and I sink onto the floor, knowing if I don't, I will fall.

Why did I even run? Why am I here? All the horrors of the last weeks, the last years, crowd in on me, shrinking my world down to just one tiny pinprick of life.

Mine. It is no life. It is nothing. I am nothing. There is nothing.

And then something warm and unyielding envelopes me.

"I don't know what ails you, little treasure," Draco murmurs in my ear. "And if I find out anything in this maze has caused you such distress, I will ensure I seek it out and you can tell me which parts you require to be removed. I will do your every bidding."

I want to keep my eyes closed, pretend nothing is happening, pretend nothing has happened. But the scent of Draco, all smoke and musk, is strong. Stronger than ever. So, I open them and find I'm pressed up against a heavy wall of scales which shine like they've been polished.

"So, you've shed then?" I hear myself say.

Maybe it was enough of a distraction to help me recover my wits, although I still feel numb, as if all of this is happening to someone else.

"All I needed was a bath and a female," Draco says, with a voice as smooth as silk.

"Who knew?" I laugh, but it comes out weird, and somehow, I can't stop it.

Until he dips his head into my neck, and I feel his lips on my skin, a rough forked tongue lapping at me.

"You taste of a promise I need to break, female," he growls. "But first I want to get you back in my quarters. Then we need to talk.

I don't know why, but his desire to talk is maybe the scariest thing Draco has done so far.

And the sweetest.

DRACO

I don't know what to do about this female in my arms. I shouldn't have her at all. I shouldn't be rutting for her, and I shouldn't be desiring her.

She shouldn't be my *szikra,* my heartsfire. But everything within me tells me that she is.

And yet again the words 'worst possible moment' cross my mind. She is a piece of treasure held out to tempt me away from my mission.

I have to go on this run. I have to make it to the end. There are no more chances left. And I know Draxx won't survive much longer without being able to shift.

But when Amber ran from me, it was as if my heart was split in two. Even my mating gland faltered. Half shed, it took me far too long to shrug off my remaining scales and get out of the pool, to follow her.

To catch her.

At the same time, I heard a commotion outside the pool room. A commotion which could only ever be made by Xicop guards.

I've led my female right into a trap. Or I've been led into one.

No one traps Draco.

Amber seems contrite when I reach her, unable to look at me. She's floppy in my arms, and yet again, my heart is beating out of my chest when I see her. I know I have to harden it, to make her tell me what she knows, but as I hold her, I'm unable to stop myself from tasting her. My tongues swipe over her skin, and I already know too much.

I gently place her on her feet and take her tiny hand in mine. Humans are so nevving delicate, it's amazing they survive at all.

Only Amber has survived, despite all the odds against her, which arouses even more suspicion. Even as my mating gland restarts and my veins fill with the mix again, I tamp it back as much as I can and lead her over to the back wall.

"Here you go, my little key," I croon at her.

If I've been given this female, I might as well use her. Amber looks up at me, blinking away the water in her eyes. "I've always believed there was another way out of this place," I say, to motivate her. "Can you find it?"

She turns back to the blank surface and runs her hands over it for a while. Behind us, I hear the sounds of the stone being slowly rolled back. I know the guards can move it, if they want to, although generally they don't want to disturb a shedding Sarkarnii, collared or not.

Today, they want to move it, and if I want to get back to the relative safety of my quarters, I need my key to work for me.

Finally, one of her long, clawless fingers finds something, and she pushes it in with a click. I reach for her as the nevving ground opens up under us and we fall into a long shaft.

"Nev this nevving maze!" I pull Amber into me, enclosing her soft, fragrant, and damp form, as we slide down.

I don't want to go down at all. Down is not good. Not for the first time in the Kirakos, I'm wishing I had a weapon, any weapon, because I'm going to need it.

Amber clings to me, and it's all I can do to attempt to hold back the mating gland, which is pumping harder than ever. Her proximity makes the rut even harder to resist.

We spin in the tube until she is on top of me and I'm descending, head first to whatever fate is coming our way.

"I'm so sorry, Draco!" she cries out, face filled with anguish. "I should have known it would do this!"

Yet again, there is something more about Amber, more about what she is, and I need to find out. I was a curious male once, a long time ago, when being curious was all I needed to do other than train and learn about leading my armies.

When life was simpler.

When I didn't need to be the hardest, baddest inmate in a prison maze.

But I do now, or we'd all be dead. All my den warriors, my brothers.

"Which is what we need to talk about," I say, just as an opening speeds into view, and I brace myself for the inevitable exit. My scales are still soft from the shed, and this is going to hurt...

I hit the ground hard, bracing myself and ready to protect my little treasure, but as we slam into the floor, she is thrown off me, and I watch with horror as she bounces onto her shoulder, crying out in pain as she slides across the floor and hits a wall, where she lies deathly still.

I'm on my feet with a snarl of feral need on my lips, just

as my collar buzzes and fires an electric shock through my system, enough to put me on my knees, even with the rut filling my veins.

"Ah, Draco." The nasty, nasally voice is instantly recognizable. "I see you have a new toy."

"Warden Noro." I grit my teeth and manage, just, to raise my head.

The skinnier version of Warden Gondnok has decided to attend on me in person. This doesn't bode well for anyone, especially me, as it means I'm in a part of the maze controlled by him.

But it's not the warden I care about. It's Amber, who still hasn't moved. I'm completely incapacitated by the initial shock I was unprepared for, and all I want to do is get to her.

A pincer grips my jaw, and my head is turned one way, then another before I'm shoved away again by the hard shelled Rak guard who also doubles as Noro's personal protection.

"She helped you shed anyway. I know you needed it."

"The state of my scales is of no concern to you, Noro."

"On the contrary, everything in the Kirakos is my concern, Draco, especially you."

He leans in, but the shock they gave me is wearing off, and I snarl, snapping my teeth, causing him to retreat quickly.

"You're doing this next run, aren't you?" he asks, attempting to appear nonchalant.

"What do you think?" I'm free of my skin, no longer irritable and distracted. I have my Amber to protect and my mission to accomplish. The last thing I'm going to allow is Noro to cause me any problems. "Of course I'm going on the run. When did my brothers and I not run?"

"I'm so pleased to hear you say that, Draco." He grins horribly at me as the Rak sidles over to Amber and lifts her limp form up.

Before I can go completely insane, another shock runs down my spine from the collar, stopping my lunge towards her and leaving me lying on my side.

I watch helplessly as the Rak fastens a smaller version of the collar like mine around Amber's pretty neck, then adds two cuffs to her wrists.

"If you take her from me," I growl, unable to stop myself, "I will find you all, and I won't just kill you, I'll grind you into dust, piece by nevving piece."

I'm attempting to get the feeling back in my limbs, but the Rak is already towering over me. He takes each arm in turn and clips on matching cuffs.

"I'm absolutely sure you will. A Sarkarnii in rut is an unstoppable force, or so you were, I understand"—Noro smiles nastily—"before you had this." He taps at his neck as an indication of my collar. "Such a shame, as I believe you were virtually invincible in your true form.

Still too far from me, Amber moans, her head falling to one side, and my attention is completely captured by her. The Rak drags me bodily across the floor, and her scent fills my nostrils.

Then they are filled with another scent, one which is disgusting at the best of times, but in rut, it is downright unbearable. Noro is crouched next to me, obviously feeling that this time, he's safe.

"Not that it's easy to stop you now, Draco, so I'm going to do my best. Humans are, according to the scientists I bought them from, the most compatible species with the Sarkarnii." He shifts position, and my nose is assaulted again. "Something about their ancestors, which I'm sure you'll appreciate. I had this one treated with a little something to make her more interesting to you, but apparently that wasn't necessary."

Then he grabs hold of both her wrist and mine, and, before the snarl even leaves my lips, he clips them together with a laugh.

"I want to make this run a little more interesting for my clients, given you are the most likely to be successful. Let's see just how easy it is for you to run with your little female in tow."

AMBER

My wrist is wrenched almost to the point of breaking as the slimy centipede alien pulls it up against Draco's, and with a weird clunk, the cuffs we both wear stick together.

"The female's collar contains an explosive which is primed to go off if it detects the cuffs being removed or tampered with, just in case you were thinking about attempting to get free, either of your cuffs or hers. The collar will also deploy if you try to get it off." The centipede alien displays a dark mouth filled with rotten teeth in a grimace which might be a smile.

He's getting off on this, enjoying it even.

"And if you were thinking you could just dispose of the female and be done, there is enough explosive in her collar to make a mess of any Sarkarnii in the vicinity."

Draco huffs out a long curl of smoke from each nostril, his pupils just narrow slits and fixed on the other alien, who steps back in what seems like quite a hasty manner.

"Once you're quite recovered, you'll find the way back to your quadrant through that door, although it will be quite the trek, I suspect. Maybe you'll have time to prepare for the run, or maybe you'll just give in to my demand."

My big alien says nothing. His gaze flicks away and onto the ceiling.

If the centipede guy was expecting something more, he isn't going to get it, and I suspect I'm the only one close enough to see the muscle ticking in Draco's jaw as he attempts to control his temper.

I just wish I hadn't come around at the point the centipede told him I'd been *given something* to make me irresistible to him. The thought makes my stomach churn. Not only for Draco but because, somehow, something deep within me, something I thought long hidden, long lost, is nipping at my heart.

I want Draco to want me. All of this is overwhelming, but he has become my constant. If he's been tricked into wanting me, it means he doesn't and inexplicably, it makes my heart hurt.

A heart which can't possibly be touched, I caged it so thoroughly. I never gave it to anyone, least of all my ex, but by the time he'd trampled all over me, I already knew.

No one was having it ever again.

The centipede alien and his friend who looks like a cross between a lobster and an octopus beat a retreat through an open doorway, while Draco lies still, presumably contemplating whether it is possible to divest himself of me with a minimum of injury to himself.

And I wouldn't blame him. He thought I was one thing, and I turned out to be something completely different.

I've been there too. I know how it rips at your soul.

But with Draco, I'm more concerned about how he will react—to me and to everything else. Which is why his stillness and silence is worrying.

Eventually, he slowly stretches out a leg and grumbles a low growl. "Finally. I thought the nevving feeling would never come back."

The second leg shifts, then one arm. Then the arm attached to me. Without meaning to, I squeak in alarm.

"Looks like you're not getting rid of me after all, treasure." Draco pulls me closer to him and examines the cuff.

I'm treated to a very up close and personal view of his new scales, which I only caught a glimpse of earlier. These ones seem to be full of stars, twinkling with light under the surface. I'm not sure if I've ever seen anything more beautiful.

Draco also smells completely amazing, like the best wood smoke, with undertones of musky sweetness I can't help but inhale.

And I realize he's stopped inspecting the cuff, and his intent gaze is on me entirely.

"I don't want to be rid of you," I say. "We made a bargain, after all," I add and immediately regret the words as Draco narrows his eyes.

"We did make a bargain, but apparently there was no need. You were always to be mine."

He displays his impressive set of fangs and then carefully gets to his feet. I have no option but to follow suit, and every single muscle in me cries out. I hiss in pain. I might have bounced in on Draco when we hit the ground, but after that, every other bounce was on my body.

"Amber?" I have an incredibly handsome face in mine, a clawed hand under my chin, a pair of eyes staring into mine. I can't deny I'd like to lose myself in those eyes, filled as they are with fire and ice.

"I'm fine. Just a few scrapes," I say.

"And I made a bargain to protect you, little creature," Draco says.

"I didn't know," I blurt out. "About being given something to make you want me. I just woke up in a white room and had to run and run, that's all. I ran for such a long time. Weeks, maybe, I don't know, just long. I've always been running, always. It seems like it will never end."

I don't want to cry, not again, but the tears flow regardless of my wishes. Draco swipes a thumb over my cheek.

"I thought this was from the pools, but this water comes from you." His brow furrows. "Why?"

"It's called tears. Something humans do." I use my free hand to wipe at my tears, but it's batted away by Draco. "When we're sad, or angry, or happy."

"Seems like a strange thing to do for all those emotions." He puts the pad of his thumb to his mouth, tongues lapping at it with a considered expression on his face.

"It is." I gasp out a soggy laugh.

"I meant it, Amber. I meant every word. Everything I said. A Sarkarnii only ruts for their true mate, their heartsfire, their *szikra*. You are my *szikra*. No narcotic can fool the mating gland. You belong to me, and I will dance for you to prove it."

DRACO

Why did I promise her a dance? The rut has taken over my rational mind. I should be heeding all the warning signs. Warden Noro and the unsaid indication he might be responsible for her being in the maze. The possibility she has been somehow enhanced to send me into rut, the timing of her arrival with my desperate need to shed.

Only the rut doesn't lie. The mating gland doesn't lie. Very few species understand Sarkarnii physiology, and there's nothing Amber could have been given which would send me, or any other of my kind, into a pseudo-rut.

Which means what I am feeling is completely real, and I really, really don't know what to do about it. The indecision burns within me like unused accelerant.

I have a mate. I am in rut.

And because Noro wants the map as much as I do, I am now, quite literally, bound to her.

"A dance?" Amber sniffs as I wipe the remainder of the *tears,* as she calls them, from her face.

I lick at my fingers and taste her salty sweetness,

marveling at how she can taste so different between the liquid from her eyes and the moisture from her gorgeous cunt.

"It's nothing, *szikra*. Forget I mentioned it."

Amber cocks her head on one side, and the delicious boldness I witnessed for such a short while seems to reassert itself.

As does my cock, pushing out from my pouch and running with pre-cum. The only saving grace is I was able to pull on my pants before we left the pool, and she can't see how she affects me.

"I am going to mention it."

I release a snarl of delight as I pull her against me. She shivers, squirms, and pants out a breath as I hold her wrists in my hands, marveling at just how tiny she is.

"A Sarkarnii dances for his mate, but I don't have time to dance right now, so unless you want me to mate you insensible right here on this floor until you run with my seed and cannot see straight, I suggest we get out of here before something else finds us." I give the wrist which is bound to mine a little shake. "This makes us vulnerable, and we need to get back to my quadrant as soon as possible, where my brother can release us."

Amber sucks in a breath. "But the centipede guy—he said if you try to get free, we'll explode."

"Warden Noro has tremendous faith in his tech builders." I grin down at her. "But I have greater faith in my brother, just as long as we can reach him before the run."

"What is a run?" she asks, and the innocence which flows from her nearly convinces me she shouldn't be in the Kirakos.

"You know." I'm unable to keep the snarl from my voice. I shouldn't have told her about the dance. I shouldn't continue to entertain the pretense she is here against her will. Amber knows things, she has to. Females were always our strategists. And I am a fool for thinking otherwise.

Her eyes are wide. "I don't know anything, Draco."

"Really?" I hold up our cuffed wrists. "Then how come you were given to me by Noro?"

She pulls away from me but can't get far. "I wasn't. I told you, I didn't have contact with anyone, as far as I can remember, before I met you."

"Oh, I think you do, little morsel. And you can't get away from me, even if you want to." I spin her, slamming her body against mine, making sure she feels my strength and arousal, because despite not knowing what Amber is, I am in rut for her.

"I'm a prisoner here, Draco, just like you, only I've done nothing wrong," she says, and her eyes are defiant, her voice blazing, a finger poking into my chest. "And now I'm also attached to you under a shadow of death, so how about you explain to me what the hell is going on here, and maybe we'll both get through this with our body parts still attached."

By the ever nevving bones of my ancestors, an angry Amber is completely glorious. I might still be suspicious as to how she came to be in my presence, but nev it, I don't even want to deny how she sends me wild. Her body is tense against me, and it's making me even harder.

"I think you're right, *szikra*."

"And another thing..." she fires out, then her face turns confused, her body relaxing slightly. "Wait. I'm *right*?"

"Absolutely. I'm sure you are just a piece of deliciousness released to distract me."

Amber bristles with annoyance at the suggestion, and if I thought it wasn't possible to get any harder, it turns out it is. She is so easy to tease, and at the same time the scent from her promises so much.

Promises of mating, promises of protection, promises I will get to my run, and I will complete it.

And I'll give her everything she's ever wanted and more.

"Well, maybe that is possible. I can't think why else I would be here," she concedes. "But that still doesn't deal with the explosion issue, does it?"

"Not yet. First we have to return to my quadrant. Get Drega to have a look at these collars." I poke at mine and get the usual warning signal.

The one around Amber's neck looks tight, her skin reddening underneath it.

"Good." She looks around us. "So, which way?"

"Ah." I lift my arm to rub at the back of my neck, some vestiges of my shed still remaining just at the very top, but it's the arm attached to hers, and Amber squeaks. I gently lower it and wrap my other arm around her waist. "That is where I'm hoping you come in, little mate."

"Why?" Amber looks confused, but she doesn't try to pull away from me.

"You are a key."

"A key?" she repeats. "What do you mean?"

"You have an ability to find the hidden doors in the maze, the shortcuts. If you are what I think you are, we should reach my quadrant within a tick or two."

"You mean we've got to spend the night out here? In the maze?" Amber says. "Stuck together? What if something tries to eat us?"

I'm not entirely sure why any of those options are a problem. I incline my head and look her over.

"The only thing likely to eat you out here, *szikra*, is me."

AMBER

I know Draco thinks I have more information than I'm letting on, and I wish I did. I wish to god I knew why I ended up here, and I'm still fucking running or at the mercy of everyone who wants something from me.

Now he's looking at me in such a way I feel like he wants me to perform, and suddenly a bone-aching tiredness floods through me. I'm just not sure I can do any of this anymore. I certainly don't want to spend any more time out in the maze than is strictly necessary.

"I'm very well aware of what you can do, Draco," I say, attempting to keep any heat out of my voice. "I'm just wondering how well you can make good on our bargain, now we're out of your quadrant?"

I don't want him to forget how I ended up with him in the first instance. I'm taking a risk, I know I am, but we're handcuffed together, and it can't exactly get any worse.

Draco leans into me until his lips are right next to my ear, a curl of smoke wrapping around my throat. "If anyone or anything dares to touch a hair on your head, I will remove theirs from their body and offer it to you as a gift. Will that do as an assurance?"

For a second, I don't want to move. I don't even want to breathe. If Draco wanted to remind me of just how vicious and feral he is to those who displease him, having him this damn close, his heat swelling from his skin, the scent of him, all fiery and smokey, does it. If I inhale, I'm back to where I was at the pool.

At his mercy.

"Will it do, female?" he growls, and I feel myself growing very hot in a very specific place.

Aliens don't do knickers, so I don't have any to destroy, although Draco is very clearly a knicker demolisher when he wants to be.

I'm not sure I've ever been as turned on by anyone in my entire life as I am with him. It's completely insane. He's a seriously dangerous alien, with two tongues, a cock I just daren't think about because under the water it was magnified to a proportion which had to be entirely wrong, claws like a grizzly, a temper on a knife edge, and he has to be no good for me at all.

Plus, as I watch the smoke whisper out of his nostrils again, he's something I can't even fathom. I can't use any of my coping mechanisms to even start to unpick what Draco is.

All I know is he made my body sing like no one ever did on Earth, and for a moment, I was truly alive again. It's the reason I ran.

It's the reason we're bound together by this ridiculous cuff, and I have a collar around my neck which feels like it's cutting off my circulation.

But he also offered to dance for me. He said I was his heartsfire, his 'mate', and another word which didn't translate, and I don't know what any of it means. From the serious look on his face then and now, every single bit of what he said was true.

And yet, how can I trust anyone, anything, when my life for the last three years has been a living hell of running and hiding from a man who also told me I was his and who wouldn't take no for an answer.

Only when Draco says it, when he calls me his, I don't die inside. Instead, a little tiny spark flutters as if it's trying to become a fire.

And I don't know what to think anymore, but I don't want to get burned.

"Are we good?" Draco leans back a little, nonchalantly, as if he hasn't just offered to kill for me.

I consider my responses but think '*Hell, no. You're a stone cold killer*' probably won't help anyone. Instead, I nod.

Draco wraps his massive hand around mine, and we exit the room by the same open doorway the weird centipede alien and his lobster friend used. I'm pushed behind Draco's super shiny scaly body as he checks for, presumably, a neon snake or his equivalent, then I'm ushered out and into a dank corridor.

W e have been walking forever, and nothing seems to have changed other than us taking the occasional left turn, which makes me think we're going around in circles. Draco remains, as far as I can tell, confident we're going somewhere, but my feet are in a state. I have several blisters, including one on the side of my little toe I think might have started bleeding.

"Can we stop for a while?" I ask Draco and try not to sound whiny.

"We need to get to the main maze before nightfall. We don't want to be caught in the undercroft for any longer than necessary."

"Does it really matter? It's not like there's actually night and day here," I grumble, but at least Draco has stopped, and I can drop down onto a large piece of what appears to be concrete to rest.

The passageways we have been using are decrepit. Green mold on the walls which are crumbling in dust, incessant drips of cold water (or at least I hope it's water) constantly hitting my head or running down my neck, stones I keep tripping over or stubbing my toes on. It's grim.

I lift my foot to inspect my skin and discover one enormous blister running down the side of my little toe, filled with fluid. It needs to burst, but the filth in this place has me worried about infection.

"It does matter...ugh." Draco is on his knees next to me and grabbing at my foot. "What is this?"

"This is what happens when you drag a woman around for hours," I growl. "She gets blisters."

The grimace on Draco's face is pretty impressive. I wonder if he's ever seen anything like it, given his skin looks so tough.

"So nevving delicate," he grumbles. "Looks like I'm going to have my work cut out with you." He hitches a lip over a fang in a semblance of a smile as he gently turns my foot one way, then the other in a careful inspection.

"I survived you, didn't I?" I slap my hand on his chest and feel the rumble I create underneath his shiny scales.

I use his huge bulk to get back on my feet and slide my shoe back on.

"Not for much longer if you continue to behave like that, Amber," he says with a huff of smoke. "I'm still in rut."

"And you told me you'd dance for me." I look up, keeping my expression even but knowing the reminder will irk this huge, muscled alien. A muscle ticks in his jaw.

I'm beginning to think I got the best end of the bargain after all.

DRACO

The competing desires inside me are almost as bad as not being able to shift. I've been used to getting my own way for a long time, especially in the Kirakos. I didn't need to protect my brothers beyond the usual. I didn't need to protect anything other than my seat of power.

And now I have Amber. A female I rut for, I want to dance for, I want to protect with my entire soul. But then there is the run and the plan I've been working toward for all these ev's. We have endured the maze in order to get to the map, to get to the heart of the Kirakos and to take it all. Draxx for one has nearly lost his mind.

I can't give it all away, for her, can I?

Her soft, lush body is pressed against mine, still in the filthy rags she wore when I found her, and I hate I haven't been able to properly provide what she needs. Even her delicate feet are evidence of my failure.

I never fail because I am Draco. Yet my female still has sore feet, and she still needs food and rest.

And this is not my quadrant.

"I am sorry we have had to walk so far. I want to put as much distance between Warden Noro and us before venturing back up into the maze itself as possible. The closer we get to my quadrant, the better the chances are of finding assistance," I explain to Amber.

I don't add that they will expect payment because nothing on Kirakos is ever free.

"So, the centipede guy was one of the wardens here?" Amber asks, holding herself like any creature in pain.

But she is refusing to submit to it, in the same way she doesn't submit to me. For some reason, her defiance—of her own delicacy, of me—it makes my heart pound.

Fortunately her description of Noro pulls me back to the present.

"Warden Noro is a Belek. Only Belek can be wardens."

"And the other one, which looked like a lobster?"

I shake my head, unable to stop the smile. "I have no idea what a *lob-ster* is, my Amber, but his species is a Rek. He's just the hired muscle."

"Didn't look much like muscle to me, more shellfish," Amber grumbles incomprehensibly, looking at our cuffs. "That's something we have as food on my planet," she adds as an explanation.

"Wouldn't fancy a Rek as food. Far too bitter," I reply, and Amber laughs.

The sound is a little tinkle in the dim light and musty scents of the undercroft passageways. It's a delight which creeps under my scales, my brand new scales, and settles itself in my skin. I have pleased my female with my tongue but in another way.

She finds me amusing, and I never thought I'd like being found amusing. But I want to make Amber laugh every tick, every seccari.

"Little key?" I stop in front of an incongruous blank wall. "We should be far enough from the warden-controlled areas. Do you think you could find a way through?"

I set her down on her feet, and she holds the injured one up gingerly against her leg. Nev it! I want to get her to Drega, get her feet seen to. I want her back in my quadrant, back in my quarters, so I can pleasure her again.

"I don't know, Draco," she says, looking at the wall. "I don't know why you think I'm some sort of key. I've just been lucky."

"Luck doesn't exist in the Kirakos." I tell her, staring at the wall. "It is made. For whatever reason, you are able to find the hidden doors where others cannot."

Amber hums to herself and then moves forward. As she lifts her hand, she takes me with her, and I follow her movements as she tracks over the surface.

"Nothing," she says, her beautiful eyes reaching mine. She bites her bottom lip with concern, and my cock jerks hard against my pouch.

"Try over here." I help her a little farther down the wall, where it turns into a small alcove.

"I don't think there is anything, Draco. It's just a..." Her hand pauses. She looks at the ground and then at me.

"I'm ready, *szikra*," I tell her. "Wherever it may lead."

Her free hand grips mine, and she takes in a deep breath, and her tiny, clawless finger presses itself into the wall.

There is a whirr and a click.

I feel her tense.

And the wall folds forward, swinging away from us, just as there is a sound at my back. I swing around to see a shadow, and I immediately grab for Amber, pull her against me, and barrel through the doorway, slamming the thing closed behind us with my foot.

"Wait! What's going on?" Amber says, her voice muffled.

"Yeykok. We need to get as far away from here as possible."

Of all the nevving things we could have encountered in the undercroft, the last thing I wanted to attract was the shadowy yeykok. But my little *szikra* doesn't need to know the details.

All she needs to know is she's safe, with me.

AMBER

Draco picks up the pace, which should be fine, only it jostles our respective cuffs together and causes them to pinch and rub. I feel like a burden compared to him, with his strong, beautiful scales, body, and mind. Draco's never been afraid a day in his life, I can tell.

And yet, I don't feel afraid of him either. More than ever before, I'm beginning to wonder who made the bargain with whom.

Branches whip past me as Draco continues to move swiftly through the maze. Above us, the light is fading, so, like he says, there is a night and day in this hellish place. Which would explain the foliage in this part at least.

It's completely different from the other area, the place Draco calls his Instead of smooth stone walls, these look ancient, as if made out of carved stone or weathered brick and dark colored mortar. The vegetation sticking out of it is blackened as if it's been burned.

"Nev! Nev! Nev!" Draco chants to himself.

"What's wrong?"

"Nothing, my *szikra*," he says, and I fold my arms, tugging at his and making him look down.

"I'm not an idiot, Draco. I'm also able to run too, if you put me down."

"But your foot?"

"Humans are tougher than we look."

His eyes dart right and left. "We're not so far from my quadrant, but we'll have to use the maze. There are no secret doors here. This is the yeykok area, and they don't like being disturbed."

"So, when I was reluctant to use my so called abilities to open another hidden door, basically I was right?" I suggest.

Draco lifts his head, attempting to look inscrutable.

But I know I'm right.

"It's not far to the edge of my quadrant. We should be able to get shelter," Draco says. "Some food and something to tend to your wounds."

A strange slithering noise behind us has Draco speeding up. "Just put me down," I exhort him, as I'm bounced all over the place. "I can run. It's the one thing I'm good at."

He winces up his face, but he knows I'm right. It's not like he can throw me over his shoulder, cave...man, style again, not while we're bound together the way we are.

"No," Draco says, his jaw set. He clamps his arms around me, but it twists at my wrist, and I can't help but cry out.

When I'm released, the look of anguish on his face, for a second, is so intense I'm not sure my heart can take it. But then it's gone, to be replaced with the stern handsome face of stone.

"You will run, but if, for any second, you are unable to keep up, I will carry you." He checks behind us and slows his pace, dropping me down his body until I'm on my feet.

My blisters are agony, but it's an agony I can put up with, given that even Draco doesn't want to contend with the things he calls yeykok, and I'm immediately keeping up with him as his hand is curled around mine.

Without my body in his arms, he is light footed and swift.

"Don't look back." He exhorts me onwards.

I might be in pain, but the way he moves makes me want to move faster, work harder, and even though my feet and lungs are burning, running alongside Draco gives me something I haven't felt in forever.

I feel free.

Admittedly, it might just be free to have my limbs ripped out at the base and then sucked clean of flesh while I watch, but for this one tiny moment in what has generally been a pretty terrible experience, being with Draco, all poise and presence, I am alive.

"This way, little mate." Draco has my hand in a death grip as we jink to one side, and a blast of light so bright it's almost painful hits us.

I'm still blinking as I'm thumped against a hard wall which yields just a little against my knackered body and heaving chest. Above me, with the light behind it, I just about make out something dark towering over me, and I feel hot breath on my skin.

"Draco?" I whisper, my voice hoarse with our exertions and because, although I'm still bound to him, for an instant I'm not sure this is Draco.

Smoke fills my lungs, and the dark shape dips to me, a pair of lips on mine. A tongue sweeps over them, parting them, delving inside, splitting, and then both parts entwine with mine. He tastes like a good, sweet bourbon, smoky and delicious. His free hand is in my hair, cupping the back of my head as he dominates my mouth, taking all of me, all at once.

I have my hand on his chest and the one bound to his on his waistband. His skin is smooth, warm and silky to the touch, but it is the kiss to end all kisses which takes me away. When he finally releases me, I'm not entirely sure my knees are going to hold my weight and instead I find myself falling against him.

His heart is racing in his chest, far faster than I would have expected from this giant.

"Amber," Draco rumbles.

Just the way he says my name, rough, like he's smoked a thousand cigarettes but dripping with honey—it's enough to send my knees buckling, only this time I'm caught by a pair of strong arms and, with my feet in shreds, I'm only too willing to allow him to carry me.

This time, his pace is slow and measured. I put my arms around his neck and lean into his warm skin, the flight having taken any final reserves I might have had out of me. My vision is stupidly dim and my head muzzy.

"Come with me, *szikra*. I have found us shelter for the night."

I don't have the breath left in me for the effort of speaking. Draco already took the last of it with a kiss to end all kisses.

And the last thing I think is to wonder how an alien ever got so good at kissing, while my body warms with the additional thought of what else he can do with his tongues.

DRACO

"I require food and medical supplies." I tower over the three Jiaka in the doorway to their quarters. "Now."

They have carved out a reasonable living area in one of the maze walls on the very edge of my quadrant. Made it pretty comfortable for themselves too.

Maybe I've been too nevving generous. Especially when I need weapons and instead these creatures grow fat on my benign rule.

"Yes, Draco." One of them hurries away into the rear of their dwelling.

Amber is still and quiet in my arms. It reminds me of how she was when Warden Noro found us. My heart is thumping in my chest and my foot tapping incessantly. My skin doesn't itch any more, but it feels like my bones want to escape my body because I don't know what's wrong with her.

This isn't the rut, it can't be. Rutting is about mating, about sheathing yourself in a female and entwining your body with hers. It's about enjoyment of her womb, being hooked together, and enjoying every seccari within her, being tamed, being at her mercy.

But to feel like I will die unless I'm by her side? It can't be right. The warden must have done something to me when he had me insensible to make me feel this way.

I prowl around the dwelling, back and forth, unable to keep still, my tail swishing, catching at my feet, my Amber insensible in my arms and my heart thumping in my chest.

A strange squeaking sound brings me back to the remaining Jiaka.

"What the nev is that? Make it stop," I growl.

The smaller of the two Jiaka sidles over to a moving bundle, resting on a cushion.

"It is my young, Draco," it says, bowing low. "And she doesn't understand how to be quiet yet." The Jiaka youngling blinks its...her...three eyes in sequence at me.

The Jiaka have young in the maze?

The concept blindsides me. I open my mouth and close it again. She goes back to fussing over the young who quietens despite her earlier words, a little tentacle shoved into its mouth. It sucks furiously, three eyes not leaving mine.

"Draco." The third Jiaka has returned. He bows low to me, offering up a bag marked with medical insignia. "We will bring you food and drink shortly." He opens a door into a large room, and I stalk over.

It's plain, white, one wall hung with a large tapestry of sorts in a swirl of blues. There's a large bed which should take both me and my *szikra*.

I snort out smoke and step inside.

"Make sure it's something palatable, not the muck you eat," I half snarl as I go to kick the door shut. "And I want a communicator," I call over my shoulder. "Don't tell me you don't have one, not if you want your head to remain on your shoulders."

I slam the door, the weirdness of what I've just witnessed fading as I lay Amber down on the bed. Her long hair, flecked with all the colors of fire and lit by the artificial lights, spreads out over the coverings, and her chest rises and falls gently, evenly.

I pull open the medical kit with my claws, clumsily with only one hand free, and half of it falls to the floor, causing me to curse.

"Draco?" Her soft voice, a little weak, but there all the same, takes away all my fears. "Where are we?"

"In my quadrant, somewhere safe," I grumble as I pick up the fallen items.

There is a swishing sound, and when I look up, she is sat up on the bed, her knees drawn to her chest and her eyes too haunted for my liking.

"Let me tend your wounds." I reach out for one of her bloodied feet, swallowing hard at the sight of my injured mate.

She shuffles away from me, hissing a breath at the pain in her feet, and my anger rises. I promised to protect her.

I did not.

Firing out an arm, I grab her ankle and pull her back to the edge of the bed, and she squeaks in alarm.

"I need to treat you, female. Stay still." My voice is a rasping growl intended to strike fear into my enemies.

Amber makes a sound which twists my heart in two. It gets past the roar of the mating gland, past my anger, past everything. It spears me like nothing else has in my entire life, other than finding my entire species wiped out. But even then, her fear, not of me, but of something else, makes me want to burn the universe.

"Amber?" I'm curling myself around her, using my body to block anything which might hurt her, making sure she is enclosed in my arms. "Whatever it is, I am here for you."

She sucks in the air between her teeth. "It's nothing. Just do what you need to do. I won't move again."

She stills in my arms, her warmth not like mine, not a heat born from fire within, an actual warmth, seeps into me.

I don't want to let her go. "Do you fear me?" I ask, the words breaking.

"No."

"Then tell me what you fear, and I will destroy it."

"So, you will destroy me."

I bend my head down to her, a single claw under her chin as I lift her lips to mine. "Never."

AMBER

Draco teases over my mouth. I don't want him to kiss me because I've already lost my mind once. Except I can't stop myself. I can't stop my back from arching to reach him, the feeling of his clawed fingers on the exposed skin of my neck, tracing over my throat, making my core quake.

I wanted to get away from him because this can't possibly be right. When I opened my eyes and he was there, slightly disheveled, slightly off balance, and yet, absolute perfection, my heart did a thing it shouldn't have.

It let out a beat for him.

And my body wanted to run.

Only this time, I can't run. Not only are my feet shredded and my wrist bound to his, but he holds me. As he tells me he will never let me go, my stupid heart wants to believe him. It wants...him.

I'm lost in his kiss, where his forked tongue caresses mine in direct contrast to the hard, scaled outer part of him. Draco is dominating, possessive, caring, and needy.

"Let me take care of you, *szikra*," he murmurs over my mouth. "Let me be your protector no matter what."

I can't do much more than release a soft moan and then a further sound of disappointment when his lips leave mine and he gently moves me onto the bed and slides down so he can inspect my feet.

After carefully removing my shoes, he goes through the bag of items and inspects each one as he looks over my bloodied feet, then he gets up, tosses me into his arms, goes to the door, and shouts for cleansing cloths and water.

Once I'm back on the bed, Draco kneels in front of me, his bound arm resting beside my thigh, and he stares at me with a gaze so intense, I feel like something small and squeaky being spotted by a hawk.

I have to break the silence. I can't stop myself.

"There was a man...a human man..." I rush out seemingly unable to stop myself. "He thought we should be together, and when I disagreed, he wouldn't leave me alone. I've spent the last three years running from shadows, from him, then I end up here." I attempt to blink away the tears forming in my eyes.

"With me," Draco intones. His voice is velvet with a faint rasp, a hint of smoke releasing from his nostrils.

"With you."

"So, perhaps you are fated after all." He cocks his head to one side, eyes not leaving mine.

I'm about to ask him what he means when there is a knock on the door, and my big, bad alien is on his feet, smoke and...*flames* huffing from his nostrils. My arm dangles in the air, still attached to his.

"Come," he snarls, obviously wanting to put himself between me and the door.

Another alien is there, much smaller and dressed in

what looks like multi-colored rags, three dark eyes blinking discordantly in a pale blue face. It holds up a basin like an offering in the first set of four arms, bowing behind it as Draco is approached like an angry lion.

Behind it, another similar but slightly taller alien stands, with a platter filled with food. The scent wafts through to me, and my stomach rumbles a growl Draco would be proud of.

There are quite a few eyes on me. One of the pale blue aliens makes a shrill sound, shoves the basin into Draco's surprised hand, and scurries away. Draco snarls, and the second alien's multiple eyes widen. The platter is pushed into the other hand, the one with the cuff attached to me, and the creature darts out of the door.

I now have a puzzled Draco looking at his full hands. He looks so comical, all big, brawny, and dominant, with a white chipped basin in one hand and a large platter of food in the other, his brow all furrowed as he attempts to work out what to do with both whilst still wanting to maintain his cool.

In the end, there's a long snort of smoky breath, and he puts the platter down on one side and the basin, which it turns out is filled with warm water, he puts at my feet.

"Put them in."

I obey, and although it stings like mad, I bite on my lip in order not to make any noise. The other aliens are already terrified of Draco, and I don't want to make him mad.

Draco gets back on his knees, and with infinite care, he steadily washes my filthy feet until they're clean enough to be put on the white cloth. Even with our bonds, he manages to make the whole process not so awkward.

I inspect them. "Not as bad as I thought," I say, while he grumbles something under his breath. "It's not your fault whoever brought me here doesn't understand the human need for footwear."

Draco doesn't reply. Instead, he sets about applying a gel like substance over the damaged parts of my feet. After an initial pinch, the stuff is cool and soothing, drying to a slight sheen.

"I'd prefer to have Drega look at your injuries," Draco says. "But we're only just on the edge of my quadrant, and with the maze changes in advance of the run, it will take at least half a tick to get back to my quarters." He looks up at me. "And you need to rest."

"I can make it," I lie.

"What if, little mate, I don't want you to make it?" Draco says, his voice filled with a smoky purr. "What if I have other plans for you?"

This time, the blue skinned aliens don't even knock, one of them instead bustling in with a proprietorial air.

"I brought clothing for the mistress," she says, or at least I make the assumption it is female, given her voice is soft.

Draco initially looks like he's going to actually bite her head off, but then, when he sees the clothes, his demeanor changes. He inclines his head, still looking predatory, and gives her a curt nod.

"Leave us," he growls, rather spoiling the effect. "My female will rest here. We'll be gone in the morning." His eyes reach the clothing again. "I will remember your hospitality," he adds with a slightly more benign tone.

She backs out of the room, keeping all three of her eyes on him, and closes the door. Draco strides over to it, and after a brief inspection, he shoves a large chest which seems to be made of metal and plastic in front of it with a grumble of annoyance.

"'I will remember your hospitality'?" I laugh as he turns back to me. "Where did you learn that line? Villain school?"

Draco whips around, and with more than just a jump, he's in the air, and then I'm flat on my back, my wrists encircled by his huge hands, those slitted pupils just slivers of blackness in his incredible whirling irises.

"I'm your villain, Amber. And I am going to teach you just what a Sarkarnii in rut is willing to do to his female."

DRACO

Amber trembles under me, but not from fear, from anticipation. She uses her unforked tongue to wet her bottom lip, and my cock pushes its way forcefully out of my pouch and is instead constrained by my pants.

By the bones of my ancestors, I want this little female. But not just to rut, although my cock is straining to be sheathed in her. I want her all, every single piece of her.

"Draco," she breathes. "What is this?"

"This is me worshipping you." I nuzzle my head into her neck, gulping down the scent of her skin like a half-starved warrior.

She shifts, raising her hips to bump mine, and hisses a little as she encounters my un-pouched cock, still clad but most definitely interested.

"I don't think you'll fit, Draco," Amber says, biting down on her gorgeous bottom lip.

That she's even contemplating taking me causes more pre-cum to spill freely.

"Sarkarnii males are big." I gaze down at her. "Even for our own females. We have a few tricks to help."

Amber's eyes widen, and she coughs. "Tricks?"

I lean in and brush my lips over hers. "Your pleasure is what makes mine, Amber." Using a single claw, I slowly rip away the remnants of her clothing. She murmurs something in surprise. "You will not be needing garments for some time, little one. What I have planned will take us through to morning, I promise you."

"So, this is how you intend to fulfill our bargain?" Amber's eyes are bright, jeweled perfection as I gaze down at her body.

Her skin is so completely unlike a Sarkarnii, covered in a slight fuzz in places, like between her legs. Every single part of her looks edible, and my dragon form has never wanted to escape the collar more. Instead, to appease it, I dip my head and capture one of her delicious nipples between my teeth, making her squeak as I bite into the sweet flesh. I already love that she is not like our females, that she is something different and exotic.

The fact we are bound together makes this experience even more enticing, and as I take in our bond, Amber's eyes are on me, the perfume of her arousal heady in the air.

"How does this work?" she asks, gently shaking our cuffs.

"This is how I prefer my mating," I rumble, and I'm rewarded by yet more perfume.

Sitting up slowly, I draw her with me before releasing the catch on my pants with our joined hand. My cock springs free, and I can't help but release a stream of smoke in relief. It aches now with the need to be in her, not from being trapped.

Amber tries and fails to repress a gasp as her small hand

strokes over the weeping head of my member, making it look even bigger than it already is.

"Oh, Draco." Her voice is rough. "That is *not* going to fit."

I rub my thumb over the slit, gathering up my pre-cum. I coat my fingers.

"Open," I order as I hold the cum-slick digit up to her mouth.

And when Amber does as I ask but doesn't take her hand from my cock, it bucks beneath her touch. Her eyes sparkle.

I push my thumb between her lips, and she closes her mouth around it. The way she sucks at me causes my cock to jerk hard in her hand.

"Good female," I growl as she laps over my thumb. "You look so good licking up my spill."

Amber moans softly as I withdraw my thumb and trace over her nipples, descending down her stomach. I push her onto her back as my fingers reach her sweet pussy.

"So, you think this little cunt can't take a Sarkarnii cock?" I ask, coating my fingers in pre-cum again before slowly sliding my digits through her slippery folds and dipping inside.

By the bones, she is tight! Almost too tight to even get a finger inside her to deposit my spill and let it do its work.

Her hips lift up at me. "Needy female," I growl. "I think you want to take me, all of me, let me hook you and fill you. Tell me that's what you want." I lift our respective arms and grip at her hair, pulling back her head so her neck is exposed to me.

"Yes, Draco. That's what I want." Her voice is brazen, her eyes glaring at me.

I trail my hand back over her throat, feeling the heady

thrumming of her pulse as her hand clutches mine. Then her eyes go wide, huge, and her hips lift off the bed involuntarily as I dip to nibble her skin, just over the throbbing artery, hot and delicious. She writhes beautifully, her breath coming in short, glorious breaths.

"What have you done to me?" she gasps out. "Draco?"

AMBER

I've never been more turned on in my entire life. I didn't even think it was possible to crave someone in the way my body craves Draco. The lightest of his touches has my skin on fire and my thighs slick.

When he tells me to open up, I do. I want his orders. I want his dominance, his possessiveness in a way which should terrify me.

But it doesn't because this villain just treated my feet as if I was the only creature in the universe. And then he shredded my clothing as if it was nothing before trailing those vicious claws over my skin in the most gentle way possible.

The taste of him! Smoky, sweet, completely delicious, his flavor exploding in my mouth like nothing I've ever had before. But when his finger enters me, thumb working at my clit as he attempts to ease the huge digit inside me and then...

As if it's been waiting for precisely this moment in time and in space, my body convulses with an orgasm so enormous, my mind goes completely blank, and my vision dims to a pinprick. In the distance, I'm sure I can hear someone screaming a name, but I'm enjoying myself too much to care.

Surfacing, as if from a deep sleep, I blink up at Draco. He's hardly touched me, and yet he's just sent me so far over the edge, I wasn't sure I was going to get back.

Above me, his breath is coming fast and shallow as his head drops into the crook of my neck, and I feel his sharp teeth on my skin.

"What have you done to me?" I get the words out in a rush. "I've never experienced anything...what was that?"

"My spill has properties to aid a female," Draco murmurs, not lifting his head but continuing to nip at my neck. "It makes the way easier, so she can take all of me."

He moves over me, carefully, slowly, so I can take in everything he's doing, and notches the head of his cock between my folds.

"And you will take every inch," Draco rasps, his voice deepening to a hundred-a-day. "I'm going to sink my cock into you, and you are going to take every ridge, every part, like the good female you are."

His scales are almost dazzling, having him this close, and I see the beads of sweat on his brow as he tries to hold himself back.

"Yes," I whisper because all of me is on fire with the desire to feel myself sheathed over him, and that enormous cock pushes at my entrance.

I'm wet and ready, but it's still an incredible stretch until he breaches me and then, with a low groan, the rest of him slides inside. Draco lifts himself up and huffs out a curl of smoke.

"Look at how well you take me, my beautiful mate, stretched so tight around my cock," he murmurs.

I can feel every part of him. His cock isn't smooth. It's covered in undulations which scrape over my walls as he slowly withdraws, releasing yet another moan of pleasure which seems to pool in my stomach and has me clenching.

Something touches my side, and I see his tail, all iridescence, glowing gold scales. It caresses me, sliding over my breasts as Draco pushes back into me.

"So tight, so gorgeous," he rumbles. "This cunt is made for my cock." He props himself on one hand, the hand bound to mine, and takes one of my thighs, lifting it up until I hook my ankle over his back, his scales smooth and warm against my skin. "Perfect," he says as his hips drive even deeper.

Something bumps against my clit and teases it with what might be a kiss or might not be. Either way, it sends me spiraling as Draco picks up the pace, pumping into me with a growl of pleasure.

With every stroke, I can feel his cock and the incredible texture which seems to hit every part of me in just the right way. He gazes down as his sinuous body continues to rise over me, plundering me, his eyes glittering before he drops down in order to take my lips with the same intensity. His double tongue flicks around my mouth like he owns it.

And he does. I don't have time to process how amazing he is or how he keeps me in the very center of everything before another blinding orgasm explodes through my body. I pulse over him, my channel gripping at his cock as Draco lets out a whine of both pain and pleasure. The lights under his scales within his skin flicker and glow bright. He speeds up, slamming into me hard, over and over. I grasp for him, pulling his head down so I can kiss him but losing myself in the climax which is overwhelming my vision.

"Scream for me, little mate." Draco has his lips next to my ear. "Scream my name until you can't scream anymore."

Another flood of delight spikes through me, and if I thought he couldn't wring any more out of my convulsing body, I was wrong. Draco rumbles, and it becomes a roar as he thumps into me. The kisses on my clit are almost painful because I'm coming so hard, and, with a pinch, I feel him flood me with his orgasm. His hips continuing to twitch, his tail still caressing me and his hand in my hair.

I shudder as yet more pleasure flows through me in stuttering waves, my pussy gripping at his cock, wanting him, desiring him, taking from him, until finally, finally, it gives way to slow, lazy pulses which leave me spent and sleepy.

Draco swipes a thumb over my cheek. His amazing eyes are half lidded as he shifts his bulk to lie next to me, taking my leg with him as...

He doesn't withdraw. It seems like he can't withdraw as something pulls inside me.

"Draco?"

"I am hooked, *szikra*. You are my fate, you are my heartsfire, and my body has claimed you."

"I-I don't understand," I stutter out.

Draco's breath is long and languorous, and his smile is one of a cat which has the cream. "I can only hook my fated mate, Amber. It is the one pleasure above all others afforded those who are destined to be together." A tiny curl of smoke and an intoxicated smile follow. "My barbs have deployed, and I am deep within your womb, hooked so my seed will take root."

He wraps his unbound arm around me, pulling my still twitching body into his, all scales and light, his heat seeping from him. He is not the feral creature from the maze, not the cool bad boy villain.

This is Draco, curled up, his head shoved hard into my neck, his hand in my hair, his nose against my skin as he breathes in and out.

"Mine," he murmurs. "All mine, forever."

DRACO

The complete and utter calm which fills me is like nothing I've ever experienced before. My mating gland has settled, no longer causing my heart to drum like I'm about to shift. My barbs hold my cock in place while the tip is hooked in her womb.

I feel like I've taken all the illegal narcotics Drega had me smuggle one time and the scent of the cargo had my entire den of warriors acting like idiots. But I also feel like I want to mate my Amber over and over, just as soon as my hook has subsided. Although, given I'm still pumping her with seed, that might take a while.

I never want to let Amber go.

"Hooked?" she queries as I lift my head reluctantly from her skin. "You mean we're stuck together?"

I give her a smile which I know is predatory, but I can't help myself. "Yes."

"How long?" she whimpers.

"For as long as my body will hold you. Until your belly swells with my seed." I growl with enjoyment.

"You're still...coming?" She gasps.

I circle my hips, groaning at the deliciousness of my barbs clinging to her walls, of my hook in her womb, our state of complete togetherness, my balls continuing to empty into her. "Yes," I reply with gusto.

"Oh," Amber says.

I brush my lips over hers, making sure she is tucked into me, so she can take what she needs from my body too. She pushes herself into me, and I relax even more.

"Do not worry, my *szikra*. It will subside soon." I'm rewarded by a soft sigh. "When a Sarkarnii finds his true mate, he binds to her in this way." I wiggle our bonded hands. "Not this way." I grin at her and get a small smile back. "Although"—I tilt my head—"I'm not sure I mind so much. It's an interesting way of mating."

At my words, Amber's face lights up, and the tinkle of her laugh fills my ears. "Trust you to like this, Draco."

I feel a fresh rush of seed. "Say my name again, mate," I growl. "Say it like you screamed it."

Her face flushes with red, which must be some sort of human response to an order by her mate as I've seen it often enough on her, but never this close up. It's quite beautiful.

"Draco," she whispers.

My head falls back as yet more spill fires from me inside her.

"Draco," she says again, a little louder.

I'm not able to speak as the desire to pump more and more spill into her grows along with the thrumming of my mating gland. Instead, all she gets is a groan and an involuntary flick of my hips, causing her to hiss in pleasure.

"Something tells me we're going to be here some time." Amber smiles, and for the first time, her eyes are bright as she does so.

"I wouldn't want to be anywhere else." I nuzzle at her,

shifting her body so I can cover her entirely with mine and my tail which is stubbornly refusing not to shift back. "And I love the scent of my mated female. You smell of me."

My voice is slurred as sleep wants to claim me, and it's only my mating gland which is keeping me awake, or at the very least, alert to any danger which might cause my *szikra* harm.

Because if anyone or anything does something to her...

The sound of Amber's voice jerks me awake, even though I'm not sure what she said.

My arm is stretched above my head, and I have to twist to see her. "Are you hungry?"

She has covered her gorgeous form with something fluffy, save for her arms, and has pulled the platter the Belek left in front of her.

"How long?"

My head is filled with drowsiness, my balls ache, and my tail is still very prevalent, as if it doesn't want to miss anything. I couldn't be more uncomfortable unless I had a need to shed. And, as I attempt to look alive, I discover my arm, the one attached to her, is not particularly responsive from being stuck in one position.

"It was a while. I slept some, but then I needed some food." She puts a slice of pink tralu meat in her mouth and chews.

My cock pushes at the inside of my pouch.

I growl.

"What?" Amber licks at her fingers, and I'm struggling to hold it together.

"Nothing." I snatch a sliver of tralu off the platter and shove it into my mouth, chewing furiously.

"Doesn't seem like nothing," Amber says, picking up some pickled zold.

She sticks out a pink tongue, testing the mottled green and blue food with a brief lick. Her face scrunches, and she puts it back carefully like it might explode. I immediately grab it and gobble it down.

"I just thought the rut would end with a mating," I grumble. "But it seems like all I want to do now is mate."

"You don't know?" Amber's sweet brow furrows as she takes another slice of tralu and drops it in her mouth.

Which means she finds herself under me very swiftly, my teeth at her neck, my cock pressed against her leg.

"No." I can't stop the rasping growl escaping my lips. "I've never been in rut before." I droop my head and roll off her.

"I'm sorry, Draco." Amber puts her little hand on my arm and traces her fingers over my scales, every touch causes my bioluminescence to follow, bright lights pricking at the places her hand has vacated. "I wish I knew more about you and your species. It seems all I've done since coming here is run."

"I love it when you run." I can't help myself, but the memory of her alongside me, ahead of me, it makes my cock want to emerge from its pouch once again. I growl at myself.

Amber looks at my warily. I take a deep breath.

"The rut is not something I've experienced. I don't know if it is the same for humans, but my species only ruts for their mate. As the Sarkarnii have, as far as I know, lost all our females, I never expected to go into rut, ever."

AMBER

I study Draco. His eyes are on mine. He has never lied to me, or even sugar coated the truth. He is a male who will absolutely tell me how it is, unfettered. Bald. Terrifying. Or sad.

"You lost your females? I don't understand."

"My species settled on a planet, Kaeh-Leks, many generations ago. We made it our home, despite not necessarily being welcomed by the inhabitants. But our skills in mining ore and ship building won them over eventually, even if they rather disliked our ability to change our forms."

Draco picks up a slice of the meat which tastes like a cross between bacon and beef. He puts it to his lips but doesn't eat it.

"Kaeh-Leks was attacked by parasites called the Liderc who claimed to be able to save the planet from the failing sun. The Sarkarnii argued for caution, but those in more abundance decided they were worth trusting." He drops his head, removing his gaze from mine. "We were right, but it meant nothing. Whilst we were evacuating our people, the Liderc destroyed all the ships. My brothers and my den warriors were off world at the time, and when we returned..."

His normally strong voice dips in volume. I see his chest shift, his breathing quicken.

"They were all gone. Everyone we ever knew, our families. Gone. And we couldn't even return to claim their bones because the Liderc had overrun the planet."

I can't see his eyes, but I can see the hollow of his cheeks, the droop of his shoulders, the defeat and the despair.

"How did you end up here?" I whisper.

Draco lifts his head, lip hitched in a bad, dangerous smile to show a white fang. "How do you think?"

Draco has done his best to present as big, bad, and dangerous to know, but now I understand how he's suffered. There has to be a reason why he ended up in the Kirakos, and from everything I've seen, it's not because he was bad.

Even if that's what he wants the rest of the universe to believe.

I fold my arms. "I don't know."

Some of the bravado slips away, and for a second, I see the male who has lost everything again, before he rallies.

"How does one find themselves in a prison unless they've done something wrong?" he says smoothly, while gazing at the bond around our respective wrists.

"I haven't done anything wrong, and I'm here," I retort.

He raises his eyebrows, scales flickering over his brow. "What makes you think I'm not here by choice?"

I pull at our wrists, managing, just, to lift both up. "Oh, how about this, and the collars we're wearing, in particular the one which will blow my head off? And the fact that anyone with half a brain would have left by now if they didn't have to be here, what with the shadow monsters and human-eating neon snakes?"

"Or could it be there's something here I want?" he suggests with another fang hitch. I reel back from him, although I can't get far, obviously. "Not just you, *szikra*. Something before you, something which might, just might, help me find any of my other kin."

"You would voluntarily come here? On the off chance there is something which can help you find other Sarkarnii?" I hiss out.

Draco cocks his head on one side, the glitter back in his eyes, smoke curls from his nostrils. "Perhaps not *voluntarily*," he says. "Sarkarnii have never really played well with others." He shrugs. "And without our females, let's just say things got a little out of hand and we ended up here."

My heart drops from my throat to my boots.

"You need females?" I can hardly get the words out.

He says he has never rutted before, but it doesn't mean he didn't have someone he wanted to rut for.

"Our females kept us on the straight and narrow. They were our strategists, our anchors. They controlled us in rut, and they ensured we behaved like good warriors." Draco says, "Without them, we are somewhat feral. The rest of the galaxy wasn't too happy about it."

He studies his claws. I feel more out of my depth than ever. I did the unthinkable. I let Draco in where I always vowed to myself I never would. Not after John. Not after everything he did to me.

I closed the part of me off which could ever care for another, and now, somehow, Draco, his shining scales, his dark gravel voice, his huge form, so vicious and so gentle, has somehow got in.

"*Szikra*, I am an honorable male, I promise you. Yes, I have done things which are not strictly legal in some parts of this galaxy, but only so my den and I could survive. But if it bothers you, I will give it all up in an instant."

I look up into his strong, handsome face. A huge clawed finger and thumb catch my chin as he stares back, and I know he means it, every single word.

But it doesn't stop me pulling away from him, unable to keep my eyes on his. "No, Draco. Don't do anything for me."

Because I know what happens next. It becomes 'look what I gave up for you' and more. Until you're too scared to leave the house.

My chin is gripped again, and this time Draco is not letting go. "What happened?" He growls deep in his throat.

"It doesn't matter." I refuse to meet his gaze until his grip tightens and I have no choice.

"I am not like other males, Amber. I do not accept anything less than complete and utter trust in me. My brothers know this, and my fellow warriors and I want it from you too. You will tell me who hurt you."

"Does it matter, Draco? If he's back on Earth, a million light years from here? What can you do?" My voice is hoarse as he gazes at me with a look so intense, I feel like I might burst into flames.

"I can make you mine, beautiful mate. I can make you the center of my world, so you never have to think of your own again."

DRACO

The snarl which rises within me is like nothing I've ever felt before. My Amber has been wronged, and all I want to do is destroy something, anything in order to make it right for her.

I'd even find her blasted planet, wherever the place may be, and destroy the male who dared to treat her so badly she can't trust her mate.

Or maybe humans don't mate the same?

Female Sarkarnii don't rut, but they do become fertile when they meet their fated mate. Amber smells fertile. She smells like I can fill her belly easily, but I'm still not entirely sure if that means she can feel the way I do.

She drops her head against my chest, and I shove my fingers into her hair, releasing more of her fragrance, which entwines with that of our mating. I can't wait to get her back to my quarters, for all the other males to scent what we have done.

For me to perform my dance for her.

A knock on the door brings me back to the present. I

can't dance until I've done the run, and once the run is over, can I still keep Amber as my mate?

I shove the worry and concern back down deep inside.

"What is it?" I growl.

"I have your communicator, Draco."

"About time," I grumble as I lift Amber's head and brush a kiss over her lips. "I need to speak with my brother, Drega, about the run, and we need to get back to my quarters," I explain. "Do you think you're up to it?"

Amber looks at her bandaged feet. "If I can get some suitable footwear, I should be okay."

"Bring it in," I call out, and the female Jiaka hurries in. "And find some boots for my female," I bark out.

"Draco!" Amber slaps me on my chest. "Be nice!"

I purse my lips and jerk my head to one side. "Please find some boots for my female." I snarl and then look at her.

"Marginally better," she says before turning to the Jiaka and adding, "Thank you."

The Jiaka makes a noise which could be laughter. It elicits another growl as she puts down the communicator and scuttles out of the room.

Amber has no such issues and giggles at me with her hand over her mouth and her eyes bright with light.

My light. My bioluminescence, reflected in her. I don't remember a time when I have glowed as much after a shed, but from what I can see, I'm lit up from within.

This is not going to help the run at all. Especially if I need to be stealthy.

I snatch up the communicator and have to fight the desire to turn my back on Amber, which will be virtually impossible, given we're joined at the wrist. Instead I glare at the comm and attempt to remember the frequency Drega uses, which I punch in with excessive force.

"Draco?" His voice is strangled and metallic, with a significant amount of static.

"Drega. Do you have my bones?"

"I keep them for you, commander. Five Six."

"What?" Amber is staring at me as if both Drega and I have gone mad.

"It's a code, my mate."

"Oh," she says, her gorgeous mouth making a perfect round shape which goes immediately to my cock.

"Draco, where are you?" Drega asks.

"I'm back in the fourth quadrant, no thanks to Warden Noro. I was ambushed at the aquium."

"As long as you've finally shed, I don't really care, because you're a grumpy never when you haven't shed. When are you coming back? The run is in five ticks, and we need to prepare."

"Yes, I am well, Drega, as is my mate," I snarl. "What's the position with weapons?"

"We still don't have any," he replies.

I curse loudly. "Then I'll have to see what I can scare up on my way back. Make sure you have some gear for disabling prison bonds when I get there."

I turn off the comm before he can reply and just manage not to throw the thing at the wall.

"Draco?" When Amber says my name, my mating gland flips, and my heart rate slows. "We have a problem."

I put the comm down carefully and pull her lush form against me. "I have you, and I do not have a problem, little one."

"Unless you want to parade me naked through the maze, we're going to have to figure out a way for me to get dressed," Amber says, and her voice is full of laughter as she twists within our bonds.

She is, unbelievably, happy, and it has my heart in a strangle hold.

This is not the rut. This is something else entirely. I just wish I knew what it was.

And I nevving wish there was not a run in five ticks' time which is now going to be even more difficult than it should have been.

Oh, and I also have a very naked, very tasty female I need to handle. A fact which already has my cock emerging from its pouch. Something else we don't really have time for.

Amber sits up, the sheet covering her falls away, and her glorious globes rise, tipped with red which means I have no option but to lean in and gather one in my mouth, sucking on her like I'm a Sarkarnii starved. Amber moans gently and pushes herself farther into me.

"So sweet, so delicious, little mate," I rumble. "But you are too much of a distraction."

"I know," she says.

What a bad little mate! I must be rubbing off on her.

There is another knock at the door. Amber grabs at the sheet, but I hold it away from her.

"Maybe you should go naked in the maze?" I rasp. "Maybe I want to show all the inmates what a delicious little morsel belongs to me."

Amber's eyes widen, but the perfume of her arousal tells me everything I need to know.

"Come," I call out, and as the door opens, I release the sheet, not taking my eyes from hers.

She huffs out something which sounds like a curse as she covers herself, except I see the hint of a smile at the corner of her mouth.

The Jiaka shoves a pair of boots at us and grins.

Nev it to the ancestors! This little female is going to be the death of me.

AMBER

From the first moment I saw him, I knew Draco was a very bad...alien. But from the way my body reacted when he suggested I go naked, I know one thing.

He is making me bad too.

And he knows it.

Once he's finished barking orders at the smaller aliens, he turns to me with his very sinful smile. "Let's see about getting you dressed, little one."

I bristle at the "little one" epithet, and it just makes Draco's eyes glitter more. So, I snatch at the clothing left out for me and quickly pull on the pants provided.

At least the smaller aliens are around about my size and have two legs. Although it seems they like their pants tight. Skin tight. Draco rumbles.

"What?"

"I think I preferred it when you were wearing your old clothing." He does the thing with his head, inclining it to one side, the way he always does when he's thinking.

Usually when he's thinking something wicked. "Although this look is pleasant enough."

"I'm not wearing anything on my top half," I exclaim.

"I know." The smile, all fangs and pleasure, is back.

I pick over the remaining garments. There's only one which is going to work. I step into the stretchy item, which can only really be described as a 'boob tube', and hitch it up over my hips and around my waist before finally hiking it over my boobs.

It does something weird. It constricts until I'm... encased. It's become more like a corset and certainly is giving me plenty of support.

It's also shoving the girls up and out in a way I'd never have risked on Earth. Not that I wanted to draw attention to myself, but while everything is covered, nothing is left to the imagination.

Which is presumably why Draco is sporting another hard on. The massive bulge in his scaled crotch area is one indication, and the fact that I can see the tip pushing out from a dark colored slit is another indicator.

He rumbles deep in his chest, then grabs his pants and awkwardly pulls them on.

Something comes over me, something bolder than I've felt in a very long time. I grab hold of the waistband and bat his hands away. Slowly pulling the heavy leather like fabric up over his hips, I let my hands graze the beautiful scales at the top of his thighs, and I allow myself a great, up close view of his muscled physique.

The tip of his cock is still emerging, a drip of pre-cum, a light beige pearl, beads, ready to drop. I swipe at it with my finger and pop it in my mouth.

"Fuck!" Warmth spreads through my body, and I want to pull off my clothes.

"My seed makes you ready for me, little Amber. Do you like how I taste?" Draco rasps.

"Your...your cum has *aphrodisiac* properties?"

"If you mean it makes my female horny and ready for me? Then yes, that's what it does," he says smugly. The heat dies away somewhat, and my mind clears. "Female Sarkarnii are venomous. If a male does not subdue her with his spill, make her ready, he could be out of action for several ticks," Draco adds.

And just like that...my mind is completely blown.

Draco's species, his entire society, is predicated on the fact females are inherently dangerous.

And yet he would protect me at all costs. He would care for me like I'm the only thing he has.

"Humans aren't venomous," I stumble out.

"But you are dangerous, *szikra*." Draco leans into me, his body heat incredible, his pupils thin slivers, and a wisp of smoke rises from his lips. "More dangerous than any Sarkarnii female, because you have stolen my heart."

I can't get away from this mountain of alien muscle. The collar around my neck and our bonded wrists remind me I'm stuck with him, no matter what.

"I need my boots," I say, not wanting to break the spell, but not wanting to deal with all the emotions piling in on me.

After all, I don't know what I feel about Draco. My head has been spinning since the day I woke up in the maze. Not only are there aliens—many, many aliens—there are ones who think humans are bait, or food, or a commodity.

Is Draco any of these? I don't believe so, but can I put my entire trust in this huge, scaled beast who continues to surprise me at every turn? My heart drums in my chest to a beat I learned a long time ago.

Draco smiles with a curl of smoke as he hands me the boots and then busies himself with doing up his pants. I've yet to see him produce anything but smoke and a few sparks, but where there is smoke, there has to be fire, and it's another reason why I need to be wary.

I'm sure I've only seen part of what he's capable of. He's alluded to being able to change his form somehow as well, which takes being an alien to a whole new level. I'm no longer keeping afloat in all of this. I've drowned, and I'm descending to the depths of newness where I can either not trust anything...

Or I can trust him.

Draco picks up the silver tube he was talking into, about the same length as a cigar case (the irony of this is not lost on me) and puts it into his waistband where it grows a silver appendage, hooking itself onto his clothing. He also grabs the last two slices of meat from the platter and hands one to me.

"We have a journey today, so you need to be nourished." He lowers his head, fixing me with a dark gaze until I put the meat in my mouth and take a bite.

At which point he rumbles gently, deep within his chest, and warmth blooms inside me. I eat, and Draco is pleased.

And this is the reason I cannot trust my heart!

I gobble the rest down as he puts his head back and drops the entire piece into his mouth, swallowing it in a single gulp. He swipes the back of his clawed hand over his lips and gives me the dirtiest grin.

"Time to go, little morsel. Time to get back to reality."

DRACO

Nev the bones of my ancestors! I don't want to leave the hollow I've carved out for my *szikra* and me, a bubble where we could forget everything.

The rut has addled my mind. It doesn't help no one has ever explained it doesn't end with a mating. When does the nevving thing end? When I dance for her? When she accepts me? When I fill her womb?

When I get free of the Kirakos?

Anger volcanoes inside me. The Sarkarnii were a proud race of feared warriors and learned scholars once. We might not have existed in harmony with the other species on Kaeh-Leks—our fiery nature always made such a thing difficult— but we lived, we bred, we had a home.

Now I'm trailing through a prison maze with the most beautiful creature who ever existed, in the vain hope my plans are enough to change our fortunes.

"What exactly is a run?" Amber asks as we walk down a broad avenue between two huge walls. "I've heard you mention it a few times." She looks up at me from under long eyelashes.

It's early and the place is currently quiet, the occasional Jiaka giving us three scared looking eyes as they hurry from one hole to another. A large male tralu, all horns and shaggy hair rattles in the distance, his dark stone colored fleece dull in the morning light. But they know who I am here, and nothing bothers us.

No one would dare.

"Approximately every half to every quarter ev, the wardens give us the opportunity to run for our freedom."

The tralu seems to be getting closer, but he isn't any threat, not before his body has warmed through.

"Really?" Amber has hold of my hand, and I love the feel of her skin against mine. "Seems like an odd way to run a prison."

"They don't do it for the good of our souls. Each run is entertainment for whoever is prepared to pay the price to watch and participate by placing obstacles in the way of those who risk it."

My tail has, yet again, without my bidding, shifted into existence. It curls around Amber's waist in a proprietary manner. I scowl at it.

"Each run makes the wardens richer. Each run makes the inmates more hopeful of success." I grit my teeth, my jaw aching. "The victors are transmitted live to the rest of the Kirakos, celebrating their win. Of course, they are simply killed for attempting to escape, but then the rest of the poor fools in here refuse to believe it."

The tralu is definitely getting closer and my scales bristle.

"So, why try?" Amber kicks at a stone which skitters away until it hits the maze wall.

"Because I don't want to escape." I lower my voice,

bending into her. "I want what is kept in the heart of the Kirakos, and I want the maze to be mine."

A roar comes from the tralu and below my feet is the rumble as it starts to pound towards us. There's nowhere for us to run and anyway, I don't run in my own quadrant.

My comm crackles to life, and I hear Drasus calling, but I'm fixed on protecting my *szikra* from the creature which is stomping up a storm, tucking Amber behind me as the tralu lowers its four horns and starts to charge.

I'm already at a disadvantage, having only one hand free, but I'm not going to let any inmate in my quadrant behave like this to me, let alone my mate.

I suck in a breath, allow the accelerant to fill my fire sacs to brimming, and as he approaches, I let rip with everything I have. A wall of flame sheets up, blocking the tralu from view for an instant, until I cut it off and get ready to fight.

"For nev's sake, Draco!" a familiar voice calls out.

Sat on the back of the tralu is Drega. He holds one horn and leans forward on the big beast's head.

"What the nev are you doing riding a tralu?" I wipe at my mouth to rid it of the remnants of accelerant.

"I came to get you and thought your mate might need a lift."

"One hundred percent, I am not riding on that thing," Amber says, stepping out from behind me.

"Hello," Drega says, sliding off the tralu, a big smile on his face.

I snarl, feeling my fire sacs filling with accelerant. Again.

"Ah, come on, Draco, she's awake and upright this time, plus she's survived you. Are you not going to introduce me to your mate?" he says, holding his hands out flat, claws sheathed in supplication.

"Fine," I growl through gritted teeth. "Amber, this is my brother, Drega." I step a little in front of her, unable to help myself, my shifted tail winding around her feet. "Drega, this is Amber, my *szikra*."

"Your *szikra*?" Drega stops in his tracks, his eyes moving from her to me immediately.

I shrug.

"But?"

"I know."

"That's not possible."

"It is, apparently, possible."

"What is possible?" Amber moves between Drega and me.

"Sarkarnii are only expected to find their fated mate amongst our own females. We are not able to mate with any other species. We are not compatible," Drega says before I can stop him.

Amber turns her head, but I capture her face in my hand, dragging her back to me and dropping my gaze to meet hers. "My brother knows nothing. If I say you're my *szikra*, you are," I growl, before looking up at him. "We need weapons for the run, and we need to get out of these bonds."

I hold up our joined wrists.

"But, if we try, I'll explode," Amber says swiftly, her teeth chattering a little.

"Yes, it is rigged to go off if tampered with," I add with a shrug to Drega.

"Not if I have anything to do with it." Drega approaches me hesitantly, as he should, until I incline my head, and he gets in close, holding my wrist and exploring the cuffs attached to each of us.

"Well?" My patience gives out after a few seccari. "Can you get them off or not?"

Drega sighs, squinting one eye as he looks up from our wrists. "Of course I can. What sort of Sarkarnii do you take me for?"

"One who hasn't been able to get our collars off?"

"I told you, I'm working on it," he says, and there is a clicking sound.

One by one, the cuffs fall to the ground. Amber stumbles back from me at the sudden release. Her eyes are wild, and she clutches at the collar.

"The explosives!" she says, her voice ragged.

"Ah, Draco's *szikra*, do not fret." Drega takes hold of her arm, despite my snarl, and pulls her to him. Shoving her head to one side, he presses a long metal tool seemingly into her neck.

"Ow!"

Her cry of pain is enough to have me leaping for him. Brother or no, Drega will not harm my mate. I catch hold of his shoulders and send him spinning to one side to get to Amber.

She has her hand at her throat, but there's no sign of the collar. I spin on the spot, seeing Drega getting to his feet, a smile on his face and the collar in his hand.

"Drega!" I rumble in warning.

"This thing is live, Draco. I suggest you stand back." He grins at me insolently.

"Nev you, Drega." I cover Amber with my body and lift her off her feet, putting the tralu between me and my idiotic brother with a death wish.

AMBER

I don't get a chance to even think before I'm scooped up into Draco's arms. There's a flash of blue scales from his iridescent brother and then the most enormous explosion which leaves me gasping for air.

"That could have been us," I gasp, my ears ringing as the shockwave passes. "Your brother!" I squirm in Draco's arms, but his grip is iron.

"Drega is fine," he says. "Drega is always fine. He lives for this sort of zar."

Dust and larger stones rain down on us, Draco has a light covering on his shoulders which almost looks like snow. He looks absurd and I fight not to laugh.

It comes out as a snort.

"Hey, brother." Drega appears behind Draco and looks completely unharmed and dust free. He claps his hand on Draco's shoulder, and a cloud of white leaps into the air.

Honestly, if looks could kill, Drega would be dead the way Draco glares at him. I cover my mouth with my hand and feign a cough to hide the laugh.

"Do I amuse you, little mate?" Draco intones.

My attempt at deception has not worked.

"Not at all." I swallow down my laughter as he leans into me, eyes penetrating slits of danger. His scent, all smoky and musky, envelopes me. A fang glints, and there's a clawed hand in my hair.

I hold my breath for the inevitable, wanting to close my eyes but unable to do so.

But Draco's do close. His lips hit mine, and he takes possession of my mouth in the most achingly glorious kiss so far. His hands cup my face, and he dominates me in a way which means I'd fall to the ground if he wasn't holding me.

"You are safe," he murmurs when he lets me up for air. "No matter what my tralu-brained brother might attempt do to us," he adds with a growl.

"I got the collar off, didn't I?" Drega grumbles.

"And attracted every guard within earshot." Draco straightens to his full height, his scales shining gold next to Drega's bright blue.

"We've always lived dangerously," Drega says, displaying an impressive set of fangs.

Draco huffs out some smoke, and he strokes a thumb over my cheek, before turning to survey the damage.

"Well, what do we have here?" He steps forward past the massive creature Drega was riding, which is also covered in dust but singularly uninterested in its surroundings.

In the wall of the maze, there is an opening. It's not jagged, like there was a hole blown in it, but as if it were a doorway.

"Looks like my little key worked again." Draco gives me an indulgent smile.

"Key?" Drega looks between us.

"My mate is able to access the hidden doors within the

Kirakos," Draco says proudly and pulls me to him as he inspects my wrist and my neck before pressing a kiss to my temple. "She is truly a gift from the ancestors."

"I'm not sure it's that simple," I reply. "After all, I did drop us into a trap."

"Trap?" Drega queries.

"It might have been a trap, or it might have been luck on Warden Noro's part," Draco says with an indulgent look at me. "But regardless of what my mate might say, she is able to find the doors in the Kirakos which no other being can."

He stalks off to the hole in the wall, leaning in to inspect it further.

"Interesting," Drega says, his gaze raking over me, and for a second, I see a different male, one which is more contemplative and less...explody.

It makes me feel odd. Not bad or scared, but I've not been the centre of attention for a long time. I drop my gaze from his and hurry over to where Draco is standing.

"Yes, it looks like this might be an interesting run, after all," Draco says as I reach him.

Inside, all I can see is blackness, but Draco puts in a hand and takes hold of something long and slim. It sits snug in his hand, and although I might be a human and a stranger to this place, I can tell a weapon when I see one.

"Why do you think these are here?" Drega asks.

"Someone stashed them, a long time ago. And they've been here, all this time, right under our noses," Draco growls. "I hope that beast of yours has some carrying sacks."

Drega hurries back to the big hairy creature.

"Are all of these weapons?" My eyes have become accustomed to the gloom. There are several racks of matte black tubes and a couple of boxes containing silvery weapons like the one Draco holds.

"They are." Draco's gaze into the hidden place is intense, a muscle ticking in his jaw, and I can see how tense he is. "And we need to take all of them."

Drega returns, and the pair of them empty the room before loading up the creature, slinging the bags under its belly where they are hidden by the fur.

Draco has hold of me by the waist and is shoving me up onto the back of this foul smelling creature which wriggles and shakes underneath my body.

"Hey! Wait! No!" I call out, but it's no use, I'm on top of the thing, and it starts to move.

"Do not worry, the tralu will not bolt, unless I ask it to," Drega calls up to me.

"Thanks for nothing," I mutter.

There are no reins, nothing, and it's all I can do to hang on and hold my breath, trying not to catch a further whiff of the thing which smells like decaying vegetation, sweet and sour at the same time.

It's not easy. The creature sways from side to side as Draco and his brother walk ahead. Draco's tail has disappeared, and I'm wondering how it gets out of his pants when we turn a corner and find a small crowd has gathered. It consists of the smaller aliens like the ones which gave us shelter last night, some others who are taller and slimmer but covered in fur, save for small patches which are scaly. They have elongated faces like raccoons and beady black eyes hidden behind furry bandit masks.

Also among the crowd are more of Draco's species, head and shoulders taller than the rest, broader and almost as exceedingly well muscled as him. Their scales glitter in a myriad of different colors. All of them have the same slit pupils, and I see the occasional puff of smoke rising up.

Draco reaches up an arm and helps me down off the

creature. It has a huge, dark eye with long eyelashes which blink slowly at me.

"Er...thanks," I say and give it a pat on the neck, which raises a cloud of dust.

Drega releases the packages slung over it, and the thing makes the weird lowing sound again, then turns away, shambling off in a different direction with no clear aim.

Silence falls as the small crowd stares at Draco, Drega, and me.

"Unless you have something of use for the run, nev off," Draco says, his voice low and dangerous. "This is Sarkarnii business."

DRACO

F inding the hidden weapons has unsettled me. Admittedly, we don't have access to explosives under ordinary circumstances, as the Sarkarnii are the most likely candidates to cause havoc if we did have them, so the weapons stash could have gone unnoticed for an eternity.

Only someone knows it was there, and the fact it was, right under my nose, doesn't sit right.

Also, I don't like not being bound to my *szikra* in a way which is completely unexpected. I like the fact her life is not at risk from her collar, but I want to be close to her, touching her, unable to get away from her. If I thought the need to shed was uncomfortable, this has to be worse.

At least until I have her by my side again, then I feel as if I could take on the entirety of the galaxy. I breathe in her scent until my head spins.

"Sarkarnii, with me." I stride past my den of warriors, the rest of the crowd which greeted us having disbursed at my not so subtle suggestion.

My quarters are as I left them, only with fresh food and

ale-wine laid out. Drega is through the doors first, his arms filled with the carrying sacks from the tralu.

"Put them down here." I point at the foot of my chair. "Get the rest of them in here. Any sign of Draxx?"

"No," Drega says as he leaves.

"Draxx?" Amber looks at me as I take my seat and hold out my hand to her.

When she takes it, I sweep her onto my lap, and she squeaks beautifully. "My other brother. Somewhat of a liability. He's taken to spending much of his time in the pit, fighting those long forgotten by anyone in some sort of attempt to atone."

"For what?"

"For the loss of the female promised to him." I sigh. "We all lost much when the Liderc took our home, but to lose our parents, the female he cared about"—I shake my head—"it nearly broke him."

"That is so sad," Amber says.

To my surprise, her concern for another—which I would expect to send me into a frenzy at the idea of her even thinking about another male—instead makes my heart beat a steady rhythm.

Despite the mating gland being in overdrive, my desire to please my *szikra* is overwhelming.

"Do not be sad. If I can find happiness, then he can too." I curl my hand around hers.

Amber's eyes find mine, and I feel her body go tense. She opens her mouth just as my den of warriors clatters through the door, unbidden.

"Draco!" they hail me, before descending on the aforementioned food and ale-wine like a plague of batiz flies.

I roll my eyes as Drega joins them. Only the nevver

doesn't break things up. If anything, I think he makes it worse.

"Enough!" I roar, and with plenty of elbows, the occasional tail, plus I'm pretty sure I see a wing, the scrum disentangles into the rag-tag den of what's left of the entire Sarkarnii species.

Or at least that's what we've been told.

"Draxx?" I ask Drega.

He shrugs and shakes his head.

"I need him. Someone will have to go to the pit to get him."

Drega looks over at Daeos. His red scales darken, but he's the only one I know we can send to the pit who will return intact.

After Draxx, the only other warrior as unhinged as my brother is Daeos. And other than me, I can't trust anyone else to go and get Draxx, if he is, indeed, in the pit.

Daeos bows briefly, swallows the goblet of ale-wine he's holding, wipes the back of his hand over his mouth, and heads out of my quarters.

"This next run is the one," I tell the remaining assembly. "The wardens do not want us to be successful, and it's because they know we will be."

"How?" someone asks.

It's Drelix. He's picking at his teeth and leaning against the wall with a show of insubordination and insolence. Smoke curls up from one corner of his mouth. He's always been a contrary warrior, and I know he was at the heart of the scrum for food, despite the fact I make sure they always get plenty.

I kick the bag at my feet. It rolls open, and the weapons tumble out.

The scrum reasserts itself as every warrior leaps for his favorite, or three.

No one ever said the Sarkarnii play nice. Or play well with others.

"Hide these wherever you need to, but you will need them for the run." I look over at Drega. "The likelihood is we'll be getting a visit from the guards beforehand, and I don't want to lose a single one. This will be our last run, regardless. This time, we run or die."

All of my warriors straighten and slam their left hand against their chest three times. My tail has, yet again, escaped, and it thrashes against the chair.

"This is my *szikra*, Amber." I stand and place her on her feet. "I will protect her with my life, and I expect you to do the same."

"Draco," they chorus loudly, some raising goblets at us, eyes roving over my mate in a way I dislike intensely, but my name is their bond.

My mate is as safe as she will ever be, not that I will let her leave my sight.

"Do what you need to do, my warriors. In five ticks, we run, and this is the run to end all runs." I toss Amber into my arms and step off the dais.

Because it's been long enough. And being surrounded by other males has sent my rut into the stratosphere.

"If I don't bury my cock inside you within the next ten seccari, I will not be responsible for what happens," I murmur in her ear.

AMBER

I'm not entirely sure what I've just witnessed, but whatever it is, Draco is rampant.

No, strike that. He is desperate. I'm not allowed to stand. Instead, he lays me down and begins scrabbling at my clothing.

"Hey." I put my hand on his face, his delicious scruff scratching at my skin. "It's okay."

He lifts his head from where he's pulling at my top, his pupils, usually slits, are wide open.

I'm not sure I've ever seen anything more adorable. I lift up and press my lips to his. Draco slides his hands into my hair, holding my head as my tongue sweeps his mouth, my fingers on his chest, feeling the warmth of him and the hardness of his scales. He kisses as if he's never kissed before, and when I am released, I'm panting with the loss of him.

"I'm in rut," he says. "I don't think I can hold back."

"I don't want you to hold back," I whisper, trailing my hand down, over his pecs, over his hard abs until I reach his pants. Draco moans and shivers at my touch as I run a finger around his waistband, feeling the bulge at his crotch, hot and getting larger.

I don't remember a time I was this bold or felt this in control. I have a huge alien who is absolute putty in my hands, willing to do anything for me.

Willing to ask all his warriors to protect me.

I release the catch on his pants, and his cock drops into my hands, heavy and already slick with pre-cum. For the first time, I get to explore him, stroking up the length, feeling a tingle on my skin as the slippery liquid touches me.

Draco has psychedelic cum. It sends my head into the clouds and my body to oblivion. It is incredible. *He* is incredible.

I want him. More than anything, I want this huge, gorgeous male who has his eyes closed, who has surrendered himself in his entirety to me. And when I say entire...boy, is Draco *big*.

How did it even fit before? It has to nearly be the length of my forearm. Along the top is a defined ridge which dips and rises like the ridge on his tail. It's as hard as his cock, giving just slightly as I squeeze, and he moans again, more cum spilling onto my hand.

"That's perfect. Do it again," he rumbles.

And now the eyes are open. He's gazing down, and I can see myself reflected in the blown pupils, black like the night.

A woman stares back at me, a smile like she is happy spread across her face, with just a hint of wantonness, her hair wild, all of her wild in this alien prison with...him.

"Don't hold back," I whisper at the woman, at Draco, at the universe.

"Never hold back," he replies, his voice a mere rasp on the air.

Clawed hands strip the rest of my clothing away and then explore my pussy, thick fingers swiping pre-cum then dipping inside me, and my channel clenches around him.

"So needy, little one. Your cunt just loves Sarkarnii cock," Draco croons, his lips brushing over mine as his fingers leave me, and I whine in protest.

He shifts his body, moving sinuously between my legs, and my whine is replaced by a gasp as he presses his cock against my entrance and then, in a single smooth movement, he is inside me with a groan which comes from his belly.

"I want to always be in you like this, *szikra*. I want to take up residence in your sweet pussy and never leave," Draco murmurs into my ear, his voice as velvet as his cock as he moves with slow, shallow strokes until I adjust to his size.

He puts a hand under my thigh and lifts me up so he can drive deeper. The other hand clasps mine as he holds it over my head. I'm pinned by him, impaled by him, being railed by him, and I wouldn't want it any other way.

My free hand trails over his angular cheekbones, down across his jaw as he doesn't move his intense gaze from mine, pumping at me with delicious circular strokes which end in a hip flick that seems to be designed to drive me wild. I trip over his chin, the scruff tickling at my fingertips, and down onto his throat, tapping over the collar which I hate because it doesn't let Draco be his true self.

And there's nothing worse than not being able to be the person you want to be.

Something pushes at my bottom hole, circling the tight pucker and testing it.

"Draco?" I pant, my hips lifting involuntarily and allowing his tail even more access as my hand slides up around his neck, still on the collar.

"I want to fill all of you, sweetness, and I don't think I can stop my tail from taking you." He grins.

His tail is as slick as his cock as it pushes, gently, into me, breaching the ring of tight muscle but not insistent, just pushing slowly as I give a little each time with a soft moan.

"If you continue to make those sounds, I will have to mate you much harder."

I whimper some more, clutching at the back of his neck, the feel of his scales and the metal of his collar somehow heightening the way he's driving into me. Under my fingers, a catch depresses, and the collar springs free.

Draco growls, and the sound reverberates around the room. My breath catches, but he doesn't stop plundering me. Instead, I think he's growing larger, the scales on his body becoming more prominent.

"Little mate," he says, fangs elongating. "You have set me free."

I'm scooped up against him as he thumps into me, his cock scraping over every part of my channel, the node at his pubic bone hitting my clit in perfect harmony. His tail seems to expand inside me, and it's all I can do to hang on to Draco's angular form as he increases his pace. I'm being held against a body which shines with gold and black, and as another growl rips through his body, and through mine, it tips me over.

I convulse, my pussy strangling his cock, my dark channel pulsing, every part of me undone, flying apart at his touch. I'm dimly aware that Draco is somehow everywhere as he thumps into me, over and over, keeping my orgasm rolling and rolling.

My body is giving out. The pleasure is just too much, too right, too perfect. Before my eyes roll back in my head, I see Draco, but I also see something else, something monstrous.

And beautiful.

DRACO

I can't shift.

I can't shift.

I can't shift, not while I'm inside Amber.

My cum will ensure she is able to take all of me, even while I am Sarkarnii, but if I hook her in my shifted form, we'll be tied together for too long, and as much as I want to fill her, see her belly swell with my seed, feel the incredible calm she brings to my unquiet soul, it might not be the best idea, not for our second mating.

And then her pussy clamps down over me. The wave after wave of tightness means I'm no longer in control—of my body, of my shift, of anything.

The roar which escapes me is one of a true Sarkarnii, and as my cock hooks into her and my orgasm slams me like I've flown into a wall, I explode inside her, my spill immediately plumping her, my shift ignoring any attempts to hold back. I become my other form, the one I've been unable to be since we arrived in the Kirakos.

Amber calls out my name, her body shaking as I continue to shudder, my massive form cradling her in my claws. My name dies on her lips as her body goes limp, but I cannot stop. I continue to climax, hooked as I am inside her. The rut is a mystery, and the one Sarkarnii who might have been able to tell me what it's like is missing in action, his brain so addled as to be only capable of violence.

I should shift back. I need to give Amber time to understand my different form. Only it's been dormant so long, stretching out my wings, my tail, and my limbs as my cock continues to fire cum into my mate—it is pleasure in the absolute.

I don't want to stop. But I don't want to scare her. All I've done is allude to what the Sarkarnii become. If she opens her eyes to see me, all the time I'm hooked in her?

"Lights off," I call out, and the entire room is plunged into darkness.

"Draco?" Her sweet voice is even better while I'm shifted. It makes the beast in me feel as if he is home.

"Do not be afraid, sweet mate. You removed my collar, and I have changed my form."

I can feel her hands, tinier than ever against my scales.

"I want to see, Draco," she breathes. "I want to see all of you."

My chest swells as I fill my lungs, unsure of what to do next. If I'd been able to shift before I met her, before...I fell in love...

"No." The word is out of my mouth before I can stop it.

"Please." She is undeterred.

"I am not as you might expect."

"Nothing in this place is what I expect," she says. My eyesight is excellent in pitch black, and I can see her eyes are open as she searches for something, anything which will give me away. "Least of all you, Draco. Let me see you."

I'm still hard, my cock still weeping its spill inside her. I feel like I could take on not just the Kirakos, but the entire galaxy.

But I don't want to scare her.

I've never wanted acceptance more in my life than right at this moment. And if Amber doesn't accept me, I don't know what I will do.

"Lights up," I say, my voice hoarse and unwilling, not because of my shift but because this is the last thing I want to do.

We are illuminated slowly as the lights come on. As a human, Amber's eyes are obviously not as good as mine, and she blinks a few times to clear them before looking up at me.

She has to look a long way.

"Draco," she breathes. "Wow, just wow." Her fingers trace over my scales, over my claws, up the hard plates covering my breast until she reaches my jaw.

"You are not afraid?"

"I am not afraid. I am in awe."

"Do not be." I dip my head to rub my muzzle on her hair, releasing her scent, which I suck down deep inside me, so I can keep it forever. "I am yours, *szikra*, I am only yours. My heart beats for you, my flame burns for you, my desire will dance for you. Now and always, my heartsfire."

"About that dancing." Amber closes her eyes again and snuggles her little body against my huge form, her voice slurred with sleep. "I'm still waiting."

"I will dance for you once the run is over, *szikra*. It is my promise to you, and my word is my bond."

But Amber is already asleep, cradled in one of my claws. I am bound to her in so many ways I can't even fathom, but I don't want to miss a single seccari of being with her. So, I keep my eyes open, even after my body finally shifts back, even after my hook softens and I can release her. Amber sleeps on, and I watch over her.

Because I will always watch over her.

She is mine.

AMBER

I think I had the strangest dream. I think Draco turned into a dragon, *while we were having sex.* He was the most beautiful dragon, with massive scales, a huge, haughty head, and sprinkles of light covering him.

It has to be the cum. I can feel from the way my abdomen aches with a delicious dull pain he filled me up with it again, and I already know it has unusual properties. Maybe it made me hallucinate?

My head clears of sleep, and I look down at the tail curling over my leg.

Draco was a dragon!

His eyes flicker open, dulled with his own slumber, and his mouth slides into the best, baddest smile.

"*Szikra,*" he says in his hundred-a-day habit rasp.

I cup his face in my hand. "Was it real? Was it you?"

"If you want."

"How?" I study him, almost as if I expect him to change before my eyes. Instead his tail tickles over my thigh.

"How?" Draco hasn't lost his smile, and his eyes sparkle as he trails a finger down my bare arm. "I am able to morph between forms, something my species has been cultivating for eons, until I can become what you saw."

"Does it hurt?" Given how big and dragony he became, I can't imagine it was easy.

"Not now. When I first shifted, yes." He rolls onto his back and puts his arm behind his head. "We are born with the ability to shift, but we are physically unable to hold the shift until we reach the moment of change when we become adults."

The way he talks, his eyes on the ceiling, not looking at me, it's as if he wants to remember but he doesn't at the same time.

And for the first time since I came to the maze, I feel truly afraid.

Afraid of losing Draco.

"What is going to happen on this 'run'?" I ask.

I want to shield him somehow. My heart thumps in my chest as I try to deflect, or I hope deflect, his feelings. For the first time in a long time, I want another person to feel good. I've spent so damn long in survival mode. Thinking about anyone else has been impossible.

"The wardens will do anything they can to stop us reaching the centre of the maze. They won't just use the guards, they'll use the creatures from the pits or the lower quadrants," Draco answers in a matter-of-fact tone. "Their aim is to tear us apart."

"And just how many of these have you done?" I prop myself up on my elbow.

"Three or four," Draco says, turning his head towards me.

"And you survived."

"Survival is not the object. Completing the run is. I

failed, that's what I did," he rumbles, his pupils slitted to thin slivers.

"Survival is not to be underrated," I say quietly.

All of a sudden, I have a huge Sarkarnii bearing down on me, my wrists caught in his hands, pupils blown.

"Who hurt you?"

"Everyone, everything. It's what I am."

"No." I feel the word in my chest rather than hear it, Draco growls so low. "No one touches my *szikra*, no one hurts her or scares her. No one even thinks about her unless I permit it."

My heart is drumming so loud in my chest, I'm sure everyone, not just Draco can hear it. My lungs are only just working under the intenseness which is Draco.

A Draco who wants to make things better by offering violence.

"Let me guess. You'd burn the Kirakos for me." I smile wryly because I know it's the sort of thing Draco would say.

"No, my *szikra*, for you, that is not enough. For you, I'd rend the universe in two and offer you the pieces to do with as you please."

My smile dies on my face. My heart slows. When I look in his eyes, all I see is the truth. All I see is Draco, and he means every single word. The heat which flows from him should make it hard to breathe, but I can breathe so easily with his huge form dominating me, vibrating with the desire to make the universe bend to my will.

To make me the center.

To give me the all.

I lift up, arching my back as my lips reach his jaw, and I brush them over his scruff. Draco groans, leaning his head into my touch.

A loud thump breaks us apart. It comes again from the door with a loud 'Draco!'.

"Nev these nevving warriors," he grumbles, pulling away from me and flinging himself off the bed.

I pull a blanket over myself as he stomps to the door and slides it to one side. "What?" he fires out with more force than is strictly necessary.

I hear Drega's low rumble, even though Draco's muscular form blocks my view. Not that I'm bothered. His arse is a thing of complete perfection. It looks like someone has carved it from marble, which glitters with gold flakes. Surely there is not an arse in the universe like his? Gorgeous hollows give way to hard muscle, and I lie back, thinking I could probably look at it forever and never get bored.

"My mate requires cleansing, food, and care. I don't care about the run until her needs are satisfied." Draco growls loudly.

Whatever Drega says, it doesn't impress Draco. "Just bring me food," he snarls. "Then we'll discuss the run."

"Don't let me get in the way of anything," I say as Draco snaps the door shut and turns back to me.

I might miss the arse, but the acres and acres of delicious abs on display more than make up for my loss.

"You come first," Draco says. "Drega and the others know this." He seems pensive, less intense than a few minutes ago, more distracted.

"I've looked after myself for a long time without you, Draco."

Apparently, that was the wrong answer. With a growl, I'm scooped up, blanket and all, with no ability to do anything other than wriggle wildly.

"I will mate you, little one, if you continue to make

those noises," Draco rasps, stalking towards another door at the rear of the bedroom.

"What noises?" I ask innocently, with an added squeak which elicits a groaning growl from him.

"Bad female."

The door opens, and I find we're in a rather luxurious bathroom with a large square tub more than big enough for several Dracos and me. It bubbles up with water which steams slightly.

"Why did we have to go all the way across the maze when you needed to shed, and you have all this right here?" I admonish Draco as he puts me on my feet and pulls the blanket away.

"Because I am a big male, and this is not big enough for a shed," Draco says with a dismissive wave of his hand.

I have to dip my head to hide the smirk. I suspect it's more like he *thinks* he needs bigger and better. There are noises behind us, and Draco turns with a snarl, leaving me in the bathroom.

I slowly lower myself into the bath and let out a sigh as the hot water washes over my aching muscles. I hurt, partly from all the damn running, but also from the positions Draco and I enjoyed. Plus the dragon.

Can't forget the dragon.

I don't know what's going to happen, but I do know whatever comes my way, I want it to be with Draco. My gorgeous, scaled hunk who thinks a bath the size of a swimming pool is 'too small' for him.

Who doesn't want to burn the world. He wants to give it to me instead, in pieces.

I think I might have lost something to Draco, and it's the last thing I was expecting to lose.

My heart.

DRACO

"What the nev do you want?" I snarl as I enter my bedroom.

Drega puts down the platter of food and folds his arms. "How did you do it?" he asks. "You know I've been trying since we got here."

"What?" I drop next to the food and devour half of it in what seems like an instant.

Turns out mating *and* shifting works up quite an appetite.

"Your nevving collar, Draco!" Drega grumbles. "When were you going to tell me you'd found a way of getting it off?"

My hand flies to my throat. Everything up until now has seemed so natural, so right, I'd almost forgotten Amber removed my collar last night.

"My mate," I stutter out. "She was able to remove it." I swallow and gather my composure. "I told you she was a key."

"And you were going to tell all of this...when?" My brother is annoyed.

He's annoyed because I've given him zar so many times about the collars, even recently, and he thinks I've been keeping this new development from him.

"I found out last night."

He snorts out a cloud of smoke.

"I did. During our mating..."

Drega holds up a hand. "I don't need all the details. Some of us haven't mated in a long time, Draco." He huffs with frustration.

I grin at him. "During our mating, my mate touched me..."

"Really?" Drega stomps a foot. "We're really going to do this, are we?"

"During our mating, my mate touched me just as I drove my cock into her sweet cunt..."

Drega puts his fingers in his ears and glares at me. I am enjoying myself, but I do need to get to the point.

"She found the catch on the collar and disabled it." I dig around in the bed and pull the thing out, dangling it from a single claw.

Drega slowly takes his fingers out of his ears and stares at the collar, before snatching it from me.

"This is it, Draco!" he says, his voice filled with enthusiasm. "This is what we need for the successful run. If your mate can get the collars off us all, we'll be unstoppable."

It makes me happy to see him happy. Drega has always been my second, not just because he's my brother but because he's always been supremely capable. On Kaeh-Leks, he was a commander in his own right of the healing corps, sensible and level-headed and incredible with tech.

It's only my influence which has turned him into a male who will destroy as much as he can heal, and who has developed an ability to go off on a tangent.

"We can't take our collars off, Drega," I sigh "and that's even if my mate can remove them from every warrior."

Drega drops his arms by his sides. "What do you mean? What about Draxx?"

"If she can take the collars off, we have to keep this as our secret weapon. It can't be used straight away, even on Draxx." My chest hurts as I think about my other brother, my immediate sibling, the one who is near enough insane with the need to shift.

Drega folds his arms again, managing to get his excitement under control. "Then we need to see if she can remove collars from any other warrior." He lunges forward, and before I can stop him, I hear a click as the collar reengages around my neck.

"Drega!" The snarl comes from the very depths of my soul.

Immediately I feel weaker, heavier, and, frankly, angrier. It's been so long since I was a full Sarkarnii, it's like my mind has forgotten. But my body hasn't. No wonder Draxx is struggling.

"We need to find out if she can get it off again and if she can take others' off."

"My mate is not touching another warrior." The growl which accompanies my words is probably overkill, but it doesn't bother Drega in the slightest, given he's always had the thickest skin.

"Why don't you get her now and see if she can take yours off again," Drega continues, oblivious to my glowering.

"Why have you put it back on?" Amber's sweet voice is filled with dismay.

I turn to her. She is wearing nothing but a simple drying cloth which barely covers any of her lusciousness. With a growl which could shake the very foundations of the Kirakos, I'm across the room and in front of her.

It seems I'm still not great with other males around my mate, despite our joining. Must still be in rut.

"Drega put it back on. Apparently, he wants to check it wasn't a fluke," I say, putting my hands on her upper arms to comfort her.

Amber leans to one side, around me, and glares at Drega. My heart skips.

The organ actually misses a beat while my mating gland goes into overdrive. My little *szikra* is looking at my brother like she wants to kill him with her eyes. My stomach squirms as I capture her chin between my finger and thumb, bringing that fierce gaze back to me.

"Try again for me, Amber."

"What if I can't?" she whispers, eyes filling with water, and something about her human *tears* sends all my insides into a slow, unpleasant squirm.

"I'm used to it. It is no hardship if it stays on." I study her face until she blinks away the water. "Whatever happens, you gave me a few hours of freedom, and that is more than enough."

I dip my head down, and she runs her fingers over the collar, searching and searching until she reaches around the back. Here she stops, and I can feel her little body going rigid. I put my mouth next to her ear and gently swipe my tongues over the little pink shell.

Amber gasps, something on my collar clicks, and the thing slides to the floor with a thump. Her stunning eyes with their round pupils, huge and black, meet mine. I slam my lips to hers, consuming her mouth, feeling my cock pushing from its pouch because there's virtually nothing between us, only the thin drying cloth, and I want her so, so much. I want to be inside her, taking her, devouring her.

Drega coughs.

"Any chance your mate could try my collar?" he asks.

I snarl loudly, but Amber puts a hand on my chest, pushing me back as she walks purposefully over to him.

"Down," she orders.

Drega eyes me and then drops to his knees. Amber doesn't waste time feeling around. This time, her sure fingers go straight to the right place.

For a seccari, I think nothing has happened until Drega rears away from her, his hands at his neck, and then, he lifts them away, collar in his palms.

"She can do it!" His voice is hoarse, his tail already extending and smoke curling from his nostrils.

I leap for him, grabbing the collar and clipping it back around his neck.

"No!" It's his turn to snarl.

"I can't have you shifting in my bedroom," I retort. "Or at all. Not yet."

He huffs, hand on his throat, knowing I'm right.

"You do know what this means, don't you, Draco?" he says with a smug smile twitching the corners of his mouth.

I narrow my eyes.

"It means your mate is coming with us on the run."

AMBER

fter Draco's brother told him I would have to go on the run, hell broke loose. Draco didn't snarl, growl, or roar. He just picked Drega up and threw him out of the room. He looked at me for an instant with a haunted expression, then followed the other hapless Sarkarnii, the door snapping shut behind him.

I look down. Draco's collar is still on the floor where he left it. Outside, the silence is broken by a low, guttural, slightly metallic croon which rises into a crescendo, followed by a number of loud crashes. I hurry to get dressed, but by the time I've found all my clothing which is scattered around the bedroom, the noises outside have gone, and what I can't hear is ominous.

Just as I'm about to attempt to work the door, it flies open, and Draco steps in. He's breathing hard, one shoulder red with blood.

It's not his blood.

He doesn't meet my eyes, only grabs the collar from the floor, and with a click, it's around his neck once again. Only then does his breathing slowly return to normal, but he still refuses to meet my eyes, simply sitting down on the bed with a curl of smoke, his hands in his lap, claws clacking together. They are also red with blood.

It's not his blood.

"Draco, what happened?" I ask, my voice like a mouse.

"Drega needed to know never to ask my mate to touch him again," he says, head still dipped. "He needs to know his place."

The sadness in his voice matches what I saw in his eyes earlier.

"I know you don't want me to come. Is it any consolation if I say I don't want to go on the run?"

"No."

This is different. This is not the Draco I know, but then how much do I actually know about him? I've been dragged through this alien prison by him, stuck together literally for a while, but other than being in close proximity and enjoying all the delights his body has to offer, do I really know this male?

He continues to stare at the floor, and I feel awkward. And then I feel uncomfortable. And then I feel scared.

I wasn't always like this. Once upon a time, I would face down the world. Until John, until he made me question my very existence. He turned me into a wreck who was unable to believe in herself.

"*Szikra?*" Draco looks up at me. "Why do you smell of fear?"

I'm not sure what to say. Instead, I take a step back from him.

Draco rises. He is so damn huge it seems to take him forever, but then he is towering above me, his scales flickering with light, his pupils mere slits.

"Why?" he thunders.

His default emotion.

"Because I am afraid, Draco. Sometimes I feel like I have always been afraid."

"You are my mate, and she has no fear."

"Have you any idea how ridiculous that sounds?" I fold my arms and look up at him.

"Are you afraid, little mate?" The words rumble through my chest.

And I am not afraid.

Somehow, I don't know how, Draco has stolen my fear from me. With the gorgeous eyes, the glass cut cheekbones, the dark scruff, the completely and utterly handsome Draco looking at me like I am the only thing in the entire universe, I am not afraid of anything.

Not anymore. Even if he is covered in someone else's blood.

"You belong to me, Amber. We are going on this run together, and nothing will pull us apart. Nothing will harm you, and nothing will touch you. Have no fear, not now, not ever, because you are mine."

The way he growls, it hits my core as if he's slid his tongue between my thighs again. No being deserves to be as sexy as Draco, but he owns it with every atom of his being. He inhales deeply, and as he exhales, that ever present curl of smoke rises from his nostrils. My mind flies back to last night when I found myself in the arms of a monster.

Not a monster, a dragon. An actual dragon.

"Can you breathe fire?" I ask and immediately have an inner cringe as I sound like a child.

The very corner of Draco's mouth twitches upwards. "I can."

He slowly extends the claw from his index finger and swipes it through his mouth, then he holds out his hand at arms' length and sucks in a shallow breath before his head jerks back, and he blows out his cheeks.

And a little flame dances on the tip of the claw, yellow with a blue center. It's mesmerizing as it lifts into a long thin streak and finally winks out of existence.

"Do humans make fire?" he asks innocently.

"Not like that," I say, warmth returning to my limbs because I have the hot body of Draco and all his fire. "But humans have made fire for thousands of years."

The smile which spreads over Draco's face is something else. It chases away the sadness I saw in him, and my heart speeds up.

"I'm glad," he says. "If you can make fire, you can control it."

"I can't control you." I laugh at him, one hand on his smooth, scaly chest, needing to feel his warmth, to be anchored by who he is.

The big bad alien who most likely got the wrong end of a bargain when he picked me.

"You have me, *szikra*. You have all of me in the palm of your hand." He holds my hand in his huge one, pressing his thumb into the center, and I close my fingers around it.

Tears roll down my face. I hadn't thought it was possible to feel so much, so hard, here, with Draco.

"I mean every word, little one. This is not the rut, not the mating gland." He lifts my hand up and places it on the right side of his chest. Beneath his skin, I feel the soft, slow thud. "This is me. You have set me on fire, and now the flames will never be doused."

DRACO

I've never wanted to dance for anyone in my entire life. But I want to dance for Amber, right here and right now. I want to prove to her she is my mate, and as is correct, I live only for her. I wish I hadn't had to fight with Drega, but the second I saw her putting her hands on another male, I knew it.

Amber is not just mine, she is part of me. She is what the ancestors give to us when we preserve their bones, and while all our culture is gone, I cannot deny fate.

I cannot deny her.

The rut is simply something which directs a Sarkarnii's heart. This is not the rut.

I love Amber.

It's the reason I slammed Drega to the floor. It's the reason I threw all the warriors crowding my ante-room out, slashing at them indiscriminately. It's the reason I'll do the run and succeed.

"Hey." Her soft voice draws me back. Her hand is on my jaw, gently scratching through my scruff.

"You need to eat," I grumble.

I want everything to be simple and nothing is simple. But feeding my mate is easy. I sit on the bed and pull her onto my lap, dragging the platter of food with me, I pick my way through the items until I find something I think she will like.

"We must eat, my mate," I say as I offer up the morsel. "The run is long. I need you well-nourished before we start."

Amber looks at me for a short while before opening her mouth and letting me put the food in. She chews with a thoughtful look on her face.

"That's good." She smiles. "What is it?"

"One of my favorites." I smile back, finding her another choice piece. "Roast tralu."

"The big hairy thing?" Amber stutters, her eyes blinking rapidly. "From yesterday?"

"Not that one, I don't think." I furrow my brow as I look at the platter. "Another one. More tender, I would say."

Amber hums, but I'm not sure if it's approval or not.

"I guess we eat stuff we ride too," she says to herself and holds out her hand for the piece I have.

I shake my head. "I do this for you, my mate. Let me."

Offering up the piece of food to her mouth, I watch her eye me for a second before again opening up and letting me put it in. As she chews thoughtfully, my cock stirs within its pouch. We need to eat, not mate.

It clearly hasn't got the message.

I want to mate, very much. But I want to be able to shift, to use my wings, my tail, all of me to please my female. And while the collar stays on, I cannot shift, and I cannot be the male she deserves.

So instead, my cock will need to remain sheathed, and my balls will have to remain hopelessly constricted in my pants. I will feed my female, and then we will prepare for battle.

I stride into my ante-room and get a baleful glance from Drega. He's cleaned himself up along with the other couple of warriors who got in my way. I know he could have fought back which only served to irritate me more.

He knows I wouldn't attack without reason, even when I'm in a rage. It's all about my mate, and somehow it makes it worse he didn't choose violence when I did.

I am Draco, and I need his respect.

"Draxx?" I fire at him.

"Still waiting," he replies.

"Weapons all good?"

"Some."

Now he's really starting to nev me off. "Show me."

Everyone throws themselves out of my way as I follow Drega who, I'm sure, will shove them aside if any of them try to follow us. We descend into the underground part of my quarters, which functions as a center of operations when we're preparing for a run. It's a place we hollowed out by hand and claw to ensure we had one place the wardens could not penetrate.

"One in three doesn't fire," Drega says as we enter the largest of the rooms. A target has been set up at the far end. "And I don't have time to fix them all."

"Why not?"

"Because you're busy rutting or kicking heads, and there's other things to organize, Draco," he says through gritted teeth.

I fire out an arm, grabbing him by the throat, but Drega knocks it away easily.

"We don't have time for this," he snarls.

"We don't," I agree. "And I don't have time for you to question my authority. This is my quadrant and my run." This time, I do get hold of him by his collar.

Drega glares at me. I'm glad of it. He was always the best of us. I want to see his fire again.

"We have a new weapon, but we need these. Do what you need to do, brother, and I will take care of the rest."

"Your mate?"

"She will come with us." It hurts my very soul to say the words. "But I want my time with her first, before the nevving run and without interference."

I want nothing more than to stay in my bedroom, curled around my mate, breathing in her scent. But I can't, and it's grating on me that I cannot do what I want and I have to take her into a dangerous situation, albeit with a large group of warriors who will protect her, and me, with their lives.

Why is my gut twisting at the thought? Why is everything suddenly so nevving hard? I give Drega one last snarl and make my way back to the ante-room.

Stood in the center, dripping with what looks like black slime, are two warriors. One is panting hard. The other is stood like a statue, and I'd recognize him anywhere.

"You ready for the run, Draxx?"

He turns, eyes burning with pain and anger. "Always," he rasps. "And if it kills me this time, I welcome it."

Great, now I have both a mate to protect and a brother with a death wish to go with the barely functioning weapons and a group of warriors who have long forgotten their training.

But I'm promised to my mate, and I will not allow this to be a disaster.

The run is in five ticks. I have time. I'll make time, for her.

And then we go.

And then nothing will ever be the same again.

AMBER

For five of what passes as days here in the maze, Draco has fed me, curled around me, and made love to me in so many glorious ways. It's a bliss I can't even fathom and I'm not convinced I deserve.

This morning, he rose before me and when I woke, there was a platter of food, but no Draco.

Why does it even bother me? I got used to being alone.

In fact, as I think about him, my heart does a long, lazy flip over in my chest, enough for it to mean I have to rub a circle there. I can't be falling for this alien bad boy, who has secrets he's not going to let me in on, even if he needs me.

I can tell Draco definitely has a plan, and while I wasn't part of it, I am now.

And I don't know how I feel about that. I miss him feeding me until I'm uncomfortably full. I can snap at him, lick his fingers, behave like a brat, and all he does is smile and smile, fangs on display as if he could eat me at any time. I want to prolong the time with him.

I want to spend time with him.

Without Draco, I get dressed slowly, luxuriously,

because I can. Because here, the only thing that wants me is Draco. Because while I have to run, with him, I don't need to run from him. The thought settles in my head like a hen on eggs as I comb my fingers through my unruly hair and look for any reflective surface to see if I can make myself look tidy.

Draco, predictably for a creature so damn cool he's arctic, doesn't have anything resembling a mirror, but there is a large, polished gold colored dish (or shield depending on your point of view) propped against the wall. I stare into it and what stares back is a woman I don't recognize.

My heart is gripped by an unseen fist, squeezed in my chest as a realization hits me. This woman looks happy. She looks relaxed, the lines around her mouth smoothed, a little smile around the lips. Her eyes sparkle with life.

I'd stopped looking at myself on Earth. Sure, I'd use a mirror, but I wasn't looking. I couldn't even meet my own gaze. I thought who I was had been stripped from me, and I blamed myself for letting that man do it. I couldn't even bring myself to blame him.

Except he was the one who made me run. He was the one who took my confidence, made me the shell of myself, all because I said no.

But the woman staring back at me will say no. She has a confidence I don't remember feeling. She's been dropped in an alien prison and survived.

She's found an alien and fallen in love with him.

Wait. What?

I'm in love with Draco?

But while I know he wants me, is it the same as love for him?

And why would he want me anyway? He's huge. He can turn into a dragon for god's sake. I'm nothing compared to him. Sure, he says he's in rut, but that could just be sex, couldn't it?

Before I get even a second to process the thought, there is a loud noise outside the room, part bang and part scraping sound. My flight or fight response is tripped, and I grab at the shield, then look around wildly for something, anything I can use as a weapon.

For a vicious dragon alien warlord, Draco's bedroom is devoid of anything useful. I feel rather silly holding the shield, so I put it down and approach the door. Whatever is out there, it's only going to be another Sarkarnii, surely?

The door snaps open, making me jump, but the corridor outside is empty. I stick my head out as slowly as I dare, but other than a few unidentifiable noises which seem far off, there is no sign of any Sarkarnii or Draco. A feeling of unease creeps over me. This is too like before. My need for him is wrong. I need to anchor myself to something else somehow. While I'm in an alien prison with so many things which want to kill me, I can't....

Voices!

I've already ventured out of the bedroom, and the door has closed behind me. On the one hand, I'm hoping it's Draco. But if it isn't, I don't know how the others will react to me. Or how Draco will react if he finds me alone with any of them.

After all, he damn nearly killed Drega and that was after he agreed I could touch his brother!

I look around, trying to find anywhere I can conceal myself, my heart beating like a drum as I back away down the corridor until I spot the conduit running along the side of the wall at ground level. It looks like there is just enough room for a tiny human woman to squeeze underneath. I dive for the floor and shove myself under as I spot several pairs of boots stomping around the corner. They come to a sudden halt, and someone calls out 'Draco' in a voice I don't recognize.

Further scraping and another pair of boots appears, followed by a long swaying tail which I do recognize.

"Warriors!" Draco's voice booms in the small space. "I trust you are ready for the run?"

"We came to collect our weapons," the unfamiliar voice says. "Drega advised they were ready."

"My brother has fixed everything up, as you would expect. He knows his tech," Draco says genially.

There's a low snort, and suddenly one of the pairs of feet disappears, only to reappear dangling six inches over the floor accompanied by a sound of choking.

"Is there something amusing about this run, warrior?" Draco snarls. "Something amusing about me or my brothers?"

"No, Draco." The words are strangled.

"I expect every single one of my warriors, my *den*, to be ready. This is the last run we will do." Draco sounds as if he's struggling to get the words out, his voice low and dangerous.

"How is it going to be like any other run?" the other unseen warrior asks, a somewhat ill-advised question given his feet also disappear for an instant like his colleague's, before they reappear, several inches from the ground in a similar position with similar noises.

A fear seizes at my gut. Draco has been nothing but gentle with me, nothing but protective, and even though I know what he can and what he will do, this situation reminds me of my past in too many ways.

"I have a secret weapon this time, warrior." Draco growls low. "A female who is a key, who can do things no other being can. She is the reason we will be successful this time and no other." Boots thump to the floor, a knee appears as coughing fills the air. "I brought you this success. I found the female. Me, and don't you forget it." He snarls.

My heart is ice.

Draco has a plan. It involves me. I am something useful.

What happens when this is all over?

DRACO

Five ticks was not enough. I promised my mate forever and instead all I got was five nevving ticks. Now I'm run off my feet, hating every second of being collared and having to deal with warriors who, like any Sarkarnii, are questioning every nevving thing I ask of them.

But we've failed on every single run up until now, and all I can do is try to give them hope, any sort of hope I can. I'm grasping at anything, the weapons, a myth, anything, just to ensure they are as focussed as possible. Even telling them about my Amber being a key.

Because my mind is made up. As much as I want to take my precious, my beautiful *szikra* with me, I cannot expose her to such danger. It will make things twice as hard, harder even, but I love her too much to put her at risk. She can stay in my quarters, barricaded in, and once we're successful, I'll come back for her.

"Is everything okay, Draco?" Amber asks as I pick at nothing on my pants.

The run will be announced at any moment. I need to get to my warriors, but I still haven't told her she will be staying here. Words have always come easily, violence even easier, but explaining to my mate she will have to stay behind while I undertake the run, something she already knows is highly dangerous? I can't work out what I should say.

"Just running through some last-minute details." I tap the side of my head.

Even mating hasn't been quite the same because I want to be able to shift, but I don't want to do it again until we are free. Until I can be the mate she deserves.

I take her hand. "I haven't danced for you."

"There's still time, and I won't let you forget it anyway." She smiles. "I'm looking forward to it."

All I want to do is enclose her in my arms, hold her, breathe in her scent, never let her go. Amber is my end and my beginning. She is what I'm really fighting for. I should have told her my plans.

I should have told her everything. About the map, about the Kirakos. About why we're even here.

But it's too late.

"We need to go." I get to my feet, and she joins me as I walk through to my ante-room, where Drega is waiting.

He throws me the cloak and the handheld pulsar before pulling his on.

"Is everything ready?" I ask.

"As it will ever be," he replies, his jaw set.

"Draxx?"

"I haven't seen him."

"Nev!" I snarl, mostly to myself. "I told him this was the one."

"Then maybe you should have told him your mate could remove collars."

The way Drega looks at Amber has my fire rising faster than it should. When I breathe out, sparks fly. Drega doesn't back off. He looks between us both just as the siren sounds.

"We don't have time for this, Drega."

"We have all the time," he retorts. "If this is the one, this is the one, and I'm as desperate as Draxx to get out of here and out of these collars."

"You've made this place your personal playground," I fire back. "I know what you do for the wardens. This is my run, and we will do it my way." I curl my hands into fists. "Don't make me hurt you, Drega."

It's his turn to snort. Amber is stood, staring between us. She folds her arms.

"What if I don't want to come? Did either of you think about that?"

All of my attention and all of Drega's is concentrated on her.

"*Szikra?*"

"What if I don't want to be a part of it?" Amber is shaking on her feet, two red spots appearing on her cheeks.

She looks like she did the day I first set eyes on her. It's as if nothing at all has passed between us, nothing.

The second siren sounds.

"I don't want you to come," I blurt out, the bald statement hanging in the air.

"Draco! We don't have any choice. She has to come. Without her, we will fail." Drega's hands splay as his head now swings between Amber and me. "Please, little female, come with us, help us," he pleads.

"Go!" I snarl at him. "Go and be seen. I'll be with you shortly."

Drega's shoulders slump. But then there is another sound. Not a siren. Not a viewer. It's the sound of laser fire.

Without thinking, I'm racing out of my quarters. If my warriors have started shooting already, we have a problem. The wardens cannot think we are armed until we are at least close to the finish.

"What's going on?" I shout up at Drasus as we mount the stairs out of my quarters.

The big male is hunkered down behind a large pillar. A laser bolt zips overhead.

"The Xicop started shooting," he calls back. "Just after the second siren."

"Is anyone shooting back?" I grind out.

"No, no one has returned fire, just like you ordered, but we're pinned down here, and we can't start the run."

I see a few more streaks overhead. "Anyone injured?"

Drasus shakes his head.

"Nev," I grind out, looking behind me at Drega and Amber.

Has someone passed information to the wardens about my plans? I've been very careful to keep the aims as close to my chest as possible, with only Drega knowing everything. I trust him with my life, with my very existence.

But it doesn't mean someone hasn't let slip about our weapons, most likely not a Sarkarnii but one of the various other inmates who think they might gain something by hanging around.

I stride out into the central square, our usual starting point, as the laser bolts zap past me and hold up my hands. High above, there is a large viewer, hovering in what passes for a sky in the Kirakos. The face of Warden Noro appears.

"Draco," he intones.

The laser bolts cease.

"I do hope you're not too surprised to see me." I grin up at him.

I see his jaw working, and I'm very pleased I got to him.

"If you've quite finished, *Warden*, we'd like to start the run."

"You have hidden weapons," he says, his voice echoing over the maze.

"Not at all," I call up. "Warriors?"

My Sarkarnii brethren step out from where they've been sheltering from the weapon fire.

"Decloak," I order.

Each one flings back his cloak. Each one displays only his teeth and claws.

"Is this satisfactory?" I put my hands on my hips and glare up at the screen.

Behind Noro, I can see the other wardens, including Gondnok. Noro seethes silently before he barks out the order. Up above us, the Xicops on their flybikes turn and head away from my quadrant.

"You have some catching up to do, Draco," he snarls out. "The run has started, and the other inmates are already closing in on the first station."

The screen goes black, and I stare at it for a short while. Until I feel rather than hear the deep rumbling beneath my feet.

"Nev it!" I grab for Amber's hand. "The maze is moving. Warriors!" I leap forward into the square as walls slowly swing.

This is not how the run is supposed to play out, but then, in the Kirakos, there are no rules.

Behind us, there is a low crunching sound as a wall which has never moved before slides over the entrance to my quarters with a grating finality.

And now I have no option but to take my *szikra* with me on the run.

AMBER

Draco seemed to have it all under control. And then he didn't. His hand is around mine as the entrance to the underground area he calls home is inexorably closed off.

His eyes darken as he looks down at me. All that stuff about not wanting me to go on the run was so obviously for Drega's benefit as I already know he fully intends for me to go with him.

I'm the 'key', apparently. He's using me like he's using this situation, this run. There's no more noble cause than Draco. I freed him and now I'm useful.

The thoughts tumble over and over in my head as Draco strides into the thick of everything, ignoring the weapons fire. He is entirely at ease.

He is entirely in control.

"Stay with me, *szikra*," he commands as his hand winds around mine, hot and dry. "We have to run now."

My guts churn. I stood up to him and yet he doesn't care. He's carrying on regardless of my feelings and what I want. So, when the maze starts to move, I'm entirely in his hands.

Doing what he wants. My limbs are frozen, but I have no alternative. I'm dragged along behind him as the rest of the Sarkarnii take up position behind us and we dive into the maze. The sounds of feet beating on the ground in harmony, the occasional grunt as one or more of the warriors takes a hit but still keeps going. They do not fire back, they do not lose focus. They run on, with Draco in the thick of it and me trailing alongside like an idiot.

If I needed to be reminded just how small and insignificant I am, because it's not something which has plagued me for the last three years of being stalked like a deer, being surrounded by these powerful warriors, albeit with their power diminished due to the collars they wear, but not so much to make them less of a force, does the trick.

My lungs burn, but a noise above me means I momentarily look up. Above us are huge screens, like the one Draco addressed earlier, only instead of the weird purple slug warden, the one who thought it was funny to electrocute Draco and handcuff us together, there are multiple faces, like an alien Zoom call, only here, our audience is screaming for blood, not wondering if they can turn off the video feed and have a snooze.

This part is not a lie. We are entertainment.

"Which way, Draco?" Drega asks as we reach a crossroads.

Draco doesn't reply, and he doesn't hesitate, taking the left fork as if he's walked this way his entire life. His tail has extended and is wagging back and forth a little like a dog.

I don't know what Draco is anymore. All I know is I let him in because I am weak. I spent so much of my life running, and when someone gives me the opportunity to stop running, I take it. I grab at it with both hands. I surrender my heart.

And I get trampled on, as usual.

For now, all I can do is grit my teeth. I want to be wrong about him, about myself, but how can I forget how he boasted about me?

"*Szikra*." Draco turns to me. "We need you."

My heart does a flip in my chest. I inwardly admonish the organ. I can't care what he wants, what he thinks of me, can I? He's just the male who saved me.

He doesn't own me.

Well aware of the scrutiny from the other warriors, some of whom still openly gaze in awe at me—or at least I think it's awe. Draco says many of these warriors have not seen a compatible female in some time. The rest feign indifference, but either way, I hate being the center of their attentions. I walk over to where Draco has come to a halt.

It's a blank wall. Of course it is.

"Little mate, my gorgeous Amber, can you find a way through for us?"

His honeyed words grate on me. This is a test, a test in front of all his den, all his warriors. He wants me to prove to him, to them, that he is as great as he says.

Despite myself, I put my hands on the wall, doing what he asks but not really trying. In the distance, there is a sound which sets every hair on my body on edge. It's not a roar, it's not mechanical, but it seems to speak to my ancient DNA as being something very bad.

Draco's head snaps around. "Drasus?"

The massive, broad warrior with the long plait down the back of his head slams his claws into the wall next to us and climbs, hand over hand, foot over foot, claws eating into the stone like butter, until he's around halfway up.

"Some of us have managed to access some of our abilities, despite the collar," Draco says in my ear, his velvet growl making me shiver. "Drasus was always a powerhouse of a Sarkarnii, as you can see."

He sounds...proud of his warrior. He sounds like he cares. Draco gazes upwards at Drasus who, holding on by one hand, looks out over the maze.

"Vesso," he calls down.

"Nev," Draco rasps. "The last nevving thing we need. They know about the weapons." He glares around him.

"What is a vesso?" I ask, feeling I probably don't want to know the answer.

"That is," Drega replies before Draco has a chance. He points up into the sky and, as I follow his gaze, I wish I hadn't.

It's full of what can only be described as a flying leech. Blunt head, filled with teeth, rotating in a circular fashion, its body's a nasty browny green and covered in lumps. The thing is held up in the air by whatever the equivalent to drones are in this place.

It is not happy, bucking and writhing in the bonds which hold it. Slime drops in huge quantities from its body, deluging the maze below.

I start working my hands over the blank wall as fast as I can, feeling for anything, anything which might give this particular place away as a secret door.

"Anything?" Draco asks, his voice even.

"Nothing." I grit my teeth to stop them from chattering, attempting to concentrate.

"Try here." Draco gestures to the other side of the wall.

"I don't think this is going to work," I say, but, with no other options, I move to where he says, again attempting to carefully work my way over the wall and ignoring the increasingly loud, increasingly earsplitting sounds of the alien leech.

And the fact that their numbers have multiplied.

A warm body is pressed up behind me, a familiar scent in my nostrils, all smoke and musk. It shouldn't ground me, it shouldn't be helping, but it is. I feel like I can see what I'm doing, and as I reach as high above my head as I can, the hidden catch slides in my fingers. Draco is my key.

With a clunk and a hiss, the wall drops back and slides, grating every inch of the way backwards, just as the drones above us release the vesso.

The huge creatures screech so loudly I have to cover my ears as I'm hustled through the entrance and we find ourselves in a dimly lit void.

"Well done, little female." Drega congratulates me as he passes.

A number of the other warriors make appreciative noises until they see the look on Draco's face and the company goes silent. Behind us, the door shifts back into position, and now we are in complete darkness.

"What now?" I ask into the night.

DRACO

If the wardens are using vesso, someone really doesn't want us to complete the run. Whether it's because they know we have weapons or something else, there's been a breach somewhere because they are throwing everything at us, and we haven't even reached a quarter of the way.

I knew there was a reason I didn't want to bring Amber, and this is the reason. If anything, anything were to harm her, it would be the end of me.

She is my fate, my everything.

But if I don't complete this run, if we don't get to the map and gain control of this place, I don't get to keep her. Everything which matters to me will be lost too.

And I'm not about to let that happen.

"Amber!" I take hold of her shoulder in the darkness.

She turns to me with blank eyes, unable to see like a Sarkarnii can.

"What's happening, Draco?" Her voice is small in this dark, confined space.

Although my warriors have backed off as far as possible,

they are all still too nevving close to her for me to feel in any way comfortable. Frankly, they could be on another planet and my blood will still be boiling.

"Lights," I growl over at Drega, and he produces, from the depth of his cloak, a fire stick. I spit a flame, and it bursts to life.

The flickering light illuminates the faces of my fellow warriors and of my gorgeous little mate. In this moment, despite being in the midst of the biggest mission I've run since we came to the Kirakos, I couldn't love her more.

Our ancestors were right to put females at the heart of everything, to cherish and nurture them, to allow them to be the strategists while we were the fighters. The look of stoic determination on my mate's face, despite the fact I can scent bitter fear from her, is evidence enough of how incredible females are.

"We need a way out, my mate." I gently cup her face in my hand. "I know you can find one."

"But the vesso?" she says, her voice trembling just slightly.

"If I'm right, the vesso will have been dropped into the wrong part of the maze, and we will not have to battle them," I reply. "But even if we do, you will be safe. Won't she, my warriors?"

Around me, there is a low murmur of agreement, my warriors deliberately not wanting to upset Amber by being rowdy, which is a surprise.

"Please, Amber," I whisper.

She pulls her chin from my hand and marches over to the back wall. I take hold of her shoulders and turn her the other way. She huffs at me, and a part of my soul feels strange. What she's radiating, her reluctance to help, to come with us—it all points to something being wrong.

I do not want my mate to hurt. I do not want her scared, or sad, or anything other than safe and secure. We might be in the midst of a run, but whatever it is she needs, she can have.

Amber ignores everyone and then begins her slow tracing over and over the rough surface, her face now a mask of concentration.

"What about the collars?" Drega murmurs to me.

"What about them?" I snarl back. He doesn't back down, and the atmosphere tenses. "We will deal with the collars when it's time."

There's a clunk at the wall next to my mate and the sounds of weights dropping, gears turning, and with a final screech, light appears around the edges of the door.

But nothing more.

"Warriors!" I bark.

My Sarkarnii jump to it, all of them straining at the partial opening as Amber stands to one side. I thump my shoulder into the wall as well, considering how much easier all of this would be if any one of us could shift.

But shifting has to be the last resort. We cannot let any of the wardens know. They managed to disable our shift for long enough after our capture before we were collared, and I know they can do it again. Until we have control, I cannot risk any single one of my warriors unnecessarily.

I need them all if I am to be successful. Although, right now, looking back at my mate, I feel like being successful is not necessarily the end of it all.

I need her. I need to understand how humans work, if they have fated mates, if she loves me too. I need her to know she is mine and how I long to dance for her, to make her a home, to see her nest and bear my young.

I've never felt these things before, and it is alien, uncomfortable, and nevving distracting. The run is everything. Without it, I cannot have her.

A sharp grinding and the door finally moves wide enough to allow warriors through. Drega leads them while I push my mate behind me and palm the pulsar, ready for anything.

"Draco." Amber turns to me, her hand on my chest, her eyes filled with water. "I know I could have picked a better time, but we need to talk."

"You're right, there could be a better time, my *szikra*." I gaze down at her, feeling the smoke in my lungs and the squeeze of worry in my belly.

I would defend her with my life.

My warriors are nowhere to be seen. I glare around, my fire rising within me because they have broken ranks and disobeyed my orders.

"Over there!" Amber calls out, and I follow her gaze.

The walls of the maze are no longer moving. The ground is. Leaving Amber behind, I race towards it, towards them, but it's too late. The crack is too wide to breach, unless I'm in my Sarkarnii form, and it's still too early to reveal what we can now do.

"Go!" I call across to them. "Complete the run. I will find you and meet you at the end."

Drega's features are set. His jaw is tight. All he's ever wanted to do is heal. All I've ever asked from him is destruction. I would be a very bad brother if I didn't know how much he enjoyed it. Suddenly, he cries out, pointing behind me, and as I turn, I see the lone Xicop, his hand clamped on Amber's arm, his face twisted in anger as he writhes at her.

She's not making any sound, but she's struggling. Her eyes meet mine as he wrenches her again, and her mouth opens in a silent scream.

My vision sheets red. I cannot use fire because I cannot risk hurting Amber, but I can use my claws and my teeth, and I can rip the Xicop's arm from his body.

And I can beat him over the head with it, and I can make sure I slice him so completely, he will never recover. I can't be a full Sarkarnii, but I can protect my mate.

I will always protect my mate, with every atom of my being.

AMBER

The second Draco sees me and the other alien fighting, he stills, flexing out his hands, claws full and sharp. He extends his neck and sinuously moves his head to one side. His pupils are mere slits as his forked tongue appears briefly from between his lips.

And then, without any ceremony, he becomes violence.

He is laser concentrated on destroying every last atom of the alien who has hold of me. While I know this maze has no room for those who are not prepared to fight back, that much has become clear to me in my short time here, what is happening before my eyes, here and now, is something else.

I shouldn't watch, but I can't not. There's never going to be a good time to see this, just like there was never going to be a good time for me to tell him what I heard, how it made me feel, how terrified I was on Earth.

And that he can't fix the past, but I want him to fix my future.

I want to be with him. I always want to be with him. Watching him lead his warriors, my brain finally caught up with my heart. He strode out into the line of fire, not because of ego but because he wanted to protect them, draw the weapons away, stop the fight until they were ready.

He tries to pretend he doesn't care, but he does. He cares so damn much he'll do anything for the ones he loves.

And he wasn't going to take me on the run because he was so scared of losing me.

Draco is covered in acid green blood as he bends over the body of the creature, as if he wants to rip its throat out, and it wouldn't surprise me if he did. Except he stills. The bioluminescence of his scales shine through the gunk covering him. It ripples in stuttering waves. He isn't even breathing hard despite what he's just done.

"No one touches my mate," he growls, his deep rasping voice ringing around the strange cavern we're in.

As I press my back to the wall, my head spins. I thought I was the key, his secret weapon.

I didn't think he'd rip another being apart just for touching me.

My heart hammers in my chest. Fear seizes at the organ, and when it seems to stop dead, I sway on my feet. I don't know if I want this.

I don't know if I want this at all. Giving up control to another, giving away my life at his whim. The time I've spent with Draco has been the best time of my life. I have felt at the center, cherished and cared for. I don't remember ever feeling this way. But also, I'm just a pawn. I'm just the mouse in the maze.

I will always have to run.

My knees give out, and I fall back against the wall behind me, red dots in my vision, breath in short, constricting bursts. I can't see, I can't hold on to consciousness, and I don't want to.

I don't want to fight anymore. Maybe I should just stop fighting? Maybe I should accept my fate?

A strange slithering, cold and unpleasant, at my back penetrates the strumming blood in my veins, the difficulty in getting air, in staying alive. I claw at the air as any support is pulled away and know whatever happens next, it's going to hurt like hell.

I hit the ground hard, all the air being expelled from my body as the hidden door I've fallen through snaps closed with a metallic zipping sound. Despite the pain, I'm on my feet and slapping my hands on the wall.

"No!" I cry, to no one. "I wasn't ready, I hadn't made a decision. I hadn't told him..."

Without any ability to concentrate, I'm running my hands over the wall, trying to find the catch, trying to find a way back. I might not have been sure, but I didn't want the decision taken from me. I wanted to be able to make it myself.

"We have her." The voice is strangled by some sort of technology.

I spin around to see three more of the heavily armored guards, pig-like snouts bristling with tusks and four piggy eyes. But somewhere, somewhere near and yet not near, there is a low, dark roar which ends in the most terrible howl.

My insides turn to liquid. There is only one creature who could possibly be making the noise.

Draco. Because I left him.

"The Sarkarnii is trapped," one guard says as the other two advance on me. "He is no longer a threat. Bring her."

His face, such as it is, has something which could pass for a smile, and it's terrible. There are no bargains to be made here.

"Such a pretty pretty." One of them fingers my hair, but then his hand is knocked away by another.

"Don't touch. She is for the wardens, and they are going to be very pleased we stole her from the Sarkarnii."

"Promotion?" The one holding me, his piggy eyes glittering with hidden menace, has some froth on his jaw.

"Promotion. So, keep your dick in your pants."

My would be assailant oinks in a way which either means he agrees or he doesn't care, but given I hear the long, low howl again, my heart hits the floor.

What have I done?

DRACO

"What's the plan?" I rasp at the Xicop under my grasp. Losing a few limbs or some of his disgusting blood is unlikely to stop the creature in the long run. The wardens have medical facilities which can all but bring most species back from the dead.

It's the reason they were able to collar us. It's the reason the collars were successful in the first place.

"There is no plan," the Xicop chokes out, but I dig my claws farther into his flesh, and he groans.

Pain still works, whatever you are and no matter what medical facilities are to come.

"I don't believe you, and you really don't want me unhappy, guard."

"I-I can't tell you, they'll kill me."

"But I can also kill you, and believe me, making it slow is all part of the fun." I grin down at him with all my fangs.

He's lost a lot of what passes for blood in these foul creatures, but he visibly pales. The stories about the Sarkarnii have travelled well. We were not known for mercy.

And yet as warriors we were always merciful.

"They know about the map. Warden Noro wants it for himself. He's going to steal your mate, the one he made sure you took, and he's going to wait until you have it before he kills her and takes what's his."

The Xicop sounds remarkably happy about this plan for a creature just about to meet whatever ancestors would have him.

"No one will take my mate from me." I don't recognize my own voice as I snarl down at what's left of this thing who threatened my Amber.

My eyes flick over to where she's standing. I hardly want her to witness this, but I have no...

She's not there.

I let go of the Xicop and look around wildly.

There is no Amber. Her scent is faint and fast disappearing under the unpleasant metallic odor of the Xicop's blood and the old dust of the maze complex.

"Amber?" I call out.

There is no response. Under my knee, the Xicop begins a throaty, coughing chuckle.

"It's too late, Sarkarnii," he says, even as I clutch at his throat. "They already have her. You put yourself right where Noro wanted. Your mate will die, as will you."

"Then why would I do anything at all, if it's already written?" I glare down at him. One eye is clear of blood and glassy.

Too glassy. I look closer. He's wearing a lens. I grasp for his ear, pulling at his head and ignoring his groan of pain. He has a comms device implanted behind it.

"Because," he gasps, "if you bring me the map, I'll give you your mate."

"Nev you, Noro!" I growl, slamming the Xicop's head

back against the ground. I stare directly at him, knowing there is an uplink to the warden. "I'm coming for my mate and the map. If you don't kill me first, I will end you."

I reach down and slowly, slowly extend a claw before I use the other hand to cover the eye and slam my hand into the side of the Xicop's head in order to make him yell.

I could just remove the eye, but then I'd get even filthier than I already am and any longer spent here is time I could be searching for Amber.

Flipping the Xicop over, I stand on his back. It's unlikely he's going anywhere, but until I work out what to do next, I can't take any risks. My *szikra* is relying on me.

She needs me and I failed her.

Blackness swims around me. My fire is almost out. It's as if I cannot feel anything, when all my life all I've done is feel everything.

I need my mate. I need my *szikra*. I need my Amber.

Without her, the run, the Kirakos, the map—they're nothing but ash and bones.

I crouch down, curling my hands into fists, breathing in and out, concentrating on the pit in my stomach, the accelerant which doesn't want to rise, the mating gland which strums out a tune I've never heard before, one which makes me want to dance, even as I'm staring into despair.

The galaxy has conspired to take my species, my family, even my ancestors from me. My den is gone into the ether, and my mate, the one being I pledged myself to protect, has been ripped away.

This run should be my triumph. It should not be the one thing which breaks me. I will not be broken.

The maze seems like it's on fire. The reflections of the flames, the old Sarkarnii tune, dance over my scales. But they are dull in comparison to Amber's beauty. The one thing I want to see and the one thing I cannot.

Warden Noro will find a way to punish me regardless of what I bring him. My den of warriors, my brothers, will never, ever forgive me if I bow to such a pseudo-tyrant, hiding behind tech stolen from a thousand other species and purchased from the foulest of them all, the Liderc.

But what else can I do? What else is possible while he has Amber? If I broke my bargain with her, if I failed in my only duty to keep my mate safe, then I have no choice. A Sarkarnii always puts his mate first.

Always.

I have to complete the run and give him my prize.

AMBER

The guard has his hand twisted in my hair. As much as I have hold of it, he's still managing to twist it so it feels like my scalp is going to come off as I'm dragged through the maze and onto a hovering platform, balancing over an abyss which drops away into a blackness the likes of which I've never seen.

Sounds and smells rise up as I'm thrown across the platform, skidding to a halt as I slam up against the sides which slope inwards. My shoulder hits first, and the pain is excruciating, exploding through me and making my stomach turn over.

"Don't damage it!" one of the other guards says, shoving at the one who had hold of me.

"It can't damage that easily. It's been mated to a Sarkarnii." He oinks and stomps over. I'm grabbed by the hair again, lifted up into his ugly face. "If it can take a Sarkarnii, it can take a Xicop."

I squirm like fuck and aim a kick at his crotch. Surprisingly, it connects, and with a bellow, he drops me and grasps at what is presumably the place he keeps his junk.

There's no respite. I'm grabbed from behind, my arms pinned painfully, and I'm thrust partially over the side, staring down into the blackness below.

"Don't try anything, Sarkarnii's mate." The words are hissed in my ear. "The wardens might want you alive, but if you happen to have a little accident while escaping, that's your problem."

I attempt to twist to look at him, but I'm shoved hard against the side, my stomach pushing painfully into the sharp edge. My head thrust downwards.

"If, for any reason, you were to survive the fall, the pit inhabitants would mince you in seconds." He snarls as a weird thumping noise rises up to me. "So, mate of the Sarkarnii, if I were you, I'd be co-operative."

I'm released suddenly and slide down onto the floor, coughing, unable to do any more other than eye the guards warily. At least I know one thing.

They don't have armor everywhere.

The one I kicked in the nuts, or the warthog alien equivalent, gives me a filthy glare, but with warning grunts from his two colleagues, he turns away and, as if by remote, because no one appears to be steering, the platform rises up into the air.

Health and safety are not a thing in this alien prison, and I can see the maze below me from the open back as we get higher. The huge walls, like concrete, shift as I watch. In places, it burns. It's worse than before, worse than the day I first saw it. Worse than the day I met Draco.

A fist grinds in my guts. How could I have been so fucking stupid as to get caught? Whatever I think of Draco, whatever my heart wants but my head is refusing to accept, I don't want to see him hurt. I don't want any of the Sarkarnii hurt. From the little interaction I've been allowed with them, they are a group of dysfunctional lost boys, posturing and fighting one minute, various parts of them turning into various parts of the creature Draco became, begging forgiveness from each other and from Draco the next.

The platform banks to the left, and the maze disappears as we fly into something like a tunnel. Pinpricks of light flash by and an icy wind whips up. The Xicops are all at the opposite end of the platform, confident I'm not going to try anything.

I close my eyes. Lean my head back against the wall of the platform and try to ignore all my aching limbs. Because the thing which hurts the most is the one thing I've been desperately, desperately trying to ignore.

My heart.

It hurts. It physically hurts in my chest. I didn't think such a thing was possible, but it is. I let Draco in. I let my big fire breathing, tail teasing monster into my world, into my life. I trusted him, I took strength from him.

The ridiculous organ doesn't want to beat, it just wants to ache. It's telling my head I was so, so wrong about Draco.

The howl. The cry of abject pain and loss I heard back in the maze. Was it him? Was he angry at my loss or angry because he lost me?

Something bubbles up inside me, something I don't remember ever feeling before. It's a desire to override my head, to make it see the heart isn't wrong.

That I'm not wrong. Not this time, not about Draco.

The platform suddenly drops, and my shoulder grates, pain spiking through me in another stomach churning bout. My vision dims, the red spots reappearing, and this time, this time, I give into it.

I let the unconsciousness take me.

"Is it still alive?"

"Oo-munz are remarkably resilient. Reviving them is very easy."

"This one was a bit broken."

"It's not now."

"But is it alive?"

"For god's sake! Yes, I'm alive!" I spit out, sitting upright with a growl.

Two of the slug-like wardens are on either side of me. These are thinner than the one Draco and I encountered or the one in the sky. One wears something which looks suspiciously like a lab coat. Both of them rear back a little at my sudden movement.

"Told you it was alive," one says to the other. "You. Are. Healed. Oo-munz," it says staccato.

"I. Am. Going. To. Punch. You," I reply, my teeth gritted.

I'm fed up of being the mouse. I want these aliens not to treat me like a lesser life form. Yes, I woke up and chose violence. Maybe I'm channeling my inner Draco.

The aliens look at each other and slither back from me. The one on my left uses his little arms to press on a panel.

"We have a code orange," it says.

I roll my eyes.

Then the door opens, and the thing from my nightmares clicks in. The lobster-octopus alien.

"It's alive?" The words bubble out as if from underwater.

"Your guards didn't kill it. But it's not friendly," one of the slugs says.

The thing turns to me, weird eyes on stalks glaring. One

pincer snips the air menacingly, and as much as I try to stay strong, to not be afraid, I feel my mask slipping.

"Then it will know pain," the thing says. "For not complying."

And it advances on me.

DRACO

There are tunnels within the maze, not just below it, although I had hoped having Amber with us would have given us an edge for what we were doing, not because she can find doors but due to her ability to remove collars.

Although, the thought of her touching any other warriors had filled me with anger. Until I saw the Xicop with his hands on her.

My concern about her touching other Sarkarnii paled into nothingness. Instead, I was blinded by pure, unadulterated rage. A rage so great I blocked everything else out.

And it meant I lost her, lost the run, lost everything.

I'm not even thinking about where I'm going as I pick up my pace through the maze. I could do with getting higher, being able to see more, but just making progress is all I can think about. Every now and then, it throws something at me, a melabuk, a yeykok looming out of the darkness—all are quickly dealt with and dispatched.

I have no time for them, no time for distractions. All I

can do is keep moving and keep thinking. There has to be a way to get to her, to my mate, my *szikra*.

Amber is all of these things, and I was too concentrated on the rut, what it meant, how it would mess with the run, to see what she is.

Heartsfire.

Warden Noro will kill her, regardless of what I do for him. My only hope is to get to her first.

It's a distant hope.

All the time I'm running, I'm thinking of what she wanted to say to me, the reason those words set my skin on edge worse than when I needed to shed.

A shed she helped with. My new scales are almost impermeable to pulsar bolts. Without her, I could not have stood up to the wardens.

Everything revolves around Amber, everything. When they gave her to me, they had no idea what had been unleashed. Not just within me, but within her too.

Ahead, I spot a set of climbing hoops which will lead me up to the top of the maze. The entire place is alive with noise, the sound of pulsar fire, shrieks of vesso and all the other creatures from the pit sent to taunt the hapless runners. But above me, I can hear voices.

Xicop voices.

As quietly as I can, I climb up and up until I'm close to the top.

"Have they stopped the Sarkarnii yet?" One Xicop asks.

"You know they have no intention of stopping them until they reach the citadel. Then the Warden is going to hit them with everything he has," another laughs. "They'll be atoms by the time he's finished. All he wants is Draco."

"Why that bastard?" the first sneers. "I'd happily put

him down myself if he ever came within range." I feel a nasty smile creeping over my face.

"He has something the Warden wants, and the Warden has something he wants," the laughing Xicop says. "But they're all dispensable, one way or another."

"I've heard those oo-munz are a perfect vessel for getting your dick wet..."

The first Xicop doesn't get the chance to finish his sentence as he's too busy wondering if he can fly when I shove him off the top, not even listening to the sound he makes as he hits the ground.

The second fumbles for his weapon, but as soon as it's in his hand, I've swiped it out, making the thing skitter along the rough surface until it hits their platform.

"Take me to Noro," I snarl, slamming my fist into his stomach and then wrapping my hand around his neck, shoving my pulsar weapon into his side. "Or I'll fire this into your guts, and you can die slowly."

"Okay! Okay!" He gasps and grunts, holding his hands up.

I must have found a Xicop with a sense of preservation which has overriden his fear of the Warden. He stumbles towards the platform and, as we get on, I grab at his wrist, ripping away the controller and pressing on the 'base' button before he can do anything stupid.

It rises up as I keep my hand tight around his throat. I'd rather not be this close to him—Xicops stink—but he'll make a useful shield if I need one.

On the pre-programmed course, we bank, and I see the maze below me. There are plenty of runners still going. Given the level of destruction I can see from high above, the wardens are doing what they can to give their paying audience a show.

It's a smokescreen any Sarkarnii could be proud of. I can only hope Warden Gondnok holds up his end of our bargain, that if we are successful in our run, in exposing Noro, he will let us free. If he doesn't, even getting to my mate, even getting the map, it will all be worthless.

I need the Kirakos.

The platform straightens, and we move through the portal from the airspace above the maze into the service tunnels. I have some idea of where the base for the Xicops is situated, and it's still a long way from any part of the Warden controlled area of the Kirakos where it's most likely they will be holding my Amber.

I tamp down the accelerant which is filling my fire sacs. As much as I want to incinerate everything I can, I need my mate. I need Amber to fill the horrible yawning emptiness inside me.

Then she can tell me what she wants to do with those who would dare to part us.

We burst out into a large, dark space, lit by the many lights of the living quarters belonging to the Xicops and others who serve the wardens. My captive grunts at me.

"You'll need to send the code to be allowed to land."

"Why are you being so helpful?" I snarl in his ear.

"I want to keep my head on, Sarkarnii," he grumbles. "I'm sure you can make it look like I didn't help you."

That's the Kirakos. Everyone wants something. I punch him in the side of his head.

"True," I reply, holding him upright as he lolls back. "I could also still kill you if I wanted to. You'd better hope you've appealed to my generous side."

Looking down at the controller, it's flashing red at me. I press on it, but nothing happens. It stays lit, so I fling it over the side. Our descent can't be stopped, and as pulsar fire strafes past, I stay behind my useful Xicop. The docking station below us is empty for the time being, and as soon as we're close enough, I shove him over the side and make a leap for it.

My boots ring out on the metal as I hit it hard, my legs bending and my fist impacting, denting the smooth surface. I take in a deep breath, summoning all my fire, all my might, everything I have, everything I need to find my *szikra*, to take her back and deal with those who thought it somehow possible to steal fate away.

Something clicks at my ear. I open my eye and look to my left. A Rak holds a disabler at my collar. I'm surrounded by Xicops, armored and armed.

"Don't," the Rak clicks out.

In his other claw, he holds a small viewer which he shoves under my nose.

Amber is on her knees, in a room surrounded by guards. She glares at them, her fire filling my soul.

"Make one wrong move, Draco, and she is dead."

I incline my head. "Kill her and I will burn the Kirakos to infinity."

"I doubt that."

And just before the lights go out, I see the pulsars fire.

AMBER

One of the guards fires up into the ceiling with his weapon. The others surrounding him whoop with glee.

I roll my eyes. What a complete bunch of twats. They get off on pushing me around, bringing me into this empty room, and shoving me down on my knees.

I'm not going to be frightened anymore. For a start, it's pointless. If they're going to kill me, they're going to kill me. Fear is relative. I let it define me.

I let it get in the way of me and Draco when he's the best thing which ever happened to me. It just took an alien abduction and a million lightyears for me to realize what I was missing.

An honorable alien. A male who only ever wanted to put me at the center of his world.

"It's done!" The guard grunts. "The Rak has him."

"Sarkarnii fell straight into our trap," another one crows.

"Draco?" His name is out of my mouth before I can stop myself.

"We have your mate." One of them shoves at me. "He's ours now," he adds with some glee.

I curse under my breath, staring at the floor and willing my stupid tears not to fall. My eyes prickle with the pain.

He came for me.

Draco came for me, and I've got him caught. All around, the guards are celebrating as if they've done something amazing, when all that's happened is I led my Draco, my handsome dragon, my protector, my alien bad boy, right into a trap.

I thought I've hated myself in the past. Hated what I became on the run, hiding from him, always moving on whenever I thought he'd found me.

But it's nothing compared to what rips through me now. They have Draco, and I don't know what they're going to do to him, but it won't be good.

"Up!" I'm jerked to my feet. "The Warden wants to see you."

I struggle uselessly in the grip of the thing. It might not help, but it makes me feel better.

"He just needs to see you. He doesn't care what state you are in," the guard growls, and I recognize him as the one I kicked in the knackers earlier.

I hope it means they're out of order, but just in case, I stop struggling as I'm dragged out of the room at a pace I can barely keep up, tripping over my feet as I hold onto the hand digging into my flesh so hard I know it will bruise.

The entire place is as much a maze as the actual maze, only wherever I am, it's made up of dark metal, with strips of light everywhere. A bit like the 1980s settled here for keeps.

I'm marched out into an atrium which is filled with creatures, not just the pig like guards I've seen so far, but others, equally as burly but with heads like sharks, black flat eyes, and too many teeth. My captor swings me around in front of him and lets go of my arm as he prepares to cross the floor.

Big mistake.

Never let go of the mouse.

The only way I can help Draco now is if I run.

I can run.

I run.

I dive between creatures grasping for me as shouts go up, but the place is too busy, and they both see me and cannot see me. I slide through legs, flick myself out of grasping claws, and then I'm in an empty corridor. Behind me, there is a raging cacophony as an alarm of epic proportions rings out and a huge door shuts with sudden finality, cutting me off from the atrium. Looks like I'll need to take my chances and keep on going.

At the end, there is a 'T' junction. Left is dark, but right there is some light up ahead. With the noises behind me getting louder, I take the right hand and race towards the light.

It's a huge window, the artificial brightness pouring into the corridor. Movement captures my attention, and that's when I see him.

Draco.

Naked, he's strapped to a metal slab, hands, feet, and chest all covered by thick silver bands. I slam my hands onto the window, calling his name, but he doesn't seem to hear or see me.

His body is rigid, shaking involuntarily, his teeth in a rictus grin.

A tall, thin robot, more metal skeleton than anything else, stands next to him, a rod in one pincer, the end glowing with light. A single artificial eye, red in the center, plays over my Draco's body.

"Where is the map, Sarkarnii?" it asks, voice high and shrill.

Draco laughs, his head rolling to one side as he exposes his fangs and lets rip with a stream of fire which has zero effect on the robot.

"I don't know," he replies with the utmost insolence, and I'm almost smiling too at his defiance.

Draco continues to laugh, and the robot spins the rod theatrically and plunges it directly into where I know it has to hurt him the most. His body arcs, lifting against the bands. They bite into his flesh as he struggles against the pain.

"One last time, Sarkarnii. Where is it?"

My Draco is panting and panting, his entire body rigid. He says nothing, merely glares at the robot as if he's trying to work out how much fire it will take to melt it.

"Have it your own way." The rod spins again, but this time it's not the glowing end but the other which it shoves under Draco's nose, a separate pincer morphing into a flat sheet which is clamped over his mouth. The rod releases a gas which it seems he has no option but to inhale.

His back arches up again, the strain against the bands making it look like he is going to break them or they are going to break him. Then he drops back, his tight form suddenly appearing liquid soft as a smile, completely unlike anything I've ever seen, creeps onto his face.

"That's good," he slurs. "That's clever. Nice."

The last word is a hiss as he squirms under the bands. A long stream of smoke flows out of him as his body relaxes.

The robot leans forward. Another pincer winds out and

parts his eyelids. Draco's pupils are huge, almost round in the way they fill his eyeball.

"You will tell us," it intones.

"I love her," he laughs. "You gave her to me to incite the rut, but I love her."

"The map! The map!" the robot yells, and it finally occurs to me the voice coming from it is not actually from the robot itself, but from a disembodied interrogator. "The map or she dies."

Draco settles back onto his slab, his tail making an appearance and curling around his legs comfortably, as if he's in bed with me and not exposed and trussed up like a Christmas turkey.

He shakes his head.

"Kill the female," the robot says. "Make sure it's slow."

"You won't kill her," he says, the words slow, slurred, *easy*. "Because you know just thinking about harming her means I'll draw out your guts like aracid threads and weave them into a new garment for my *szikra* to wear."

There is a long silence, in which Draco's eyes roll in his head. Whatever it is they've given him seemingly agrees very much with his physiology as the tip of his cock is emerging from his pouch.

"My *szikra*," he murmurs, inhaling deeply, then expelling a long stream of smoke. "How I long to fill your belly with our young, delight in your changing form, so like mine, so different." He's struggling with the words now, eyelids flickering in a monumental effort to stay open which he's clearly losing. "My heartsfire."

"It is done." The robot bursts to life. "You have nothing left to lose, Draco. Tell us where the map is."

Draco's eyes open, and in that moment, I see a vulnerability I never knew my confident, assured, handsome mate had. For a moment, he believes whoever is talking. He believes I am dead. Then they close again, and his entire form goes limp.

I'm banging on the window, yelling his name, desperately wanting him to hear me, to know I'm alive, until hands grab me from behind, and I'm biting, scratching, bucking, writhing.

Nothing is going to keep me from Draco. Nothing.

"This is no good," a voice attached to the hands holding me says as a flash of blue flicks into my vision. "Get her to be quiet."

And a hand is clamped over my mouth and nose, the breath being squeezed from me until I can't see my Draco anymore.

DRACO

araxio.

    I've only had it once before, the night my den and I were on Arbuthno to close a deal for some new Caison blasters. The trading moon has always been notorious, but then we were Sarkarnii, so no one was going to bother us, regardless of what we did, or in Draxx and Drega's case, what destruction they wrought.

Then the owner of the bar suggested paraxio.

'Works on all known species.'

We were broke, but in the mood to party. The Caison had taken our eyes out over the cost of the blasters. I never usually bothered with narcotics, but then virtually nothing but fermented sugars have much of an effect on a Sarkarnii, and even then, it takes a considerable amount.

Where was the harm?

And we woke up, collared, in the bowels of the Kirakos, raging. An idiotic decision on my behalf, and one I will always, always regret.

Because out of everything I'd planned for, the collars were the one thing I had not.

The drug floods my lungs, making its way into my system, relaxing and delicious. I hear the voice of Noro but take no notice. All I can think about is my heartsfire, my Amber. Her face when I slide inside her, her pleasure, her perfection.

Her loss.

It cuts through the paraxio like a claw through flesh. It hits me with the force of a thousand suns.

Noro did not kill her, did he?

He wouldn't. He knows what I would do to him.

I shake my head, trying to clear it from the drug, from the lies I've been told, trying to open my eyes, to make my limbs respond.

I'm in a seclusion cell. Not large enough to stand up in, the walls smooth, curved, impenetrable. There's a hole underneath me for waste and another above me for food. I know from long ago, if I lick the walls, there is moisture.

Here, we are sustained life forms, not sentient, not free. We are nothing.

For a seccarii, I laugh, loud and rasping. Clouds of smoke escape me, filling the cell before being sucked away into the waste. The collar constricts, chimes a warning, but the drug is still large in my system, and I don't care.

I need my Amber. I need her like I need air and fire and life.

She is not dead. I rub at my chest over my mating gland. She cannot be dead, or I would feel it, somehow.

I know I would feel it.

I would feel it, wouldn't I?

My head swims. My eyes feel wet and sore. It has to be the paraxio making me feel this way. Like everything is over.

My claws dig into the spongy material holding me. I am not going to be caged, and I am not going to be collared anymore. I draw down the air, through my lungs, into my fire sacs, allowing accelerant to fill them.

Noro might think he's calculated everything, but he has not. He has not calculated what I will do to get to my mate, or to get to him if he professes to have harmed her.

Because if he has harmed her, then I have broken my bargain.

And a Sarkarnii commander *never* breaks a bargain.

Hate fills me. Cold, hard hate. Politics, I can do, violence is my friend, but hatred, I've never bothered with. I thought it was counterproductive.

Not now.

With every single atom of my body, I direct my flame upwards, firing and firing, despite my collar, despite everything. If I have lost her, if she has gone, someone has to pay.

And that someone is Noro.

Then I'll burn the galaxy down.

AMBER

I fire out with my right elbow. It impacts something hard which makes an 'oof' sound.

"This one is most definitely Draco's mate," a partly familiar voice says, and I open my eyes. "She's as dirty a fighter as he is."

I'm looking directly into a wall of green scales, two sets of vicious green claws wrapped around my arm and my legs.

"Put me down!" I growl.

"And as grumpy." My attention is drawn to the sparkling blue scaled back walking ahead of us.

"Drega?" I gasp. "It was you?" A coldness sears through me. "But Draco..."

"We're incognito," the big green Sarkarnii who still hasn't put me down, says with a slightly unhinged smile.

"I can assure you, you are not."

"Best put her down, Draxx. If Draco scents you on her and vice versa he will rip your tail off." Drega sighs.

With a huff, I'm dropped to the floor where for a second my legs don't want to hold me up. I slap a hand on the wall of green scales.

"Why didn't you rescue Draco?" I snarl. "He was right there."

"He was in a holo-lab. What you saw wasn't there," Drega says, as if explaining to a child and making my skin bristle with annoyance.

He gets up close and personal, despite what he said to Draxx, and I'm suddenly and surprisingly pushed and pulled as he inspects me, before releasing me with a puff of smoke.

"Then why did I see it?" I put my hands on my hips as I back away from his strange inspection.

Drega looks at Draxx. "Because we'd hacked into the system to find him."

Draxx bends forward. "I'm sorry you had to see your mate like that, little one," he croons.

"I'm not." I fold my arms and glare at him. "Because seeing Draco means he's alive, and we're going to get him."

"That's not the plan," Drega growls.

"The plan is to complete the run, get to the finish, and be ready," Draxx adds with a knowing nod.

"Oh, and just let Draco fend for himself?" I raise my eyebrows.

"He's got out of worse," Drega grumbles.

"Like that time with the spaceworms." Draxx grins. "That was fun."

Drega brightens. "It was, wasn't it?"

"This isn't funny." An anger I've never felt before is rising within me. "They're not going to stop until they break him, and we need him."

"Why?'" Drega asks, dominance rolling from him as he looms over me. But I don't care. I'm not going to be intimidated anymore.

"Because unless Draco tells me to, I'm not removing your collars."

Draxx takes in a breath, and smoke streams from his nostrils, his eyes wide.

"She can remove collars?" Draxx rumbles at Drega. "Why didn't you tell me?"

Now Mr. Dominant looks sheepish, but he quickly recovers and steps between me and Draxx.

"You didn't need to know." He fires me a look over his shoulder. "She is a key."

The big green Sarkarnii, easily the same height as Draco and probably wider, peers around Drega at me.

"Are you?" he asks, his voice cracking.

"I don't know," I answer truthfully and now hate myself for even using the supposed ability I have to open locks in the Kirakos against these Sarkarnii. "I've only tried on Draco and Drega."

There's something in Draxx's eyes, and I remember what Draco said about him losing his family. My stomach contracts. I feel awful.

"We need to get Draco." Draxx straightens. "The little female needs her mate." Smoke curls from his nostrils, even as I see one hand trembling wildly before he curls it into a fist.

"We can't..." Drega says, sidestepping the arm fired at him by Draxx, before he growls then holds up his hands in supplication. "Okay, o-nevving-kay, we'll get the big nevver, even if it's not what he wants, and he's likely to rip us both new orifices."

"I'm prepared to take that chance." Draxx gives me a big, goofy grin. "Draco'll have to catch me first."

And the thought of these three monstrous males chasing each other fills my head, making me smile.

Not as much as the thought of rescuing Draco, but I smile nonetheless and link arms with Draxx.

He rumbles a little and then very gently backs away. "Drega is right, little one. Draco should not scent me on you. It is not a sensible way to behave while he is in rut."

A foot slams into Draxx's side, and the big guy hardly moves, just gives Drega a sad look. "I'm always right!" Drega says. "Let's go get Draco before I change my mind."

"You won't be changing your mind." I flex my fingers at him, and it's his turn to huff out smoke as he stomps down a side passage leaving Draxx and me to follow.

The passage is narrow, pushing me in fairly close proximity to the brother I've only heard about. Draxx doesn't seem as unhinged as he was described.

At least until a door slides open next to us and a guard steps out. Before I can move, or even blink, he has hold of him, and with a loud snap, the creature goes limp, Draxx huffing and throwing him to one side.

"Xicops," he rasps. "Don't like them."

"What did you do?" Drega stares down at the motionless body. "You know they're all connected to the mainframe. Now they'll know where we are."

"Don't care," Draxx says, his jaw set. "He'd have killed the little female."

Drega narrows his eyes at me, as if also contemplating my demise. "We need to get as far away from here as possible. Draxx, stop killing the guards, at least until we have Draco and we can finish this nevving run."

Draxx shrugs, and I'm shepherded ahead of him until, thankfully, the corridor opens out into a larger space where Drega slams his fist onto a wall which slides open reluctantly to display a set of lights buried in a console. Drega works his way over them.

"Draco's been transferred to the seventh quadrant for further softening up," he says without looking at either Draxx or me.

"The seclusion cells?" Draxx, despite his massive size and impressive scales, shakes as if he's been punched.

"This time, we're getting someone out, not going in, brother," Drega says quietly as he gently puts a hand on Draxx's shoulder. "It'll be better."

"It will be better if I can just burn this place to the ground," Draxx says, sparks rather than smoke firing out of his nostrils.

"We can do that too." Drega grins.

I stare at them both, wondering if it's going to be possible for any of us to come out alive at the end of everything.

"Just like with the spaceworms," Draxx says, happily.

"Just like with the spaceworms." Drega nods.

Yep, we're all going to die.

DRACO

I'm running out of accelerant. I must have depleted my reserves earlier when I was under the influence of the paraxio. My body can manufacture more, but what I'm using to burn through the seclusion cell is so much I'm not able to replace it fast enough.

But have I made a hole large enough to, at the very least, get my claws in and rip it open? With some reluctance, I cut off my flames and reach up. The edges of the feeding hole are pliable, and I dig in with all my might.

The material gives. I struggle at it again, filling my mind with thoughts of my mate, of what I'll do to anyone who has harmed her. What I'll do to anyone who has threatened to harm her.

Because she has to be alive, doesn't she?

The ancestors would let me know if I'd lost my mate, as Draxx found out to his cost. My general brother always had a tenuous grip on reality, but losing the female promised to him—it seemed to have flicked off the switch. Reality is no longer his friend.

I cannot be like him. I am the last great Sarkarnii left. I

have to survive. I have to see what's out there. Find any more of my species. I have to have my revenge on the Liderc. I have to have that map and the Kirakos.

With a bone shaking roar, I tear at the hole above me, but there's nothing. The material has cooled. I'm back to where I started.

Above me, the cell wall is shiny with my flames, turning it glass like, reflecting a Sarkarnii I hardly recognize. One who stares defiantly back at nothing. One who will not be defeated even in the face of defeat.

One who needs his mate, his *szikra*, more than anything.

"Amber." Her name is a breath on my lips, but it's all I ever want to say.

I had her, right here, in my arms. She was mine at the worst possible time, at the best possible moment. And I never told her just what she was to me.

I close my eyes and thump my head back against the floor of the cell. I'm cramped, needing to stretch my limbs but unable to. I fancy, just for a second, I hear her sweet voice calling my name. My tail curls, shifting free but simply making this tiny cell even smaller. I will it to stop. There's no point in making myself any more uncomfortable because my mind is playing tricks on me.

"Where the nev is he? DRACO?"

I sit up, slamming my head on the top of the cell. "Drega?"

This time, I do hear Amber's voice, and I slam my hands on the sides of the cell as I roar out my desire to get to her. I don't care how much the collar attempts to shock me, I will get to her. There's a hiss, and a crack appears all around the edges of the cell. I scrabble at it, my heart hammering, my mating gland going wild, and the need to shift, to get to her, to be free overwhelming any sense I might have.

"What the nev?" Drega says as he peers in through the crack.

But I've already got my claws in it, and I'm wrenching my way out as Amber's scent fills the space. In seconds, I have her in my arms and my face buried in her hair. I can't speak, I can't breathe, all I have is her.

All I have is her.

AMBER

The second I heard him, the second I saw him emerge from the weird egg-shaped cocoon, my world snapped together.

It's as if all the pieces fitted perfectly as he thundered towards me, his step sure, his chest broad, his eyes a riot of desire. Draco's delicious smoky scent surrounds me as I'm caught up, and he stills. Only his fingers gently stroking through my hair are moving.

"I thought I'd lost you," he murmurs in my ear.

His cheek is wet against mine. Although it's hard to tell because I'm crying so damn hard. It doesn't matter what happened before I came here. My ex might have tried to break me, but he didn't. I might have run, but running made me stronger.

And Draco completed me. He showed me what I could do, what I could withstand, the person I really am.

I am a survivor, just like him, just like his species.

"You didn't lose me," I whisper back. "I'm right here."

"My heartsfire, I beat for you, I bleed for you. I am

always yours. Fate is nothing. You are everything." Draco's tail curls around my waist. His voice is hoarse.

"I love you." I press myself into him, wanting to be part of him. "I love you, Draco."

Tears stream down my face at my admission, at laying myself bare for this huge, gorgeous male.

"You should not. I broke our bargain," he says.

"I'm alive, aren't I?" I swirl my hands over his scales, marveling at the silky feeling and the bioluminescence which glitters at my touch. "I'd say you kept your side of the bargain."

Draco finally lifts his face from my shoulder, and his eyes search my face. "But did you keep yours, female?" he growls.

"I warmed your bed, Draco. And I came for you." I look up at him as his face cracks into the best smile.

Not the insolent one, or the charming one, or even the one he does just before he unleashes violence, but one filled with genuine humor.

"You did, my little mate. And you brought help." He swipes a thumb over my cheek, then laps at it and raises his eyebrows. "Help I'm pretty sure didn't want to come."

I trace my fingers over his strong jaw. "You're not wrong." I'm trying to burn his face into my brain. I never want to forget my Draco at this moment.

"We still on for the run or what, brother?" Drega interjects with a huff and a stream of smoke.

Draco looks at him like he's seen him for the first time, and then he sees Draxx, and the smile is briefly back.

"Oh, we're running all right. Noro has had a change of heart. He knows what we want, and he wants it for himself. He still wants us to fail in the run, but regardless, he will want the map."

"What map?" I ask.

"Starmap," Draxx rumbles.

I look between them all, confused. "So, the run wasn't a run?"

"It was. It's the only time the security in the Kirakos is reduced by enough which would make it possible for us to gain access to the undercrofts," Draco says.

"And you were going to tell me this when?" I cock my head to one side as I look up at my gorgeous but infuriating male.

"When we returned victorious, map in hand, the Kirakos under our control." Draco grins at me, before capturing my chin in his claws. "At which point, I would have you remove my collar, and I would mate you until you couldn't stand, or speak from screaming my name. You would know such pleasure, my love. Pleasure only ever dreamed of."

He hasn't lowered his voice, and I'm acutely conscious of Drega and Draxx's presence. My cheeks heat because Draco's low rumble and his promises are making me squirm.

"Draco!" I hiss, moving my eyes to where his brothers stand, Drega with his arms folded and Draxx grinning like nobody's business.

"Forget them, female. Don't even think about another male." Draco's low growl makes my insides quake. "You are mine."

I genuinely think I might combust on the spot. How has he managed to turn me to jelly so damn quickly?

"I don't want to interrupt your mating dance, Draco," Drega says, his voice dripping with sarcasm. "But if we're to get the map and complete the run, we need to do it now. Or it will all be over."

Draco ignores him, staring down like he's at once

wanting to consume me, his presence dominating, perfect, delicious. He rubs the flat of his thumb over my cheek, as gentle as a feather.

"Then we run," he says, not even looking up at his brother. "We run, and we run to win."

DRACO

My entire body is on fire. I'm burning up. Because I have her back.

This female is everything. I'm never going to let her go again. As for my brothers, who are both irritating and present, I need to have words as to why she stinks of Draxx.

The reason I had to growl 'mine'. Not that Draxx would take her from me, but the rut is not over, not until she has been danced for.

Not until I am buried inside her over and over.

I attempt to tamp down these distracting feelings as we weave our way through the mostly empty seclusion cells, each one just large enough for its intended occupant, each one round and squat.

"Still in rut?" Drega slaps me on the back. "I can see it in your eyes."

I growl at him. "You'll find it less amusing when it happens to you."

Sparks dance in his eyes. "You forget, brother, I have far more self-control."

"For self-control, make that the ability to turn himself from fire to ice," Draxx says wryly, joining us. "I'm pleased for you, Draco. Finding your mate is the best thing."

I wind my tail a little tighter around Amber's waist as I grasp at his shoulder. "Thank you, brother, that means much."

"And such a pretty one too," he adds, oblivious. "She has such lovely hair." He reaches for Amber.

"Touch her and lose it," I snarl.

"Ah, the mating dream," Drega scoffs. "I'll stick with my self-control."

Draxx gives me a hurt look, which I'll take any day over the feral, goo-covered creature I last saw. I snarl at him until Amber slaps my hand.

"Stop it!" my little spark says. "All of you." She glares specifically at Drega.

I stick my tongue in my cheek and then give him a tor-eating grin. He huffs smoke out so hard, there are flames.

I consider that a win for Draco.

"Where are the rest of the den?" I ask him.

Drega visibly swallows down a retort, wanting to demonstrate some of his "control," and, as he knows only too well, I will deal with him as I see fit, should he fail to obey orders. I'll set my mate on him for starters.

"They are waiting out the remainder of the run at the finish line until we give the order."

"Excellent." A lungful of smoke escapes as I enjoy every second of the plan coming together. "How far are we from the undercroft at this level?"

"From the seclusion cells?" Drega gives me his look, the one which tells me something I don't like is coming. "We're five floors up and at least two across from where we need to be, and that's if the map is where we believe it is."

"Hold on," Amber interjects. "What is this all about? I think I deserve to know, given I was taken from my planet and brought here specifically to intervene."

"I don't think they expected your abilities as a key, my sweet mate. They underestimated you."

"Cut the crap, Draco, and tell me."

I draw in a breath as it's both Drega and Draxx's turn to look smug.

"You know we deliberately got ourselves caught and put in the Kirakos." I say, carefully, watching her fold her arms and tap her toe.

"And?" Amber says, her voice hard with anger.

"When the Liderc obliterated our species, we heard one ark got away from our planet. We've been searching for it ever since," I explain, holding my hands out flat. "One of the original builders of the Kirakos had a starmap like no other. It's supposed to be something a god gave him."

Drega snorts, ever the Sarkarnii of science. I shoot him a look.

"Allegedly, it shows every species in the universe and their position at any time," I continue.

"Sounds fantastical," Amber says, but her body has relaxed.

I think I might have got away with it.

"We have to try," Draxx rumbles.

Her eyes soften as she looks at him, and this time my mating gland doesn't go into overdrive. This time, my heart beats in tune with his. With hers. Amber cares about my brother, and there is nothing wrong with that.

"That's true," she says with a gentle smile. "You have to try."

"If there really was an ark which made it off Kaeh-Leks, the map will show us where the remainder of our species are." I put my hand on Draxx's shoulder. He gives me his lopsided smile. "Maybe even those we are missing."

"I hate to break all of this up, but the run is on, and we need to get to the undercrofts," Drega says. "We have to secure the map before the run is over."

"The run is over when we win." I glare at him.

"Tell the Xicops that." Drega points behind us as a cohort of the guards pour into the seclusion cell area and pulsar bolts zip over our heads.

"Great shots as always," I grumble. "Do you have any weapons?"

Drega hands me a pulsar as Draxx flings off his cloak and pulls out a pulsar-rifle. Around his waist is a belt of pulse-grenades. Drega follows my gaze.

"He got it from...well, I don't where he got that lot," he grumbles.

"Just watch him, will you?" I ask as Draxx rises up and releases a volley causing all the Xicops to dive behind the various seclusion cells. "I need the right explosion at the right time."

Drega gives me a business-like nod and at once my world settles into place. Brothers who take orders, will wonders never cease?

I place my hand in the small of Amber's back, luxuriating in the proximity to my mate, regardless of the bolts sizzling past us as I hurry her to the nearest exit. We dive down and out of the way of the firing where Amber puts her back flat against the wall, breathing hard.

But her eyes are dancing with light and life, and she grins up at me.

"Where next, big guy?"

"Next, we have a maze to capture, my heartsfire. And this time, we get to challenge fate."

AMBER

Draco takes my hand, and we run down a dark corridor. I hear Drega and Draxx following behind, and a quick glance over my shoulder confirms they are intact and uninjured.

I'm running, with Draco, with his brothers, through this maze, and I couldn't be happier. I wouldn't want to be anywhere else, regardless of the danger. A laser fires over our heads and slams into the wall ahead of us, making me squeak in surprise.

Okay, so maybe I'd prefer to be somewhere with a little less danger of getting shot.

"We need to go down, Draco," Drega shouts from behind us.

"I'm trying," Draco grinds out as we turn left, then right where I see a light up ahead.

As we race towards it, I see it's a vast atrium, lit by a million pinpricks of light and where platforms, high above us, float purposefully from one side to the other. But our corridor ends abruptly. There's no platform and no bridge.

Drega and Draxx catch up with us. Drega growls with frustration at the drop.

"Now would be a good time for collars to be removed," he mutters.

"You said you wanted to go down." Draco raises his eyebrows, ignoring the comment about collars. "Don't tell me you've changed your mind?"

An arm is wrapped around my waist, and I'm unceremoniously hoisted onto Draco's back.

"Hold on, little one," he says, and in a single lithe movement, he turns and drops over the edge, his claws catching on the metal where he hangs easily as I hold on around his neck with all my might.

"Draco!" I hiss, accidentally looking down and immediately doing an impression of a spider monkey, my legs wrapping around him as much as I can, my arms squeezing hard.

He chuckles, the rich sound vibrating through him as something slides under my butt and up my back. The tip of his tail peers over my shoulder, and I relax just slightly.

"Here we go," he says as Drega and Draxx join us.

Hand over hand, foot over foot, their claws slam into the metal like butter as they climb down and down. Whenever I risk a peek, we still seem impossibly high and the likelihood of falling still great. It's all I can do not to throw up.

So, when I thought I was enjoying the danger...

I wasn't.

After what seems like forever, Draco swings us into another corridor and drops to the floor. My stomach turns over, my palms sweating like mad. But the tail gently uncurls from me, and I slide off him. The passageway we're in is not like the others, metal lined and dimly lit. This place looks like it was hewn out of rock, green algae halfway up the walls and a strip light which looks weirdly familiar.

"Are we being followed?" Drega asks.

"What do you think?" Draco snorts out smoke and sparks. "This is a run. Noro wants the map almost as much as we do."

"Why?" I query.

"Because he wants to control the Sarkarnii," Drega says, his voice dark. "He wants us to do his dirty work all over the galaxy."

Draco looks down at me, a sad smile on his face. "It's why he gave you to me. To see what I would do, to see if we are compatible as species and if he could control me through you."

I try not to let all the air out of my lungs at once. The thought repels me.

"I'm..." Words fail me, but I get a pair of arms around me.

"This has nothing to do with you. But it's the reason we were chased into Warden-controlled territory, the reason he bound us together to ensure he could observe us."

"Observe?" I gasp.

"I think we gave him a good show." A curl of smoke rises from Draco as he hitches the corner of his mouth. "He never intended for you to send me into rut or for fate to intervene, *szikra*." He puts his face millimeters away from mine, his slit pupils simply slithers of darkness in the spinning fire of his eyes. "I'm glad you did. I long to have you on my tongue once more." The forked tip slips slightly between his lips, and my core clenches accordingly. His eyes flutter closed. "I will mate you here and now, regardless of our audience, if you continue to smell quite so edible."

"Sorry." I apologize like any good Englishwoman, my

cheeks coloring at his suggestion. "What?" I add for good measure.

Draco pulls me to him, his lips on mine, his tongue sweeping and demanding of me, wanting, capturing, *owning*.

"Still in rut," Drega says in a matter-of-fact way to Draxx when Draco finally lets go and I struggle to regain my wits.

"Still in rut." Draxx nods sagely.

"Nev off, the pair of you," Draco says genially. "Have you any idea how to find this nevving map now we're in the undercroft?" he growls at Drega.

"We need to look for a specific symbol," Drega replies.

"What symbol?"

"A circle with a crescent moon above."

"Like this one?" Draxx rumbles, the big Sarkarnii shifting his weaponry from one shoulder to the other as he rubs his huge hand on the wall.

The movement reveals the sigil Drega suggested, a circle with a crescent moon over the top.

"Now what?" Draco asks.

"I guess we look for more." Drega shrugs.

"You really have this all figured out, don't you?" I laugh.

"We wing most things. It's what Sarkarnii are good at," Draco says, wryly.

I don't believe him for a moment. Draco's never done anything which could even possibly be considered to be 'winging it'. He's all about the control.

"Draxx, take up the rear," Draco orders. "We'll look for more of these marks."

We wind our way through the passageways, all three of us searching the stonework for the sigil Draxx uncovered until finally, at a T-junction, I see it, down near the floor.

"Look!" I drop next to it and reach out my hand to brush away the dirt like Draxx.

"Wait! Amber!" Draco calls out, but it's too late.

As I touch it, the symbol glows for a second, and then the ground under me gives way.

DRACO

Amber doesn't believe she's a key for some reason, despite all the evidence to the contrary. Humans must not have such things, which seems backward. Presumably they have DNA like most of the rest of the warm-blooded species which reside in the Universe. Rogue technology, a remnant of a sentient AI system, allowed certain species, or certain DNA strands, to access anything they wish. It's code which has infected every piece of tech since.

There's nothing that complicated about it.

But even knowing she's a key doesn't stop her from touching the mark and, inevitably, dropping through a hidden doorway beneath her. With a soft squeak, she disappears before I can get hold of her, my hand grasping at nothing before I get to the hole and peer down.

I'm joined by Drega and Draxx as they also look down.

Amber looks up at me.

"Makes a change," she says, and then she steps away from where I can see her.

A growl more feral than any noise I've ever made before

escapes me, and I'm jumping down into the space before my brothers can say anything.

"Draco!" Amber turns to me as I land with a thump and yet another growl.

Her hands are clutched together as she stares around in wonder, and I follow her gaze.

This place is like nothing I've ever seen before. The light is being bent somehow around the walls. Multiple images move, and static appears and shifts around as my eyes track over them. And it's not just images. There is data, so much data, scrolling over and over, everywhere I look.

"What the nev is this place?"

"It's a control room." Drega pushes past me, followed by Draxx who is seemingly as entranced by the place as my mate.

"Controlling what?"

Drega runs his hand over the wall, and the images stop swirling, resolving themselves into cohesive sets. I can see the maze, the warden-controlled areas, and some other places I don't recognize. At the same time, stars swirl over our heads and data streams past next to Drega who is flicking his way furiously over everything.

"Stop," I tell him.

He stops.

"What's that?" I point just above his head at an image which seems familiar.

Drega reaches up and with a single digit sweep, brings it down and expands it.

"Nev!" We stare at the image. "Is this live?"

"Is that...?" Amber stares at the screen.

"Yes."

Surrounded by guards are my warriors. They're being shocked by both their collars and the guards with the usual prods. How they've ended up in this situation is unclear, but they're losing the battle.

Amber turns to me, water hovering in her eyes. "We have to do something," she says hoarsely.

"Drega?"

My brother is working furiously over the wall. "I don't know if I can."

"You said this was a control room," I say evenly.

"But what does it control?" Amber walks over to the opposite wall, or at least I presume it is a wall.

She lifts a finger and touches it before I can stop her. It makes a ripple effect, like me dipping my tail in the water of the aquium. The ripples spread and spread. It's not something I like, nor do I like her being close to it. In two strides, I'm by her side, ready to protect my mate from whatever this is.

"DNA accepted. Welcome, human," a soft voice intones out of nowhere.

Amber's eyes flick up to mine, her face ghostly as the lights play over her skin. "It knows?"

I can't imagine what's going through her mind, so instead I press my body to hers, so she knows I'm here for her, ready to catch her, ready to protect her, or let her do whatever she needs to do.

"Ask it," Draxx says from just behind us. "Ask it where the map is. If it recognizes you, it might give us the information."

Amber looks at me again, and I nod, slowly.

"Have you solved the problem with my den?" I say back over my shoulder.

"Working on it, Draco," Drega grinds out.

"Um, computer?" Amber says hesitantly and somewhat

incomprehensibly. "Do you have the starmap of species?" She smiles around at me and Draxx.

"Good name," Draxx says, ignoring my growl.

The ripples on the wall roll backwards until they reach a single point. Amber reaches up, but I grab her hand.

"It's fine, Draco. I don't think it wants to hurt us," she says quietly, and I release her.

Amber places her slim, clawless finger on the wall. The light glows underneath the pad for a second, and then it's like a hundred sparks fly away from her touch. She gasps and the lights dance in her eyes.

"Do you wish to know where the other humans are?" the voice says.

"Other than on Earth? I suppose, yes," Amber replies. "And the Sarkarnii, other than those in this room," she adds.

"There are precisely five humans on this moon," the voice answers, and Amber's legs sag, meaning I catch her.

"And the Sarkarnii?" she whispers.

"Draco!" Drega interjects. "We need to go. We have to get back to the run or we're going to lose everyone."

I turn to growl at him, but what's unfolding on the wall feed is not good at all.

"I can't stop it from here, but I have some codes I can use if we can get closer which will disable the shock ability of the collars," Drega says urgently.

"We have to come back here." Amber puts her hand on my arm.

"Oh, we are coming back here, without a doubt, but we have a run to complete."

"And we have a warden to slay," Draxx growls, his eyes on the carnage unfolding on the wall. "Once and for all."

Something tells me it's time to let my brother loose.

AMBER

There are other humans in the Kirakos?

My mind is swirling. On the one hand, I thought, presumed, I was the only human here. Maybe I hoped I was. That there are others, ones I've never seen and Draco has never mentioned, is highly troubling.

But what's worse is the situation unfolding elsewhere with the rest of the Sarkarnii. I want answers, but they're going to have to wait.

Draco shoves me back up through the hole, and then he, Drega, and Draxx swiftly follow, each leaping sinuously out as if they're climbing a staircase, despite their great bulk. Once they're out, I trace my fingers over the symbol once again. To my surprise, the hole closes up.

"Come, little mate." Draco takes my hand and helps me to my feet. "I need to get you somewhere safe, and we can conclude the run."

"No."

"No?"

"You need me, Draco."

A muscle ticks in his jaw, and he rubs his claws over his

scruff as his eyes flick away from mine. I don't waver. I am seeing this through to the end.

I'm done running.

"Let's go," Draco snarls at his brothers, obviously not wanting to admit I'm right but basically admitting I'm right.

He looks at me, eyes soft, as we hurry back through the passageways until we reach the atrium. There, waiting for us it seems, is a platform.

"The one thing I could control," Drega grumbles as he steps onto the thing, and we follow.

It rises up as Draco pulls me into his arms. He gently brushes my hair back from my face, his eyes studying me as he grips my waist.

"It's going to be okay," I whisper.

He smiles. It's his best smile, the one where he's surprised by something into smiling, and it's so genuine I could weep.

"I should be saying that to you."

"Perhaps." It's my turn to smile. "Perhaps this is how it's meant to be, Draco. Perhaps everything I ever did was to put me in this moment with you."

"If I lost you..." Draco breaks eye contact to look over at the glittering green scaled back of Draxx. "If I lose you, Amber, I have nothing. Fate is incredible, and it is cruel. I cannot take another if I have you. Not now, not ever. Our souls are bound to dance among the stars and suns."

My heart beats, rising within me as if it wants to look out of my eyes, my throat constricting and tears I don't want pricking at my eyelids.

Draco dips his head, and his lips meet mine. For not long enough, I'm lost in his kiss, as always, demanding and dominant, with a hint of what he intends to do to me.

Things I want so very, very much. Because I am no longer afraid of anything, except not being with Draco.

There is a very loud cough, which means I'm reluctantly released. Drega glowers at us. The platform is docked and Draxx is waiting.

Draco gives him a very fanged smile which is as far removed from the one which played over his lips just a few moments ago as I am from Earth.

"Time to do some damage, brothers," he says. "Drega? I presume you're ready?"

We're back in the corridors with metal linings, and Drega inserts something into a nearby panel, flipping it open. He works furiously over a second black panel inside before looking back at Draco with a grim smile.

"Ready, commander."

"Draxx?"

The big green Sarkarnii pulls something from his belt and inspects it. "Ready, Draco," he rumbles with an unhinged glint in his eye.

"Stay behind me at all times, *szikra*," Draco says to me, cupping my chin in his clawed hand.

I nod as far as I am able. He stares at me intently, as if he's trying to burn my face into his mind, before letting me go and tucking me behind him. Drega and Draxx move behind us, and Draco strides forward down the corridor.

With Drega calling out directions, we wind our way through a number of passageways until we reach a large metal door.

"Hold on," Drega says and performs the same trick as earlier with the wall. "Now," he calls out.

Ahead of us, the door rises, and I can see the grey concrete walls of the maze, only now we're in a large open area.

Immediately, Drega and Draxx dive in and start firing. There is a volley of laser shots which range all around us. Draxx is hit but seemingly doesn't even notice it, stalking forward and shooting his rifle-like weapon from the hip. Then he throws one of the black cylinders from his belt. The thing rises up into the air and then zips off towards the main gaggle of guards.

They scatter as it dives and there is the most almighty explosion which causes me to clap my hands over my ears and stop dead for a second. I'm not entirely sure but I think I hear Draxx chuckling as he continues to stride ahead. Draco grabs hold of my clothing, and I'm towed along in his wake as he lets rip with highly targeted shots, hitting a guard every time.

"Over there," Drega calls out, and I look to where he's pointing.

The rest of the Sarkarnii are in the most enormous scrum of hand-to-hand combat. It seems like they are getting the upper hand, and my heart lightens a little. Whatever Drega did, it seems to have worked. One of them spots Draco and raises a cheer, which is echoed among the rest who redouble their efforts as Draco, Draxx, and Drega continue to pick off the guards and the tables are slowly turned.

"We can still complete the run, my warriors," Draco bellows.

It's then I finally see it, and I can't quite believe what I'm seeing. At the far end of the square is a wide set of golden steps, rising up and up like a Mayan pyramid. Nothing signals 'the end' more than a giant pyramid.

Although I'm reminded of exactly what pyramids were for, and it wasn't for the living.

With a roar, galvanized by their leader, the Sarkarnii redouble their efforts and the resistance drops away.

"It's time, little mate," Draco says to me, holding out his hand. "It's time to finish this."

I put my hand in his and feel the most incredible rush of warmth from his touch. His huge form is outlined in the light from the steps, and I've never felt safer in all my life than with him.

This is not about fate, and I finally understand what he meant when he said we were bound by the stars and the suns. What we have is love, and it's a love which has transcended millions of light years, bringing us here to this moment.

He looks over my shoulder and, in a smooth, easy movement, I'm lifted off my feet, twirled around until I'm stood again, and he smiles at me.

Then my huge dragon alien jerks forward slightly. His eyes are unfocussed and his legs buckle as he drops to his knees.

"Draco?" I reach for him as he falls forward into my arms, and I see the huge wound on his back. "NO!"

His eyelids are fluttering, and blood runs from his mouth as I cradle his head in my lap.

"No." The word is a mere breath, a mere whisper to whatever gods might be out there, somewhere. "I'm not giving you up."

"And you are mine." He tries to growl as I see Drega running towards us.

"Always."

He reaches an unsteady hand up to my face, but it drops away as his brother reaches us, skidding to a halt and dropping down beside me.

My eyes are too full of tears to see. I can't hear what Drega is saying as blurred hands pull at my mate.

This is not how it's supposed to end. He is Draco. He is the commander of the Hundred Legions, Captain of the *Golden Orion*, and ancestor of the High Bask. Ruler of the 4th Quadrant of the Kirakos.

And he is the male who saved me from myself. He is the male who saved me from everything. I scrub at my eyes because I don't want to lose sight of him, not now, not ever, and all I can see is the damn collar. The thing which held him to this place. My hands are red with blood as I feel for it, for the catch which will set him free.

Forever.

DRACO

I'm up high somewhere, sounds of wings rippling as I beat down. It feels good, but it seems strange. I'm trying to recall something, anything about who I am, where I am, and why I'm spinning around in a cloudless sky.

My ancestors used to do this, I know too, somehow. I turn my head, which is large and powerful, and feel my lungs fill with air.

And my belly fills with fire. I want to burn something. I want to let rip until everything is ash because something aches within me, and I'm not sure what.

I concentrate on the thought of my ancestors. They flew, they set worlds alight. It didn't make them popular, but it made them strong.

I am strong.

I release the fire building up inside me, and it feels so nevving good, I do it again, only this time with a roar. My tail flicks, and I dive down in the still air, which means nothing. I could fly anywhere. Although I don't believe I should. I need to be here, whereever here is.

Something tickling at the back of my brain, something big. Big like me.

I spin again, luxuriating in the flight, in my scales, glinting gold, in my fire, all hot and perfect. But there's still something wrong.

There's something I should be doing. It creates a gnawing feeling in my stomach I don't like.

I want to stay in the air, swooping and flaming. I want to stay like this forever.

Forever.

Forever?

My wings fold. I drop for an instant until they flap suddenly to halt my fall. There is another forever. It's just out of my reach. I can feel it, but I can't see it.

It is...just out of my reach.

Maybe it's just the need to produce more fire. I release my flames, and it feels incredible. But it's not what I want. Not what I really want.

I want to remember. I need to remember who I am, why I am, what the forever is.

Only it would be so easy to let go and just climb higher and higher until there is nothing, the pain is gone, and the need to be anywhere or anything is no more.

Except.

Except...

Amber!

AMBER

Something drags me away from Draco, despite my desperate attempts to cling to him, and I howl my protest.

My entire being has been ripped to shreds. Nothing, nothing has ever been so terrible. My soul is empty. I am a husk, a black hole.

I am grief.

"Keep her back," a voice growls, and green scales flash in the diamonds of my tears. "Keep her back while he shifts."

There is the most enormous rushing wind, the sound of a huge body uncurling, and I scrub at my face, trying to work out what is happening.

Draco is gone.

Someone grabs at my head and hair, twisting my face upwards, where I see him.

If I thought what I've already witnessed of his shift, in the confines of the bedroom, was amazing, what I see in the sky is nothing like that.

It is magnificent.

Draco is magnificent.

Scales are bright, dazzling, his form is exactly what I dreamed a real dragon would be. Huge wings, translucent, massive head, horned, vast flank of scales.

"Little female?" I hear Draxx's voice, but I cannot take my eyes of Draco as he rises higher and releases a fireball that has all the remaining guards cringing. "I need you to remove my collar too."

I blink at him as if I'm looking for the first time. My heart has no idea what to do, hammering and leaping in my chest. My lungs seem immobilized. Draco is alive!

"Please, I have to get to him," Draxx pleads with me. "His shifted form will heal him, but he will need to be reminded what he is," Draxx gently traces a hand over my cheek, "what he has here on the ground, waiting for him."

My eyes fill with tears once more, but I motion for him to come closer and, as he dips his head, I feel for the catch on his collar. With a click, it is free, and he takes several paces away from me.

With a low roar, wings sprout from his back, and before I can see anything else, Draxx is in the air and heading for Draco who is swooping down over the maze, releasing more fire.

The two meet, Draxx slamming into Draco enough that the huge golden dragon almost pauses in the air, and then they grapple, spinning dizzyingly towards the ground until their wings open and they slow their descent.

Fire rages. Guards scatter.

And all I want is Draco.

It's then I hear my name. From high above me, someone shouts...no, someone howls my name. It's a howl I've heard before, the one when I was taken from him.

"I'm here!" I start to run towards the steps, wanting to get higher, to help him pick me out. "I'm here!"

Sarkarnii part in my wake, but as soon as I am past, they are following me, injuries or no. I have an entire cohort of huge alien warriors fanning out behind me as I race up the stairs, heart hammering and lungs burning.

A dark shadow covers me and is gone, followed by another. The warriors behind me are drowning out any further calls as their battle cries ring out.

My way is kept clear by laser bolts firing over my head. I don't know if I'm going to make it to the top, or what I'm going to find when I get there, but all I can think about is reaching somewhere close to Draco, or the creature Draco has become.

Pushed onwards and upwards by the mass of warriors behind me, I stumble up the last few steps, feeling like my lungs are going to burst, just as Draco and Draxx land. The ground shakes with their presence, and the shout of triumph from behind me cancels everything out, other than the massive presence of these beasts, silhouetted against the light.

I hold my hand up to shield my eyes, and it's then I see him. Striding confidently towards me as if he's never been away.

Never been dead.

Draco wraps his arms around my waist and lifts me up, swinging me around and around. His lips hit mine just as I see a hint of a wing and the lash of a tail. Then I close my eyes and forget everything except him.

"I lost you," I murmur over the sweet, salty, familiar taste, sucking in his smoky musk like a woman starved.

"Never. I would reduce this place to ash and bone before leaving you, my heartsfire," Draco rumbles, his deep, delicious voice doing things to my insides, turning them to liquid. "You did the right thing at the right time, little key, as I always knew you would."

"The collar?" I gaze into his eyes, my eyebrows knitting. "How did you know I'd take it off?"

"Because you want to be free, just like me."

"I am free, Draco. Because I have you," I say before slamming my lips back on his and taking as much from him as I ever could.

DRACO

mber's scent, it is everything. It is the reason my
mating gland fills me with the mix, my heart
beats, and my body shifts. She is what our ancestors came down from the skies for. She is my heartsfire.

"Draco."

My name reverberates around the large open area at the
top of the golden steps, a nice touch, even if I say it myself.

"Warden Noro," I reply, not letting go of Amber. "I
believe my Sarkarnii and I have completed your run."

"You cheated!" he snarls, his already hideous counte-
nance morphing into anger.

"In what way?" I ask, evenly. Not that it matters. All
that matters is we got to this point.

"You shifted into your Sarkarnii form," he gibbers, ire at
risk of taking over his rational side.

"I do not believe there are any rules for a run. You
proved that when you attempted to hold my warriors back
at the start."

Noro snorts. From behind him, as if out of the sky,
Xicops march out in numbers. We must be close to the outer

rim of the Kirakos and right next to the warden-controlled area. They are using a hidden entrance to fill the space behind Noro.

"It doesn't matter, *Sarkarnii*," he sneers. "My clients have had their fun, and with a little tweaking, they'll not know who won this run or didn't."

"And you'll have made a sizable sum betting as well as your usual kickbacks." Drega steps up next to me, his arms folded.

"Why do you think I stay here, in this"—he waves a set of tiny arms around—"place? The credits are good, and no one cares about the scum of the universe incarcerated here."

Drega nods sagely. "That is correct, although I'm not sure it's likely you'll be making much in the future." He inspects his claws.

Noro laughs, a foul gurgling sound. "You think Warden Gondnok is going to help you? He wanted you to win to line his own pocket."

Drega looks up for an instant and then at me, the corner of his mouth lifting and a single claw extending on his middle finger.

He's pointing up. Above us is a small viewscreen. Somehow, whatever it was in that control room, Drega has managed to get one of the things working for us, or at least that's what I presume.

"Gondnok wanted me to win in order to expose you, Noro." I grin, exposing as much of my fangs as I can. "The thing is, when you're playing to win, the last thing you want to do is bite the hand that feeds you."

Noro goes silent. "Gondnok set me up?"

"Technically, he set us both up as he has absolutely no intention of giving me what I want." I laugh. "But if I have to choose an enemy, I choose him."

For a brief second, Noro preens.

"Not because you would have any success, or even have a chance of outsmarting me, Noro." I let my fanged grin grow wider, channeling my shift. "But because I trust him less than I trust anyone ever, including the Liderc."

Noro deflates amusingly, before he rallies. "This is immaterial, Sarkarnii. You will surrender yourselves, you will give me the map, and you will put your collars back on, or I will ensure your little mate stops breathing."

Ah, the last vestiges of the coward he is resurface.

"Are you threatening my mate, Noro?" I pull myself up to my full height, adding a little more with the shift. "Because the only reason you collared us is we are invincible without them, and there are two uncollared Sarkarnii here, and that can so easily be more."

As I speak, Amber quickly turns to Drega and removes his collar. It tinkles onto the golden ground.

"So, if you really think you can beat us, Noro—if you really think you can threaten my mate and get away with it —I suggest you make your move now."

As far as the Belek can change color, Noro pales significantly.

"I'd also suggest you do something, *Warden*," Drega adds. "As everything you've just said has been broadcast live to whoever was watching."

Noro shakes violently, his body twisting one way and then another as he attempts to take in exactly what has happened to him.

"It looks like I may have won after all, Noro," I say. "And because I am a generous Sarkarnii commander, especially where my enemies are concerned, my warriors and I will not sully our hands with your hide. I will leave you to Gondnok."

Noro turns his slimy body and looks back at the guards. They're melting back into the sky as if he doesn't exist, all but a black clad cohort which marches towards us.

"You'll never get out of here, Draco," he hisses. "Collared or not, the Kirakos is a fortress designed to keep any and all criminals in."

"Who said I wanted to escape?" I shrug. "Maybe I want to stay."

His jaw goes slack. I look up at the viewscreen, hovering above us.

"Time is ticking." I nod my head as both an acknowledgement of who is watching and as a challenge. "Fate is already on my side."

The guards are nearly at our position when I turn and head down the golden stairs. Behind me, Noro splutters as they take him, but I don't look back. None of my warriors do. Instead, we walk back down into the maze as victors.

"Did you really mean that?" Amber looks up at me. "About not wanting to escape?"

"I don't want to escape...yet," I say quietly. "The Kirakos has more secrets it needs to give up, my mate. But this little victory will mean we...you...are safe for the time being."

"But Draco." She tilts her head up to me, eyes sparkling with mischief. "I thought I was always safe with you."

"Ah, my little key, that is provided you don't touch anything."

She steps in front of me and puts a hand on my chest. The other skirts my lower abdomen, and instantly, my cock wants to emerge from its pouch.

"I don't believe not touching was in our bargain." Amber gives me the coyest smile, her eyelashes fluttering, my cock pushing its way out of my pouch entirely. I move closer, not wanting to give my warriors a show of exactly what I want to do to my mate. "And when I have you naked, in my hands, how can I not touch?"

I drop my head down into her hair, snuffing up her scent like a Sarkarnii starved, my lips close to her ear.

"I will mate you here and now, on these golden steps, to let all my warriors see what victory looks like," I murmur, and I'm rewarded by a slight gasp from my bold little mate and a puff of her arousal perfume.

What is she going to do?

"Then mate me," Amber says, and, with a roar, I shift into my true form, wings beating, my mate in my claws as I rise up, carrying her away to my quarters.

AMBER

Teasing Draco has resulted in possibly the scariest moment of my life, being lifted off the ground by his dragon form and the resulting terrifying rush of wind and light causing my heart to nearly leap out of my chest.

Problem is, when he lands, it seems everyone, rather than being afraid, wants to congratulate him. So, now I have a very sexually frustrated Draco and a big crowd, whose numbers have been swollen by the arrival of the remainder of the Sarkarnii warriors in high spirits, even the injured ones.

Very quickly, food and drink are brought out, along with tables and chairs. Draco flops into one and pulls me onto his lap with a tired sigh. One of the three eyed Jiakas brings us a platter of food which is most welcome.

I spot the bright blue of Drega's scales as he circulates, treating those who need it and checking over those who don't have any choice. I can hear his grumbling as he does so. A reluctant healer among the reluctantly needing-to-be-healed.

At a much slower pace, Draco is approached by the absolutely massive warrior with the long braid who climbed up the side of the maze earlier, Drasus. He bows low in front of Draco, his huge frame filled with poise.

"Draco," he says. "Your mate has freed you and your brothers from the tyranny of the collars." He risks a brief glance up at me, earning himself a growl. "Would you be agreeable to her freeing us all?"

I feel a pricking at the back of my eyes, and I don't remember ever being this emotional in the past. Maybe tears seemed pointless, weak even. But here, next to Draco, they don't seem stupid at all.

He looks at me. "Would you be willing to do this, for my den?"

I nod, my voice too choked with emotion to use. Draco growls under his breath, as if debating something internally. He taps his clawed fingers on his leg, now encased in leather.

Nakedness isn't quite the same for the Sarkarnii, but Draco has found himself some pants. I think because he likes to look cool. The same can't be said for Draxx, who remains stubbornly pantless.

"Fine," Draco snarls, but he leans forward to Drasus. "But this female is mine. She will touch you only to remove your collar. If you touch her, you will lose the limb, understood?"

"Draco!" I glare at him, the tears evaporating. "Unnecessary!"

He reaches his hand out for mine. "Absolutely necessary." His scales gleam as a tail appears, along with a pair of wings, shining in the light.

I shake my head as Drasus looks between us. "Come

here." I beckon him over, and he sidles to me with his eyes still firmly on Draco.

When he's within arms' reach, he dips his head, and I reach to his collar with a chorus of growls from Draco. Somehow, finding the catch on the collars is getting easier and easier, so it takes me less than five seconds to hit the right spot, and the metal hits the floor with a heavy, dull thud.

Almost instantly, I have a queue of silent warriors, all giving Draco fearful looks, but all of them desperate enough to risk his wrath. One by one, they kneel before me, and I start to feel like a queen. Even Draco snarls less as each one has his collar removed and the sky is full of dragons tumbling like kittens.

Eventually, they are all done, and there is a pile of collars on the floor in front of me.

Draco looks up, a smile playing over his features as he watches his fellow Sarkarnii.

"This is not how I expected things to end." He stands and offers me his hand.

I take it, and immediately I'm slammed against a hard, muscular body, a strong arm wrapped around my waist and a clawed finger and thumb cupping my chin.

"And how did you expect it to end?" I ask, defiant.

"With me buried inside you for eternity," he rumbles, lips brushing over mine, that incredible tongue tickling at my mouth, pushing inside.

"There's nothing to say this is the end," I reply as he dominates me. "Nothing at all."

"Good." Draco lifts me off my feet and into his arms, ignoring my disarmed squeak. "Because it only ends when you are mated completely and thoroughly."

For a second, I think he's going to change, shift into his

dragon form, but instead a wisp of smoke rises out of the corner of his mouth, as if he's just taken a drag on a cigarette. My bad boy sends my internal organs into a spin cycle I'm not sure they'll ever recover from.

He spirits me down into our quarters, barking at the doors to lock as we enter the ante-room and he strides into his bedroom.

I wriggle in his arms until I'm pressed against his chest, my legs wrapped around his waist, and he growls deep and low, shoving my back up against the wall.

Looks like we're not going to make it to the bedroom. Not this time. His tail whips up behind him, his wings extending. He looks like a demon, a sex demon who wants to devour me.

I am not going to refuse.

"You enjoy my Sarkarnii form?" Draco says as I feel the huge bulge in his pants pressing up against my clit.

"Yes," I say, hoarse with need.

The very thought of discovering a monster inside me has my core clenching painfully at nothing. I shift one hand from his neck to trail down his chest and around the waistband from which his cock protrudes. I trip my fingers over the tip, and he shoves involuntarily into my hand.

"I need you naked, heartsfire, or I cannot be responsible for what happens to your clothing." Draco grinds himself against me, needy and insistent.

"Then make me naked."

Claws slice through fabric like butter. I could protest, but Draco is consuming my mouth, stealing my words, if I had any, with his forked tongue flicking over mine. I'm divested of all my clothing in no time, but I've no time to mourn any loss as Draco's hard form is pressed against mine. He squeezes at my breasts and dips his head to capture a nipple and make me gasp as a tail slides between my butt cheeks.

He groans as I clutch at him, sending deep spasms through my breast and into my channel. I'm completely open to him, held fast in his arms, up against the wall. Our mutual desperation to be close, to be one, is everything.

Draco groans and shudders, scales flashing, rippling, expanding, and contracting. He spins me around, and I hang on with a laugh, wondering what he's doing, what he wants. Things clatter to the floor around us, and something slides under my arse until my back is against the wall again.

"Little mate, my beautiful Amber, I know you tease, but I cannot take this any slower. I have to be inside you, hooking you, filling you until you swell. My rut..."

His eyes are a swirl of light and dark, his lips slightly parted as he waits for my permission to take every inch of my body and make it his own.

"Fill me," I murmur in his ear, tugging at the pointed tip.

He has a hand on either side of my head, and his cock is pressed just at my entrance where my thighs part for him. The pre-cum seeps in, sending a bloom of warmth through my body. Draco gazes down at my pussy with an expression of pure hunger. His eyes shift up to my face as he presses the head of his cock just through my tight ring of muscle.

The stretch is incredible, almost impossible, until the feeling of bliss hits me and every muscle seems to relax as his pre-cum does something to me. Something utterly, utterly delicious. Draco pushes farther in and releases another mouthful of smoke.

"Look at you, little mate, stretched tight around my cock. So perfect, so ripe, so willing."

I risk a glance, and what I see floods my channel with

moisture. Draco only has the tip inside me, his scales, his bioluminescence, are glowing over his cock. I'm obscenely wide over him, and he's yet to drive the rest home.

"Mate me," I growl. "Mate me like you want to split me in two."

DRACO

I'm struggling to contain my shift. But until my cock is seated and she has taken my pre-cum, I cannot change. My Sarkarnii form wants to enjoy this little morsel so very much. Amber looks at where she has taken such a small part of my engorged cock, and her sweet cunt releases just enough I can slide all the way into her in one smooth and glorious movement.

She pulses over me, her hands grasping at my body, little claws tearing my scales, her head thrown back in wanton delight. My seed has tamed this female, but I still want her marks on me. Marks any fully mated Sarkarnii should wear with pride.

Moving slowly, I withdraw and circle my hips. Amber whimpers, her body lifting, hungry for mine. Hungry for my essence. Her body shudders as I trace a claw around the red tips of her nipples. Maybe our ancestry is similar, given Sarkarnii females feed our young with milk, although their breasts are nothing as delicious as my Amber's. Humans must do too. The thought lifts me and makes my cock jerk inside her. Could I fill Amber with a Sarkarnling?

It's not anything I've thought about before, but it brings me close to hooking her long before I'm ready. I feel like an untried warrior as I attempt to regulate both my breathing and my shift, all while she flutters over me.

And the noises she is making!

Nev it to the ancestors! I am not going to last.

I touch my lips to hers as I ease my way back inside her, luxuriating in every hot, slick inch and swallow down what she is murmuring, doing my best to quell the rising climax inside me because I want to remember every single secarri of our mating, every time I mate her for as long as I'm deemed worthy of being alive.

As long as my female deems me worthy.

Amber is all that matters, her pleasure, her sounds, the feel of her as I sink deeper and deeper, regulating my breathing, controlling my shift.

Giving her what she needs. Allowing my mating gland to fill me with the mix I need to ensure her pleasure, to give her my seed, to make her body ready to receive me.

"Draco." Her voice is hoarse.

She is so full, so at her limit, and I need to push her over it.

"What is it, my heartsfire?" I whisper at her, brushing a lock of hair off her forehead with my thumb. "Do you need me to mate you harder?"

She bites at her lip and nods. "I need...I need..." Her eyelids close, and she pulses around my cock.

Just like that, I can sink right up to my balls, right to the point my cock can hook inside her. I feel the unmistakable rising of my climax, and as I continue to spill my seed, she opens up even more with a gasp and a groan.

"You are...this is..." Amber's eyes fly open as her pussy contracts with a sudden, incredible pulse. "I love you!"

She falls back as I pound at her, my shift taking hold and my form changing, growing larger, growing scalier, wings and tail becoming fully formed as my cock hooks into her womb, taking full advantage of her orgasm to explode inside, pumping so much of my seed, so hard, so quickly, it's as if she is already carrying my Sarkarnling. My growl is thunderous, and as she sees what I have become, what I am, how I am taking her for everything and giving back all the pleasure, my tongue caressing her, licking away the salt from her skin, she cries my name.

I lose myself in her, in the way she grips my cock, holds my hook, the sheen of moisture on her skin. I want to hear her cry my name forever.

I want to dance for her.

AMBER

Draco's dragon form ploughs me until I can't even think straight. He wrings orgasm after orgasm out of me. And when he's done, he returns to his other form and carries me through to the bedroom, still with his cock hooked inside me.

I wake to him plundering my body over and over, and each time, it's better than the last. Each time, I wish he'd woken me sooner. Each time, I get the benefit of Draco and his dragon, both equally needy, both finding the exact point of my pleasure and then tipping me over the edge.

But when I open my eyes this time, the room is empty, both of Draco and his Dragon. The slow "whump whump" of his heart gone, missing and only beating in my head.

The emptiness without him is huge, hollow, echoing. All I have is what is in my heart, a bloom of warmth I grasp at, hold onto. Believe in.

There's a weird chime which has me sitting up in the bed, pulling the soft, warm alien sheets to me and yet again marveling at the absorbent qualities of the mattress below me. My whole body aches from where Draco plundered me over and over, filling me so full, my belly started to swell.

The mere thought of what we did has a smile creeping over my face. My bad boy has made a bad girl out of me.

The chime comes again and, fruitlessly, I look around for something to put on, worried the noise might indicate some sort of attack. It's then I remember what's left of my clothing is in the ante-room, shredded into pieces.

"Damn it," I mutter.

The door snaps open, and one of the four armed, pale blue skinned aliens stands in the doorway. It's a female, given I spot the long braids running from her forehead down her back, and I relax a little.

"The commander told me to help you," she says, stepping inside. "I'm Ckika."

"Help me with what?" I feel my brow furrow with confusion.

With one of her arms, she motions behind her, and suddenly there are five Jiaka in the room. They have their arms piled with packages.

"Help you dress for the commander of course," Ckika says, clasping one pair of hands together, her black eyes flashing with what can only be described as glee.

I'm suddenly very aware of my present state, filthy from yesterday's events, covered in Draco's...spend. Not just covered, in fact. I have to stink to high heaven.

"I need a bath," I announce, shuffling off the bed and taking the sheet with me.

"Excellent!" Ckika announces, and I'm surrounded by Jiaka, all coming up to approximately my waist height as I head towards the bathing area.

"No, I can bathe on my own," I protest, but they're

already ahead of me, pulling stuff out of the packages and fussing around me.

The sheet is stripped away, despite my efforts to keep it, and I get a chorus of interested noises which make me want to die on the spot. Then many, many hands are guiding me into the water. While I sink under the surface, they chatter, and more items come out of the packaging, until finally, with a huge flourish, Ckika unwraps the last thing.

It flutters like a bee's wing, an iridescent gossamer of light and life.

"Is that"—I stare and stare—"is that a dress?"

"Your mate, the commander, had it made for you."

"But how?"

Ckika laughs, the sound tinkling through the air, and it makes me smile despite my confusion. "Nothing goes unnoticed in the Kirakos, sweet one." She swirls the dress around. "But you must finish so we can make final adjustments."

I'm speechless and strangely obedient as I get out of the bath and I'm wrapped in an absorbent cloth, which dries me almost instantly. I'm hustled back to the bedroom where I'm made to sit while the others swirl around me, poking and primping, until finally and ignominiously, the towel is pulled away from me and the dress offered up.

The fabric is like silk only finer. I'm terrified of ripping it, but Ckika helps me with clucks and helpful noises as it spills over me like water, hugging every curve and rippling down into a puddle at my feet.

The Jiaka coo for a few seconds, but they're not finished with me yet. I'm turned one way and another until they all stand back, arms folded in various positions and smiles on their faces.

"Do you have a mirror?" I ask. Ckika purses her lips. The word mustn't be translating. "I want to see myself?"

"You do not have to." She smiles, the pale blue skin around her dark eyes crinkling. "You look like a Sarkarnii's mate. He will have no choice but to dance for you."

The chime comes again, followed by a thump on the door.

"Is she ready?" a gruff voice barks.

Ckika waves her hand over a small round dot next to the door, and it slides open. Drasus stands with his arms folded. His eyes move from the Jiaka to me.

His jaw drops open.

"Well, then. Are you taking this female to her mate?" Ckika asks, her voice filled with amusement. "These Sarkarnii have not seen many compatible females for a long time," she says in a loud conspiratorial whisper to me.

Drasus shuts his mouth with a snap of sharp teeth, and he growls at Ckika for a second before looking slightly fearfully at me.

"If you would come with me, my lady?" He executes a bow, his purple scales flashing with light. "Your mate requests your presence."

I am now wholly confused by everything, and I'm done with going along with it all. Sure I'm wearing a pretty dress which glitters like Sarkarnii scales, but that doesn't mean I'm just going to stop running and start following.

"Not until you all tell me what's going on." I put my hands on my hips.

"Your mate wishes to dance for you," Ckika says as Drasus draws breath. He huffs out a smoke ring instead. "He has chosen to do his dance in front of his Sarkarnii kin."

DRACO

I'm already regretting the three goblets of ale-wine I drank all too quickly without eating. My skin is itching and my head spinning.

All I'm going to do is dance for my mate. I am Draco. This is my quadrant, my den warriors.

Dancing for my female is not a hard thing at all.

So, why do I want to throw up?

"Drasus says she's ready." Drega appears by my side, and my throat goes instantly tight. I cough up a lung full of smoke. "Are you okay, Draco?" He grabs my head, pulling at my eye. "None of us have shifted for a while, so who knows what the effects are? Plus you were basically dead yesterday."

"Get the nev off me." I bat his hands and take a step back. "I need to concentrate."

"First time for everything." Draxx snorts smoke and a few embers as he joins us.

He still isn't wearing any pants.

"If you want to fuss over someone, fuss over him. He's

hardly been in this form since my mate removed his collar." I point at Draxx and retreat farther from Drega.

We're waiting in a far-too-small-for-three-large-Sarkarnii alcove just off the main square outside my quarters. Drega eyes Draxx who growls back a warning not to be touched.

Nothing ever changes.

"Did you go back to the control room?" I know I'm going to get no time to think about my dance, so I may as well try to quell the nerves rising within me.

"We did." Draxx nods. "But half of it wasn't working."

"We need your mate to activate the map again," Drega interjects. "At least we need a human to activate it, then I can change the settings to Sarkarnii."

I huff. The last thing I really want to do is take Amber anywhere but my quarters where I can mate her over and over.

"Still in rut?" Draxx asks innocently.

"I swear," I fire out an arm at him, but he dodges it, "if any of you mention the rut again..." Drega raises his eyebrows, daring me to finish the sentence with anything like a threat. "I will wish it on you both."

"Not happening to me," Drega says, confidently.

"Nor me," Draxx adds darkly.

It's my turn to laugh. Out in the square, the noise rises and falls to a hush. I swallow as I turn towards the sound.

"I need more time." The words stutter out.

"If you're ready, then you're ready," Drega growls.

"Nevving easy for you to say. You haven't had to dance for your mate."

Draxx laughs. "And it's about time you did, brother."

He gives me the most almighty shove, and I find myself tumbling out into the square in a way I did not intend, a snarl and flames on my lips. Looking smugger than ever, Drega and Draxx join me.

Drega puts his hands on my shoulders and stares into my eyes. "We're right here for you, brother." He spins me around, and there, in a pool of light, my mate stands.

The silk of her dress, the one I ordered to be made for her before I even accepted what she was, clings to her every curve. It shimmers, setting off her lush skin perfectly.

She is on fire. The silken flames lick up her body, flickering and bright.

I have never been more in love with her than in this moment.

Behind her, stood near the maze wall, is the Jiaka female and her mate, in her arms, her youngling is nestled. I nod at them both. She smiles at me, although the male looks terrified. I'm going to have to do something about that.

But I don't look at them for long. Not when I have my heartsfire, my *szikra*, waiting for me.

Waiting for me to dance for her.

Waiting for me to stake my claim.

And then she smiles, and my entire world is brought down to this one moment.

I bow, holding out my hand in the time-honored tradition to show my female I mean no harm as the beat starts.

AMBER

Draco looks at me like he wants to change into his dragon and devour me. Then, with a nod at Ckika, he executes a low bow, holds out his hand, and a deep drumbeat comes out of nowhere.

His hips sway, sinuous and hypnotic, as the beat grows louder. Behind him, his brothers mimic his movement with a switching, swaying of their bodies.

The dress I'm wearing might be nothing more than a scrap of silk, but I'm heating up from within as, with each beat, Draco sways in front of me, pelvis snapping as the beat booms out. His tail appears, and it curls around him in a way which is almost obscene but completely mesmerizing.

I can't take my eyes from him, not even if I wanted to. Everything has contracted until it is only me and Draco. He moves something within me which is not entirely human, not anymore. I find a pair of arms wrapped around me, moving me in time to the beat. Fingers with claws rake through my hair.

"You are the most beautiful thing in the entire universe, heartsfire," Draco murmurs. "Tell me what you want, and

I'll get it for you. Anything, everything, no matter what, no matter how hard or how high. I am yours to do with as you please, to direct and to mold. Let me help you burn this place or light it up."

My heart is stolen from my chest. The organ has grown wings, just like my mate, and it has taken flight above us. My head spins as I am spun around, the beat growing heady and intoxicating as the smoky scent of Draco fills my mind.

"Is that what you want, Draco, really?" I don't want my voice to be so hoarse or so lacking in confidence, but this huge male, this powerhouse—he could have anyone, any female. He doesn't have to settle for me.

"I choose you, Amber. I will always choose you. Fate might have thrown us together, but only love can make me burn like this. Set me alight and quench my fire forever, *szikra*."

It seems like the Kirakos stops spinning for a second, and I have my hand on his jaw, his scruff soft under my touch. I look into his eyes and see a reflection of myself. A girl in a pretty dress who is so in love with the male in her hands.

"I am yours, Draco. I think I always have been."

My lips are on his before the words have finished, my tongue demanding his attention, my hands raking through his hair, feeling the pulse of his scales and light, feeling how he wants to change his form but holds it down because I am in his arms. Knowing he wants to let go and yet wants to be with me in this moment and I am all that's keeping him here is so powerful, so perfect.

Around us, everything comes to life. There are Sarkarnii in all their forms. They dance too. Some wrestle with each other, their shift taking place like a scramble of fog and fire. Long tables have been procured from out of thin air and are loaded with food.

"Your warriors like a celebration." I grin up at Draco. "Is this for completing the run?"

"This is for us," he replies, squeezing me tightly as he snuffs in my hair. "I have danced for my mate, and they approve."

"They approve?" I'm smiling wryly at his joy.

"They approve." He nods firmly. "My den warriors approve of your choice of mate." I can't stop the laugh which bursts from me. "As it should be. If they hadn't, there would be trouble," he adds with a growl, slightly spoiling the illusion of gratitude.

From the corner of my eye, I see Drega and Draxx stood side by side, both with gold-colored cups in their hands. They raise them as Draco slides me past, my feet hardly touching the floor as the beat intensifies and I'm swung one way and then another as the dance consumes us both.

Draco is mine. And the only time I'll ever need to run is into his arms.

EPILOGUE

AMBER

I watch as the three Sarkarnii warriors race each other across the main square outside of Draco's quarters, before shifting and taking to the air in some sort of game, the rules of which I don't understand one bit. But it keeps them occupied, and given the entire maze is filled with dragons and the place is in a state of flux, it's probably not a bad thing.

No one dares challenge the Sarkarnii. They didn't much dare before, even the other quadrants, given these were trained warriors far above any of the other inmates scratching a living in the Kirakos. But now they can shift, become the huge dragon-like creatures, things have been very quiet.

Above me, the light is blotted out and a flash of gold fills my vision. Draco spins easily in the air before landing, and with that strange swirl of flesh, he is stood on two feet, with only a tail left of his previous form. He's naked, but then essentially, most of the Sarkarnii are, most of the time. Especially Draxx. I don't think he's dressed once since I took off his collar.

"Szikra." Draco rumbles his greeting, his long-standing whiskey-and-cigarette-habit voice flowing through me like my greatest pleasure.

It's been a few weeks since the run and since all the collars came off. Weeks which have passed in a haze of, well, sex. Draco's rut did finally break, but it hasn't stopped him wanting to fill me at every opportunity.

I am absolutely not complaining.

And this morning, after Draco and I finished with breakfast, I realized something else too. I'm late.

Very late.

He wraps an arm around my waist and pulls me into him with a thump, taking my mouth in his demanding, delicious way, forked tongue owning the kiss.

"Did you miss me, Mr. Mysterious?" I refer to the way he snuck out while I was in the bathing area, in a not too subtle way.

Draco doesn't do subtle, as I've discovered. He does growly, snarly, rumbly, and sexy.

But not subtle. He's getting a little better at saying "please," though.

"Who is this 'Mr. Mysterious'?" Draco furrows his brow, and his words are filled with a growl.

"It's you!" I slap him on his hard, muscular chest and wish I hadn't as it doesn't yield. "Sneaking off while my back was turned."

"I think you'll find, *szikra*, I do not 'sneak'."

I look up, and up again, at my massive alien warrior. He is probably the very definition of not sneaking, but I can't help playing with him.

"Okay, creeping off, then."

A growl rasps at his throat, smoke curling from his nostrils.

"I need to show you something. If you don't mind a trip back to the undercroft." His eyes are filled with concern.

"I don't mind. I believe I have a Sarkarnii bodyguard around here somewhere." I peer around Draco's bulk myopically and get yet another snarl of possession.

"Drasus is not required." He references the huge purple warrior who occasionally follows us around as presumably added muscle, not that Draco needs it.

"I meant you." I give him another playful slap, and my hand is caught in his big clawed one.

"I know," he intones, eyes flaring and sending a spike of desire right through me. "Come."

In an instant, we're in the air, and I'm carefully held in a set of enormous claws. My stomach squirms, despite wanting to be brave, and I fear I might just lose my breakfast.

But I can't be fearful for long as it is fascinating flying over the maze, looking down and seeing other creatures looking up as Draco's shadow covers them and flits away.

Without warning, he banks and dives, causing me to release a little shriek of involuntary terror, and the claws tighten around me. The warden-controlled areas have been locked down, but I know Drega took much information from the control room, including a way to access it again.

The ground rises up to meet me and then, in a flurry of wings and limbs, I'm in Draco's arms. He sets me down on wobbly legs. We're in a dead end of the maze. The floor is dirt, and the entire area looks abandoned.

"Next time, I will throw up on you," I warn.

He simply grins. "Your tolerances are so much higher than you give yourself credit for, my mate." He snuggles me into his side, and I melt a little.

It just comes naturally to him to compliment me, even

when he's not even trying, and I'm still not quite sure how to take it. So, I say nothing and just enjoy his warmth.

"We're in here." He gestures to a blank wall, then presses his hand on it.

There is a low 'clunk', and slowly, vertical cracks appear until a doorway is revealed.

"Looks like I taught you my trick." I laugh.

"Drega is full of tricks, Amber. This is just one of them, a door programmed just for Sarkarnii."

A dark corridor runs down a steep slope as we move inside. Draco clicks his fingers, and a flame appears, although I already know it's not from his fingers. The light flickers as we make our way deeper and deeper into the bowels of the Kirakos, until we finally step out into a slightly familiar passageway.

"Do the wardens know we're here?" I whisper.

"No, why?" Draco asks at full volume, and I cringe.

"Because of how we got in last time!" I hiss.

He waves a dismissive hand. "They won't bother us, even if they do know we are here." He points down to the mark near the floor. "If you would care to do the honors, my heartsfire?"

I swipe my fingers over the symbol and step to one side as the door slides open. A grinning face appears.

"Thought you two had got lost in the tunnels," Drega says. "And by lost, I mean mating," he adds unnecessarily.

Sarkarnii, as I've discovered, have virtually no filter. Draxx has none at all, to go along with his lack of pants.

"Mating comes later, brother." Draco shows a mouth full of fangs and holds out his hand for mine, helping me into the hole.

I get a better look around the place this time, given

we're not being chased by guards and don't have a cohort of Sarkarnii to free. What I thought were blank walls are a smooth, warm to the touch metal. I trail my fingers over it, getting a little static energy buzz from those which are blank.

Drega is working furiously at the standing console, pressing down on the various lit up squares as he gazes intensely at a screen filled with data, smoke escaping his mouth and being breathed in through his nose.

"I'm not sure you should be touching anything, little mate."

Draco encircles me from behind, pressing his hard, muscular form against me, and his muscles are not the only thing hard. His hands slide under my clothing.

The dress he had made for me lasted all of ten seconds once we returned to his quarters, claws shredding it from my body in a frenzy. But Draco has made up for it, and I have plenty to wear. Although today I've opted for more loose-fitting items as they're more comfortable. I've even let the girls free of the interesting underwear which is able to mould to my shape.

Draco cups me, thumb tracing over a sensitive nipple and making me shiver. The other hand roves over my belly, holding it gently as he buries his head in my neck and nips at my neck.

"Nev! I've got it!" Drega cries out, making me jump.

"Got what?" Draco growls into my skin, sending goose-bumps everywhere.

"The location of the other humans, the ones who might be the other keys to the Kirakos," Drega says, looking over at us, eyes shining. "Who might be able to unlock the map."

"I feel surplus to requirements," I mock grumble.

"Not at all. We need you to explain to them what we want," Draco says. "And I need you all the time." His hand slips over my stomach and down my pants, fingers brushing over my mound, and I lose a breath, my knees buckling and my hand planting on the wall in front of me.

"Welcome, humans." The strange soft, android voice chimes like last time.

"Humans?" Draco moves his hand away which is both a shame and a relief, given Drega's presence. "What does it mean humans?" He slowly pushes me behind him, taking up a protective stance. "What do you mean humans? Explain yourself!" he snarls.

Something appears on the wall, a little flicker of light which reminds me of the bioluminescence of Draco's scales. It grows larger until I can see something pumping, fluttering within a small egg shape. It gets larger still until finally, finally, I recognize it.

An image I've seen countless times on social media posts and on the TV. Instantly recognizable and yet every single one unique.

The answer to a question which I've been asking myself for over a week.

"What is it?" Draco peers at the thing.

"Looks like some sort of food," Drega says, looking over from his console with disinterest. "Not that I'd eat it."

"Draco?" I say softly.

"Hmmm?" He's still staring intently at the image.

"Draco."

"Yes," he says absently, reaching out to touch the screen.

I reach up and grab his face in both of my hands. "Draco!"

"Heartsfire?" His pupils are big and black as concern rolls off him at my sudden movement.

"It's our baby."

"What?"

"What?" Drega asks, his attention torn from the screens.

"Get out," Draco growls at him. Drega opens his mouth, shuts it again, and climbs quietly out of the control room. "Tell me." His gaze is on my face, lips slightly parted and just the hint of color in his cheeks.

"I don't know how long I've been here, but it's been longer than the normal cycle for a human." Subconsciously, I put my hands over my stomach. "I have been wondering if maybe it could be stress, or something else, but it can't be, and this confirms it." I look over my shoulder at the new life within me. "I'm pregnant, Draco."

Saying the words out loud brings it slamming home. Tears I didn't even think I had spring into my eyes. I don't want to cry, but I just don't know how I feel about the whole thing, any of this, and especially how Draco is going to react.

"You have my Sarkarnling in your belly." His voice is hushed and so unlike normal.

I want to look up, I so much want to look up, but I'm not sure I dare. I thought I knew him, just a little bit. He's arrogant, egotistical, gorgeous, caring, honorable, and his heart is so damn pure, the fact he's in a prison is incomprehensible. But this is very soon. A baby is very soon after everything we've been through, and I don't know how he will react.

A cool claw is under my chin, tilting my face up to him. Tears escape and run down my cheeks.

"You're giving me a Sarkarnling?" he asks.

A small sob forces its way out. I wanted so much to be strong once I knew, but I'm crumbling faster than I thought possible. "Yes."

"Then you have given me the greatest gift I could ever imagine, my *szikra*." I'm folded into his arms. "As long as it is what you want."

"I've never wanted anything more." I can't stop the tears now. They flow with abandon.

"Which makes me the happiest Sarkarnii in all existence," he croons. "And I can't wait to meet our little one, or for you to grow fat and round."

"Draco!" I lift my hand, and it's immediately caught by him.

He presses a kiss to my palm and sucks my index finger between his lips.

"Female Sarkarnii are said to be insatiable when they are with young." He gives me his best sinful look. "I very much hope humans are the same."

I am on fire, and I never want it to end.

Book 2: Draxx is available to pre-order directly from the author and will be released on Amazon in September 2023.

www.hattiejacks.com/pre-order

You can get an alert for all my new releases before anyone else by signing up for my newsletter.

Sign up for my newsletter here or you can also sign up on my website www.hattiejacks.com

And you can follow me on Bookbub, Amazon or even join my Facebook group - Hattie's Hotties!

JOIN ME!

Why not join the Hattie Jacks Alien Appreciation Society?
Subscribe to my newsletter for a free sci-fi romance novella:
www.hattiejacks.com/subscribe

You can also join my Patreon
https://patreon.com/HattieJacksAuthor
Where I post chapter serials of my ongoing work in
progress, the occasional poll and little snippets of character
art.

Additionally, if you wish, you can stalk me on Instagram:
www.instagram.com/hattie.jacks
or join my Facebook group:
www.facebook.com/hattieshotties

ALSO BY HATTIE JACKS

Fated Mates of the Sarkarnii

DRACO

DRAXX

DREGA

DRASUS

DAEOS

DRELIX

Warriors of the Citadel

SAVAGE PRIZE

SAVAGE PET

SAVAGE MINE

Elite Rogue Alien Warriors

STORM

FURY

CHAOS

REBEL

WRATH

JUST WHO IS THIS HATTIE JACKS ANYWAY?

I've been a passionate sci-fi fan since I was a little girl, brought up on a diet of Douglas Adams, Issac Asimov, Star Trek, Star Wars, Doctor Who, Red Dwarf and The Adventure Game.

What? You don't know about The Adventure Game? It's probably a British thing and dates me horribly! Google it. Even better search for it on YouTube. In my defence, there were only three channels back then.

I'm also a sucker for great characters and situations as well as grand romance, because who doesn't like a grand romantic gesture?

So, when I'm not writing steamy stories about smouldering alien males and women with something to prove, you'll find me battling my garden (less English country garden, more The Good Life) or zooming around the countryside on my motorbike.

Check out my website at www.hattiejacks.com!

Made in United States
Troutdale, OR
11/04/2024

24446369R00188